Ian and Grace

They were not driven ~~by~~ ~~unbearable urgency.~~ With age had come the wisdom to recognize the pleasure of delayed gratification and to savor each moment of discovery and draw it out. They understood the value of prolonging desire, of allowing passion to build kiss upon deepening kiss, touch upon exploring touch.

But neither were they immune to the flames they fanned in each other's bodies. Their breath heated and emerged in gasps, their hearts pounded. Grace buried her fingers in Ian's thick, heavy hair. His hands slipped inside the jacket of her silk suit.

When she felt the scald of his palms against the sides of her breasts, she drew a sharp, fainting breath and would have stumbled if she hadn't steadied herself against him.

"Oh, Jeffrey!"

They both froze. Jeffrey's name hung between them like a sudden barrier, shocking in its effect.

Grace felt as if she'd been abruptly drenched with icy water. The error utterly mortified her. "I'm sorry," she apologized in a low voice.

Ian's hands fell to his sides. "Don't apologize," he said evenly. "It's perfectly all right, perfectly understandable."

Weddings
By
DeWilde

About the author

A native of Colorado, the talented Ms St. George is the author of over thirty novels, in categories ranging from historical, to mystery, to romantic romp. Her love of historical fiction made the writing of the DeWilde family history particularly appealing, and her talents for imagining the unexpected have produced a touching and surprising love story that will enchant fans of *Weddings by DeWilde*. She brings a wealth of life experience to her writing, having served as a flight attendant for United Airlines, as well as the national president of the Romance Writers of America. The winner of numerous awards, Ms St. George is hard at work on her next project.

Weddings
By
DeWilde

PREVIOUSLY AT DeWILDES

A new Galeries DeWilde is set to open on famed Rue de la Paix!

- ◆ Megan DeWilde has realized her dream of opening another exclusive DeWilde emporium in Paris.

- ◆ She wasn't expecting to forsake competition with the rival Villeneuves, and fall in love with one instead.

- ◆ She wasn't expecting her beloved brother to forbid her marriage, or for the irritating detective, Nick Santos, to be tailing her on her romantic rendezvous either.

- ◆ And she was certainly flabbergasted to find her dear aunt, Marie-Claire, in the arms of Armand Villeneuve, who'd broken her heart decades before.

And Megan's mother, Grace, could never imagine the shocking secrets she was about to discover about the DeWildes, just as she was poised to sever her ties with them!

*MILLS & BOON and MILLS & BOON with the Rose Device
are registered trademarks of the publisher.*

*First published in Great Britain 1996
by Harlequin Mills & Boon Limited,
Eton House, 18-24 Paradise Road, Richmond, Surrey TW9 1SR*

Maggie Osborne is acknowledged as the author of this work.

© Harlequin Books S.A. 1996

ISBN 0 263 80100 4

06-9702

*Printed and bound in Great Britain
by BPC Paperbacks Limited, Aylesbury*

Family Secrets

BY

MARGARET ST. GEORGE

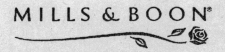

MILLS & BOON®

TELEGRAM TO: Grace DeWilde

FROM: Ian Stanley

Darling stop Time ran out before
expected stop Will try not to
leave before you arrive stop But
hurry stop I love you Grace stop
Come to me Darling stop Your Ian
stop

CHAPTER ONE

"GRACE? IT'S JEFFREY."

Pressing the phone close to her ear, Grace DeWilde lowered her head and closed her eyes. It impressed her as unbearably sad that after a marriage of thirty-two years, Jeffrey thought it necessary to identify himself by name. She would have recognized his voice from the depths of a coma.

Kicking off the sheets, she drew up her knees and pulled the hem of an oversized T-shirt down over her legs. It was six-thirty in the morning in San Francisco. She wasn't awake enough to figure out what time it was in London.

"Is it afternoon at your end?" she asked, blinking at the morning sunlight glowing against her bedroom draperies. Usually she awakened eager to begin a new day, but lately she'd found herself wanting to roll over and go back to sleep. A small alarm sounded deep in her mind. In the past, such behavior had signaled she was either pregnant or feeling anxious. An unconscious sigh lifted her breast. She certainly wasn't pregnant.

"Are you awake enough to talk?" Jeffrey inquired, brushing aside as irrelevant her question about the time in London. "You sound half asleep," he added, unable to conceal his surprise.

How well they knew each other, Grace thought, rubbing her forehead and wishing she had a cup of coffee. That is, they knew each other's small daily habits. The disastrous events of this past year had amply illustrated that they could still surprise each other.

Abruptly, she sat up straight against the pillows and her eyes opened wide. "Jeffrey! Has something happened to one of the children? Is that why you're calling?" Her mind raced. "I spoke to Kate last night, so it can't be Kate... Is it one of the twins? Megan? Gabriel? Is Gabe's wife having difficulties with her pregnancy?"

"Everyone is fine," he assured her. "I called to talk about us."

Relief loosened her shoulders, but her chest remained tight. "There is no us. Not anymore." Morning added a sultry tone to her husky voice; how many hundreds of times had Jeffrey teased her about her morning "come hither" voice? And how many times had they reached for each other, still warm and drowsy with sleep?

"Then you're going ahead with the divorce."

Grace waited before answering. How did people stand this? It was so damned hard. One minute she was remembering the sweetness of beginning the day in her husband's arms, the next minute they were talking about divorce. She drew a long breath. "We can't continue like this. It's been nearly a year since we've seen each other." It felt like a lifetime. "Things aren't getting better. We're fighting through our attorneys, and every time we talk on the phone, we argue."

"Not every time," he said quietly. He sounded tired.

Her immediate impulse was to ask if he was eating properly and taking his vitamins. She wanted to inquire if he was getting enough sleep. Instead, Grace bit her lip and waited, wondering at what point the pauses had begun to appear. Was it before she left him and came to San Francisco, as far from London as she could run? Or had the awkward pauses begun to punctuate their conversations even before she learned about his affair with a woman young enough to be his daughter?

The pain of Jeffrey's betrayal blossomed behind her rib cage like a malignant flower. Each time she thought about his affair, fresh anger seared her. How could he have done this to her? To them?

"Grace?"

"I'm still here," she snapped.

Breathing deeply, exercising the willpower for which she was famous, she fought back an army of negative emotions. For the sake of her children, she had determined to keep recriminations and bitterness out of this divorce.

"We're living on separate continents. We're building lives that don't include each other," she reminded him in a level tone. "Divorce seems the logical next step."

Bending forward over her knees, Grace covered her eyes with her free hand and held her breath. All he had to do was say, *I don't want a divorce. I love you and I want you back where you belong. Please forgive me.*

If he would bend enough to ask, she would somehow find a way to forgive. They would start over, begin again.

"If you're determined to proceed with this, there are practical matters we need to discuss."

The air slowly leaked from her lungs as hope deflated. Anger rushed to fill the vacant space, and she hit the bed with a fist. "Our respective attorneys are handling the practical matters." Resentment brought her fully awake. Was it so hard for him to ask her forgiveness? Or did he simply not care that they were about to tear apart a marriage that had been successful for almost thirty-two years?

"What do *you* want, Jeffrey?"

"I'd prefer to handle the points of contention directly between ourselves rather than risk having the attorneys turn this into an acrimonious paper fight."

That he chose to deliberately misunderstand her question raised conflicting feelings of irritation and helpless amusement. Grace had been the volatile partner in their marriage, the one who wore her heart on her sleeve in the privacy of their home. No one needed second sight to recognize when she was angry, happy, sad or annoyed. Expressing emotion came harder for Jeffrey.

"What points of contention?" Grace inquired cautiously. She steeled herself, waiting for him to mention her new store, Grace. "I thought we'd settled the nonsense about a noncompete agreement. I won't consent to anything like that, Jeffrey." She shoved at a tousled strand of blond hair and anger flashed in her blue eyes. "I have a right to use my expertise to make a living."

"You're a wealthy woman. You hardly need to 'make a living,' as you so charmingly put it." The smile in his voice increased her anger.

"I don't intend to vegetate or become one of the ladies who lunch," she said, building steam. "I'm barely past fifty. That's young in today's world. Launching Grace has been exciting and fulfilling. The store is up and running, Jeffrey, and doing well. I'm not going to give it up!"

"I'm not asking you to give up anything," he said sharply.

"Really? Then why did I have to fight your attorneys over one damned thing after another before I could get Grace opened?"

A sigh of exasperation sounded against her ear. "I should think the answer would be obvious. There was concern that you would capitalize on the DeWilde name."

"I *am* a DeWilde! That's my name, too!" The effort not to shout made her tremble. As he well knew, she had been Grace DeWilde longer than she had been Grace Powell. Moreover, her ideas and hard work had helped transform the DeWilde empire into the multimillion dollar corporation it was today.

Actually, the issue that had lit a fuse under her had been Jeffrey's insistence that she agree to a noncompete clause that would have prevented her from owning and operating any business dealing with bridal apparel, weddings, jewelry and a list of etceteras. It made her furious even to think about it.

"There's no point fighting this battle again," Jeffrey said coolly. "You won. We've settled the matter, haven't we?"

"If so, then why does this subject continue to arise every time we talk? Jeffrey, Grace is *not* cutting into DeWilde's market!" Grace paused and forced a calmer tone. "You're right. There's no point talking about this.... What did you call to discuss?"

"My attorneys say your attorneys want Kemberly."

Grace made a face and sighed. Dissolving a long-term marriage and business partnership was extremely complicated; there were hundreds of details to be adjudicated. But she was certain she and her attorneys had discussed Kemberly. She remembered the bitter taste in her mouth when she had agreed to relinquish her home.

"There's been a misunderstanding," she said finally. "If I retained Kemberly, it would remain closed most of the year. I'd rather you kept it, Jeffrey, so the children will feel comfortable going home whenever they like."

Jeffrey had proposed to her in the rose garden. Her children had grown up at Kemberly. She and Jeffrey had fought there, loved there. They had done a lot of living at Kemberly.

"I'm glad this isn't going to be a problem. If there's anything at Kemberly that you want..."

She nodded, forgetting that he couldn't see her. "I'll fly over and remove my personal items before I leave for Nevada."

He cleared his throat to fill another uncomfortable pause. Suddenly it seemed of the utmost importance to know where he was so she could picture him in her mind. "Are you at your office?" she asked.

"I'm in my den at the flat," he answered.

She visualized him sitting behind the scarred desk that had belonged to his father, his elbows resting on the leather blotter. No matter what time it was in London, he was probably wearing a jacket and tie. She hoped he also wore a waistcoat against the damp chill of late February.

"Where are you?" he asked after a minute.

"I'm still in bed," she said, trying not to feel defensive or guilty or sexy.

"Sitting cross-legged, no doubt, wearing one of those shapeless T-shirt things." Amusement lightened his voice, and a hint of something else. Wistfulness? Regret?

"Something like that . . ." she said when she could speak in a steady voice.

"Where in Nevada will you be staying?"

Grace wrapped her finger around the phone cord. "Do you remember Marsha Ingram?"

"Ian's sister. Of course I remember." He sounded annoyed that she could think he might have forgotten the sister of his closest friend.

"Marsha's husband is Nevada's premier landscape architect. I understand he's landscaped many of the lavish hotels there. Marsha and Bill will be in Europe until late summer. They've offered me the use of their home outside Las Vegas. I have to stay in Nevada for six weeks to fulfill the residency requirement before we can obtain a divorce."

"Las Vegas?"

She laughed at the shock in his voice. "I know. Originally I hoped to wait out the requirement in Reno, near Lake Tahoe. That would have been convenient for me to fly or drive back here to check on the store and handle any problems that might arise. However, I've been advised that I may not leave Nevada at any time during the six weeks. Not for a day, not for an hour." Irritation replaced her amusement. "I accepted the loan of Marsha's house because it's the farthest point from temptation. I couldn't possibly drive to San Francisco then back to Las Vegas in one day."

"Good Lord, Grace. I'm trying to imagine you in Las Vegas, and I can't."

The remark was a backhanded compliment, but it also confirmed that Jeffrey was leaving the details of their divorce to his attorneys and taking only a minimal role himself. His attorneys had undoubtedly mentioned that the divorce would be granted in Las Vegas, Nevada. It stung that he hadn't remembered.

"Was there anything else?" she asked, glancing at the clock. She preferred to be in her office before the employees arrived at the store. Today, she would be late.

"If you'll inform Monica when you'll be in London, perhaps we could have dinner...."

Notify his secretary? No, she wasn't about to beg for an appointment with her husband. Pride and sorrow stiffened her spine. "In view of the circumstances, that probably isn't a good idea."

"Perhaps you're right," he agreed after a minute.

"Well, then..."

She waited for him to say goodbye, because she couldn't make herself say the word. Instead, after another pause, he said, "It's been raining here. The tulips at Kemberly are out of the ground. Not in bloom yet, of course. But they'll be early this year."

Grace pictured the spring beds. In a few weeks, masses of tulips and jonquils would burst into a blaze of red and yellow. "Don't forget to phone your mother. Her eighty-first birthday is next week."

"The DeMarises asked after you. They're having their annual ball in Cannes in late March. I gave them your new address."

"I'll have to decline. I'll be in Nevada in March."

The reminder of Nevada stopped the conversation. Actually, Grace decided it wasn't a conversation as much as a reluctance to hang up the telephone.

"Well!" they both said at once. Grace laughed, then her voice softened. "I really do need to jump in the shower and get ready for work."

"Goodbye, Gracie. Thank you for being so reasonable and understanding about Kemberly."

Sudden tears filmed her eyes. No one but Jeffrey had ever called her Gracie.

After she replaced the telephone on the fancy electronic shelf in the middle of the headboard, Grace swung her legs over the side of the bed and bit her lip. The emotional turmoil of speaking to Jeffrey left her feeling drained. During the last twenty minutes, she had flashed through half a dozen emotions. Sadness, regret, anger, amusement, resentment and bittersweet nostalgia.

They were going to divorce. For the first time she believed it would really happen.

The bottom fell out of Grace's stomach. She reached the bathroom only seconds before a spasm of nausea sent her to her knees.

GRACE WAS LOCATED in the heart of San Francisco's shopping district near Kearny and Post. Sandblasting had cleaned the old stone facade to a mellow golden hue. Tall arched windows imparted a promise of elegance while hinting at old-world sophistication.

By the time Grace's driver opened the door for her and she hurried inside, the store was bustling with activity. All the private fitting rooms were occupied, she noted as she walked briskly toward the elevator. Two prospective brides tried on gowns in front of glistening Venetian mirrors while their mothers sipped espresso, seated in the depths of plushly upholstered settees.

The fresh scent of Grace's signature fragrance lightly perfumed the air, a soothing Mozart concerto provided background to squeals of delight as smiling saleswomen displayed one fairy-tale gown after another.

Before she entered the elevator that would take her to her second-floor office, Grace noted that all the specialty boutiques were attracting browsers except the small travel agency. The travel agency had been a mistake, she decided with a frown. Grooms made the honeymoon arrangements; Grace's clientele came from the distaff side.

The instant she entered the reception area of her office, she began issuing instructions. "Rita, the flowers beside fitting room number two are wilted. Have them replaced at once and tell the florist this can't happen again. Remind her that the store's arrangements are the best advertisement for our floral service. Also, have someone call maintenance, please, and tell them two bulbs need to be replaced in the foyer. If there's room on my schedule, find thirty minutes and tell Ms. Wares at the travel agency that I need to speak to her."

Rita Shannon Mulholland, her personal assistant and gift from heaven, followed Grace into her sunny office. She gave Grace a cup of black coffee as Grace took off her jacket and sat behind her desk, beginning the morning search for her reading glasses.

"In the middle drawer," Rita said, grinning.

"The travel agency isn't making it," Grace commented, settling the glasses on her slender nose. "Should we expand the veil boutique? Or try to come up with something else for that space?"

"Our average sale in veils runs about eight hundred dollars a pop," Rita said, sitting on the edge of Grace's large desk. "But I liked your idea about testing some trendy, untraditional gowns. We've got a designer in the wings who is doing some interesting wedding dresses with T-shirt tops and satin slacks. What do you think?"

Grace laughed and rolled her eyes. "T-shirt tops? I love it. Let's try for an appointment between the time I return from England and the time I leave for Nevada. I'd like to talk to him."

"Her."

"Her. That reminds me. I'll need a hotel in London." She rushed past the thought of booking a hotel suite instead of going directly to the flat in Chelsea.

Rita made a notation on her pad. "I'll take care of it. Claridge's?"

Grace considered. "No," she said finally. This would be a quick trip to accomplish a painful errand. "Book something where I'm not likely to run into anyone I know." She didn't intend to contact any friends or inform anyone that she was coming. Closing her life in England was something she had to do alone. "So. What's on the agenda for today?"

Tilting her head, Rita studied her. "Grace . . . are you all right?"

"Why do you ask?" She glanced up from the pile of mail on her desk.

"You look a little pale. And this is the first time since I've known you that you've been late."

A guilty flush warmed her face and a rush of defensiveness leapt to her tongue before she conquered it. The store wasn't going to collapse if she arrived thirty minutes late. Grace reminded herself that she had hired efficient people, the best in retail. And Rita Mulholland had been with her since the inception of Grace; Rita knew the store as well as she did.

A rueful smile curved her lips. "How in the world am I going to stay away from here for six weeks when I feel this apologetic for being thirty minutes late?"

Sadness and understanding filled Rita's eyes. "Then you've decided to go ahead with the divorce?"

"You're the second person who's asked me that today," Grace said softly, adjusting her glasses. "Yes," she continued after a minute. "It's definite. You'll need to clear my schedule to accommodate six weeks in Nevada. Following that, I'll need another week out to attend Ryder's wedding in Australia." Ryder Blake headed DeWilde's Sydney branch and was a close family friend. Frustration clouded Grace's brow. She supposed there would never be a convenient time to get a divorce, would never be a time when she felt comfortable being absent from the store.

"I'm sorry. I'd hoped something good would happen at the eleventh hour and you and Jeffrey..."

Grace pulled back her shoulders and made herself smile. "If we couldn't work out our differences in a year, I doubt we'll do it in the next few days or weeks. Don't worry about me, Rita. Everything happens for the best. Now...what do I have today?"

Rita consulted the notes in her lap. "You're doing an interview with Sandra Callas from the *Chronicle* in thirty minutes. You're speaking to Women in Business over lunch. Your speech notes are in the green folder, by the way. At two o'clock you have a meeting with the department heads. Your attorney will phone at three." She placed a pile of pink phone messages on the desk. "Most of these can wait. Your daughter Kate phoned. Your masseuse called. And Alex Stowe." Rita paused and her eyebrow lifted in a suggestive curve.

Grace laughed. "Alex is my niece's neighbor."

"With whom you have already had one date."

"We had dinner and went to the theater, and it was a perfectly lovely evening, but Alex is just a friend."

Rita grinned. "Oh, really?"

"Really," Grace insisted. "Good heavens, Rita. I have neither the time nor the inclination to date!"

After Rita left her office, Grace blinked into space. She hadn't given much thought to dating. The last time she'd had an actual date, she had been—what?—twenty years old? And Jeffrey had been twenty-four. Lyndon Baines Johnson had been the U.S. president, Winston Churchill was in the final year of his life, Vietnam was heating up. The Beatles sang "I Want to Hold Your Hand," and *My Fair Lady* won an Academy Award as the best film of the year.

Her last date had occurred a lifetime ago in a different world.

She was starting life over at age fifty-two. The full reality of what she faced slammed across her chest.

And she, who wasn't afraid of anything, was suddenly frightened to death.

CHAPTER TWO

THE FLIGHT TO ENGLAND seemed interminably long. Fortunately Grace didn't have anyone in the seat next to her so she was able to spread out her briefcase and papers. Catching up on reports and paperwork kept her from dreading the emotionalism that was certain to assail her at Kemberly.

"Mrs. DeWilde? Would you care for another cup of coffee?"

"No, thank you." Now that the in-flight movie had ended, Grace hoped to sleep during the rest of the flight, which crossed Canada and then the North Pole.

The flight attendant offered her a pillow and a light blanket. "I've read many articles about you, Mrs. De-Wilde. It's a pleasure to tell you in person how much I admire all you've accomplished."

"Thank you."

Her modest fame always came as a pleasant surprise. In the past, Grace had accepted accolades with pleasure and a thrill of recognition. Now, she thought, frowning, she felt a tiny edge of unaccustomed anxiety.

In the past, she'd had the cushion of the DeWilde name, the DeWilde fortune and the DeWilde Corporation to fall back on if she erred. In the future, she would be working without a net, as they said. And people were watching.

The article in the *San Francisco Chronicle* had turned out well, she thought. Her store had received glowing praise, and so had she. But she was a realist. Grace knew she was news right now because of the shock waves still reverberating through the financial world following her separation from Jeffrey and more recently, by the announcement that a divorce was imminent. The DeWilde stock had wobbled last week, and the phone had rung constantly with journalists seeking confirmation about the divorce.

Lightly, her slender fingers played over the pillow and blanket, still in her lap, and she wondered if she would be able to sleep. There was so much to think about right now.

She really didn't need to worry about the store; Grace had taken on a life of its own. Rita Shannon Mulholland was a marvel of efficiency, she could practically read Grace's mind. With Rita at the helm during her absence, everything would run as smoothly as if she were there herself. And she and Rita would speak on the phone every day.

Still, Grace was her baby; it was her idea, her money and her reputation on the line. It felt strange to think the store would function, and function well, without her. Nevertheless, it was not good business practice to abandon the store during its crucial first year, and that worried her.

Regardless, it was time to move forward with her life. She had used launching the store as an excuse to put off making a final decision; it would be so easy to continue making excuses and delay the divorce indefinitely.

She had considered that option and rejected it.

Resting her head on the seat back, Grace turned her gaze to the window. All she could see were clouds and the ocean below. There was nothing to distract her thoughts.

Launching Grace had kept her frantically busy for months, too busy to grieve for her personal situation. Now the store was running like clockwork and she could no longer avoid taking a long, hard look at starting over. But this was the point where her usually quick mind froze. She couldn't move past the *idea* of starting over, couldn't see herself facing the second half of her life alone, couldn't actually bring herself to make solitary plans.

A sad smile curved her lips. For thirty-plus years she had teased Jeffrey about his need to always have a plan, had laughed and told him that he thought *spontaneous* was a four-letter word. Now, here she was, feeling half panicked that she didn't have a plan to follow into the unknown future.

First, she had to dismantle the past. That was the purpose of this upsetting trip. But she didn't want to think about that, either. She'd deal with it soon enough.

COLD RAIN PELTED the car as the limo driver pulled away from Heathrow Airport.

Grace settled in the back seat and gazed at the dripping landscape. Despite the low clouds and gray dampness, her heart soared, insisting that she had arrived home even as her intellect reminded her that she didn't live here anymore. Although she had resided in England for more than thirty-two years, English friends swore she still retained an American accent while American friends claimed she sounded as British as the queen.

She supposed any accent she had acquired would fade now that she had chosen to make her home in the United States. Already she was saying "elevator" instead of "lift," "trunk" instead of "boot."

But it would be a long time before she stopped thinking of England as home.

A sense of wrongness assailed her when the driver stopped before the street awning of Marlow's, a small out-of-the-way hotel. The Chelsea flat was only a few minutes from here, filled with familiar, well-loved items and the scents and sounds of home. Thirty minutes in the other direction would have taken her to the DeWilde flagship store and the office where she had happily commanded a legion of people and dealt with a dozen stimulating challenges every day.

"Mrs. DeWilde?"

When Grace realized the doorman was peering into the car and had called her name twice, she started, then slid outside into the damp, chill air.

"We're having a bit of a cold spell," the doorman remarked, holding an umbrella over her head. He opened the hotel doors and ushered her inside, out of the rain.

"Thank you."

The lobby was small, luxurious and charming. A fire crackled in the grate. Rita had chosen well, Grace thought as she stepped to the counter to register. Registering in and out of hotels was the task she most disliked about traveling alone. Although she recognized her attitude as chauvinistic, it had always seemed that registering into a hotel was a man's job.

After the bellman delivered her luggage, she removed her suit jacket and gazed around the room. Victorian wallpaper and gleaming antiques offered more charm and individuality than American hotel rooms did, but it couldn't duplicate home. This wasn't the flat in Chelsea.

"This trip is going to be worse than I imagined," she whispered, eyeing the telephone.

But before she called her son, she needed something to eat.

And after room service satisfied her appetite, she decided a hot bath would further relax her.

Finally, she ran out of excuses. Sitting on the edge of the bed, she made herself dial Gabriel's private number at the store.

"Gabriel DeWilde speaking."

"Gabe? It's Grace." Their rule for working together had been that he would call her Grace in her professional capacity and Mother in private. Since she'd left his father, Gabe had almost consistently called her Grace.

"How was your flight?" Caution dampened the vibrancy that usually sang through Gabe's voice.

"Uneventful, exactly as I want a flight to be. How are you? And how is Lianne feeling?" The baby wasn't due for months yet, but Grace could hardly think about it without feeling a pang. She had never dreamed that she would end up as a long-distance grandmother. When she had imagined her children marrying and starting their own families, she had pictured herself nearby, playing a welcome role in their lives.

"Lianne's fine," Gabriel answered evenly. "How are you?"

"I'm fine."

An uncomfortable silence followed, and sadly, there seemed nothing more to say. Grace lowered her head and propped her forehead against a palm. Gabe was hurt and furious that she had left his father and fled to the other side of the world. She was hurt that he and Lianne had eloped rather than include their families in their wedding.

None of her children knew the reasons why she had left Jeffrey, and she didn't want them to. Kate and Megan were trying not to take sides, but Gabe blamed her.

"I'm calling to confirm that we're having dinner tonight," Grace said, striving to sound cheerful. "I'm eager to see both of you."

"You didn't receive my message?" She heard Gabe swear under his breath. "I'm afraid tonight isn't going to work out. Nick Santos is in town, and tonight is the only night Dad and I can meet with him." When Grace didn't speak, he filled the silence, offering explanations that were redundant. "You know that some of the missing jewel pieces surfaced."

Of course she knew.

"Nick has been trying to trace the origin of the pieces."

Also old news. "Is Mr. Santos having any success?"

"That's what tonight's meeting is about. We're hoping Nick has something to report. Though frankly, I doubt it."

The mystery of the jewels missing from the DeWilde's private collection was a family secret. The world at large did not know the pieces had been stolen and replaced with excellent replicas, but their disappearance had become almost an obsession with Jeffrey. For his sake, Grace hoped the mystery neared a solution.

"Mr. Santos is an interesting man," she said, remembering the electricity that had snapped between the private investigator and her daughter Kate when Santos had appeared in San Francisco to question Grace. "Is there another night that would be better for you and Lianne?" she asked. "Perhaps the two of you could drive up to Kemberly and we'll have dinner there. I'll be at Kemberly for a week...."

Gabe paused, and she could almost hear him sifting through possible excuses. "Actually, this is a difficult time for us...a dozen things going on at once."

"I understand," Grace said softly, plucking at her bathrobe.

"Well..." he said, and she imagined him glancing at his wristwatch.

"How is your father?"

"Don't put me in the middle of this, Grace."

"You put yourself in the middle." She'd identified the anger in his voice and responded with a flash of her own. "You chose sides a long time ago."

"What did you expect? When you cut and ran, it wasn't only Dad whom you left. You walked away from a dozen critical items that you let dangle, you left at least six fires for me to put out. You didn't say goodbye to anyone. And you've never given a reason for any of it!''

''I admit that I handled the situation badly. I tried to phone you before my flight left, but . . .''

''Look, we've been over this before. Really, I have to hang up. I'm late for a meeting with marketing. You remember marketing, don't you? The department that depended on you?''

His bitterness shocked and hurt her. ''Gabriel, please. We need to talk.''

There was a moment's silence before she heard the hint of a sigh. ''You will always be my mother, and I'm trying to respect that. I don't want to fight with you, and whether you believe it or not, I'd prefer to keep an open mind. But you've made that difficult. You deserted Dad and you deserted the company. You've begun a new life in the States, and you're proceeding with a divorce. I thought I knew you, but I don't.''

''And you won't know me, Gabe, if you won't talk to me or give me a chance.''

''I want to,'' he said eventually. And she heard echoes of the little boy in his voice. The little boy who had brought her his skinned knees and his wounded feelings, who had shared his sorrows and his joys as he stretched toward manhood. ''But you have to meet me halfway. You could begin by explaining why you're divorcing Dad.''

She swallowed hard and squeezed her eyes shut. Suddenly the fatigue of the flight and the change of time overwhelmed her.

''I can't do that,'' she said quietly. Under no circumstances would she tell her children that their father had had an affair. If they were ever to learn the truth, it had to come from Jeffrey, not her. ''I . . . it just didn't work out.''

"After thirty-two years you decide your marriage isn't working out?" he exploded. She cringed at his pain and frustration. "People don't wait thirty-two years to decide a marriage isn't working out. Especially a marriage that everyone who knew you thought was wonderful and solid! Why in the hell won't you tell us the truth? We're your children, we have a right to know!"

"No, Gabriel," Grace said with quiet dignity. "You don't have the right to know more about our marriage and our personal difficulties than your father and I choose to explain. And we will respect that philosophy with regard to your marriage to Lianne."

He was quiet a minute, then he spoke in a voice deep with frustration. "Why does it have to be such a damned secret?"

"Our reasons are private, not secret."

"If that's how you want it, then fine. But don't tell me you want to talk, because you don't. Now, if you'll excuse me, I'm late for a meeting."

"Gabriel, please. Don't hang up. I don't know when I'll return to England or when we might see each other again."

But the line was dead. Grace replaced the receiver with a shaking hand and lowered her head. Was there anything more painful to the heart than an estrangement with one's child? If so, she couldn't think what it might be.

"Damn it, Jeffrey," she whispered angrily, dashing tears from her lashes. "You're responsible for this!"

Long after she should have been sleeping, Grace lay on the bed, staring at the ceiling of her hotel room.

If Gabriel had to choose sides, then it was better that he had chosen Jeffrey's. He and Jeffrey worked together, socialized together, and both lived in London. An impossible situation would have arisen if Gabe had blamed Jeffrey for his parents' problems.

Grace knew this, but still she burned with resentment. It seemed so damned unfair for Jeffrey to allow Gabe to place all the blame at Grace's door. It was Jeffrey who'd had an affair, who had shattered their vows, not her.

Rolling on her side, she jerked the blankets over her head. But she couldn't shut out the sudden unwanted image of her husband with a younger woman—a woman named Allison Ames.

Though she held Jeffrey fully accountable for his part in the affair, Grace couldn't pretend to be unaware of what had made him vulnerable to another woman.

She did know.

After more than thirty years of marriage, she had believed she could confide a secret to Jeffrey, a secret their successful and happy marriage had made irrelevant. But it hadn't been irrelevant to Jeffrey. Far from it. Grace's revelation had rocked him to the core and set him on a path that led directly to Allison Ames and eventually to the dissolution of their marriage.

To Grace, her marriage had disintegrated because her husband had had an affair he would neither express regret for nor apologize for. To Jeffrey, his marriage had disintegrated because his wife confessed that she had fallen in love with him *after* their marriage instead of before.

Her confession had been a terrible blunder. But she could not apologize for telling the truth. And Jeffrey's affair had been a terrible mistake, but for some reason he couldn't bring himself to ask Grace's forgiveness.

Lost in the recent past, Grace stared at the ceiling and listened to the rain weeping against the windows.

KEMBERLY HAD STOLEN her heart the first time Grace saw the mellowed stone and graceful Queen Anne windows. To her eyes, the Georgian mansion had seemed magical yet solidly real, a poem writ in elegance. From the first instant, the wings angling back from the central core had seemed like arms opened to welcome her home.

Pulling her rental car next to the hedges fencing the lane, Grace braked and rested her arms on the steering wheel, leaning forward to drink in the sight of all that was right about England.

Jeffrey's grandparents had bought Kemberly in the nineteen-thirties. Genevieve DeWilde had begun the restoration of the house and the antiques that came with it, but it had been Jeffrey's mother, Mary, who insisted on adding electricity, telephones and adequate plumbing. After Mary and Charles gave the house to Jeffrey and Grace on their tenth anniversary, Grace had devoted herself to restoring the formal gardens and expanding the rose collection.

Three generations of DeWilde women had left their mark on Kemberly, but surely, Grace thought, none of them had loved the beautiful old house as deeply as she.

As she slowly wound up the steep rise toward a cobbled circular drive, she imagined the yellow jonquils and purple hyacinths that would appear in a few weeks in the window boxes perched on Elizabethan-style sills. The checkered fields below were already green and would shade toward emerald in another month. In the distance, a village church spire pointed the way to heaven.

In the early 1800s the Prince Regent had stayed at Kemberly in the famous blue room, and in more modern times, Eisenhower and Churchill had argued in the drawing room. The graceful old house brimmed with history, both public and private.

Before Grace could remove her luggage from the boot—trunk—of the rental car, Mrs. Milton's son appeared to carry it inside. Mrs. Milton herself threw open the front door and twisted her hands in a sugary apron.

"I'm glad to see you, Mrs. DeWilde, but it's a sad day nonetheless." She touched a corner of the apron to her eye, then murmured, "Dinner at seven-thirty and not a minute later."

Grace laughed and touched Mrs. Milton's chapped hand. "As dictatorial as ever, I see."

"Come inside, come inside. There's tea waiting in the drawing room, just as you like it with sugar and lemon, and a cheery flame in the grate to ease the chill."

Because this was very likely the last time Grace would visit Kemberly, no detail was too small to merit her attention. There were the grooves in the wooden floors, cut by the wheels of her children's roller skates. And there was the spot where Gabriel had landed and broken a tooth after tumbling down the central staircase.

Here in the drawing room, beneath a sprig of mistletoe, Megan had thrilled to her first adult kiss. Kate had nursed a multitude of wounded creatures in a cage in that corner.

Memories flooded Grace's mind, overwhelming her. Sitting before the fire, she extended her hands to the flames, wondering how she was going to endure this week. No one walked through life without surviving a number of crises, and Grace had found the strength to overcome her share. But it was memory that was proving a formidable opponent. Memory was a powerful, wispy thing that couldn't be grappled with, only endured.

After a time, she lifted her head and gazed at a large giltframed portrait hung above the fireplace mantel.

The portrait of Anne Marie DeWilde, Jeffrey's greatgrandmother, had been painted in 1870, the year of her marriage to Maximilien DeWilde. Grace had resurrected the painting from a pile of attic discards, amazed and delighted by such an exciting find. Her reason for hanging Anne Marie's portrait in the drawing room went deeper than paying homage to Jeffrey's great-grandmother. In the portrait, Anne Marie wore the same diamond-and-sapphire engagement ring that Grace now wore.

It had always been Grace's intention to give Gabriel the ring to present to his bride. But Gabriel and Lianne had eloped.

Grace turned the ring on her finger and studied Anne Marie DeWilde's delicate features, seeking hints of her children in their great-great-grandmother's smile. She didn't know much about Anne Marie DeWilde except that Anne Marie had also suffered an estrangement from her only son. Max DeWilde had refused to address a single word to his mother for forty years. The reason for the deep rift between mother and son was unknown, but Grace guessed the estrangement must have been the most painful incident in Anne.Marie's life.

A shudder twisted down her spine and she reached for the teapot to warm herself. She absolutely could not allow the estrangement between her and Gabriel to continue. But resolving their differences presented a dilemma. She refused to turn Gabe against his father by exposing Jeffrey's affair, yet she could think of no other way to explain her own actions.

Mrs. Milton rapped on the door and popped a cheerful smile into the room. "Mr. DeWilde is on the phone for you."

Grace had been so absorbed that she hadn't heard the ring. Frowning, she hesitated, then stood. "Thank you. I'll take it in here."

Before she lifted the telephone, she gazed back at Anne Marie DeWilde's portrait, remembering something else about Jeffrey's great-grandmother. Anne Marie and Maximilien DeWilde had separated after their children were grown. The separation had lasted fifteen years, until Maximilien's death. They had never reconciled.

Suppressing a disheartened sigh, Grace lifted the receiver. "I was just thinking about you."

"Were you?" Jeffrey sounded pleased and surprised. "I called to make certain you'd arrived safely."

Turning, she gazed out a tall, narrow window at the rainy fields beyond. "You were right. The tulips are pushing out of the ground. Mr. Pettybottom has already turned his cows into the south pasture."

"Grace..." He cleared his throat. "Gabe is having a difficult time with the divorce. The girls are, too, but Gabe appears to be having the most trouble dealing with everything that's happened. Can you talk to him?"

She pushed a hand through her hair and wished the phone cord were long enough to permit pacing. "I've tried, Jeffrey. I know he feels I left him, too. It's so frustrating! I can't explain without talking about..." She bit her lip, refusing to mention Allison Ames's name. "Gabe is determined to blame me. We can't talk to each other. He doesn't want to see me." She couldn't keep the bitterness out of her next remark. "If anyone can explain things to Gabe, it's you."

"If you believe it would help," he said stiffly, "then of course I'm willing to sit down with Gabe and explain my part in all this."

It was a huge concession, and she knew it. When she recovered from the surprise of his offer, Grace considered the ramifications.

"Grace? Are you there?"

Sighing, she turned away from the window. "I'd feel vindicated if you'd tell Gabe how you betrayed everything I thought you and I were," she snapped. "But I think doing so would create more problems than it might solve. If you tell Gabe...well, then you'd have to tell Megan and Kate. It would be unfair not to. The truth would force the children to take sides. They could no longer even pretend to be neutral."

It occurred to her to wonder if he'd offered to reveal his affair knowing that she would reject the suggestion. She threw out a hand. "You and Gabe work together very closely. The truth might damage that relationship and ultimately hurt the corporation," she added helplessly. "All in all, it's better to stand by our agreement and say nothing. Gabe and I will have to find another way to work out our differences."

"When we get into this kind of conversation, it amazes me that you reduce everything to the affair."

"Why? Because the foolishness of male middle-age crisis is such a cliché?"

"No," he said, speaking as sharply as she. "Because what I did is only part of why all of this is happening."

Grace covered her eyes with her free hand. "Jeffrey, I would give anything not to have confessed that I didn't love you when we married. I never dreamed you'd be so damned upset over something that happened thirty-some years ago. All I was doing was thinking out loud about how much we've changed over the years. In my case, I grew from a shallow twenty-year-old into a woman of strength and depth—I hope—and, more important, into a woman deeply and passionately in love with her husband. Loving you didn't take long, Jeffrey. It happened swiftly, and I thought I was the luckiest woman in the world. Why is something that ended so wonderfully so catastrophic for you?"

"You married the DeWilde name and the DeWilde fortune. You didn't marry *me*. You're damned right it's catastrophic to learn that the woman I adored would have married Quasimodo if his last name was DeWilde!"

"That's not true and you know it!"

"Isn't it? That's certainly the impression you gave."

"That's not fair! I liked you, admired you, and I cared about you. Very quickly I fell head over heels in love with you!"

"The point is, I thought I was marrying a woman who loved me from the beginning. I didn't realize I was gambling that somewhere along the line my wife might learn to love me. Let me ask you something. If my name had been Jeffrey Smith instead of DeWilde, would you have married me, Grace? If my family had been, say, plumbers instead of jewelers and retailers, would you have married a man you didn't love?"

Sagging, she rested her weight against the wall. "The point is, we were happy. We loved each other for almost thirty-two years. We had three wonderful children together. We were a business team. Damn it, we were *happy!*"

"We loved each other for thirty-two years? So you fell in love with the man you married during the first year? Or was it the second or the third year?"

"I don't know! What does it matter? I loved you! You were the grand passion of my life! And I thought that was what I was for you. I believed it right up to the minute I found out you were sleeping with a girl young enough to be your daughter!"

Instantly she felt him withdraw into the stoic silence that rose like a shell around him whenever they argued. The angrier and more verbal Grace became, the more silent and withdrawn he became. His furious silence drove her crazy. She wished that just once Jeffrey would let his emotions erupt. Just once, she wished he would shout back and throw his arms out and pace and maybe smash something. Instead, his voice and eyes went as cold as the icy silence that encased him, and he withdrew as quickly as possible to the comfort of business reports and financial statements.

"Oh, Jeffrey." Her voice sank to a whisper. "Was it worth it? Were a few nights in a Paris hotel worth what you've done to us?"

Since she didn't expect a reply, his response stunned her.

"It made no difference to Allison that I was connected to the DeWilde stores."

"Either you're incredibly naive or your paramour is a clever actress," Grace snapped. The words flew out of her mouth before she realized what she was saying. She was stating that Allison Ames, like herself more than thirty years before, had been more attracted to the DeWilde name and fortune than to Jeffrey himself. Hastily, she attempted to backpedal. "I apologize. I don't know Miss Ames. If you say it didn't matter to her who you were, then it probably—"

"But you don't believe it," he stated flatly, his voice cold. She imagined him straightening his shoulders and lifting his chin. "Well, Grace, I'm sure you have things to do. I wish you a safe flight home. Now, if you'll excuse me . . ."

Home. Already he thought of San Francisco as her home. He couldn't have said anything more telling to reveal his feelings about the impending divorce.

After she hung up the telephone, Grace walked to the center of the room and looked up at the portrait of Anne Marie DeWilde.

"Was it like this between you and Maximilien?" she asked in a husky whisper. "Did you feel angry and hurt and bewildered? What did you say to each other before you parted forever? Did you argue? Try to wound each other?"

A flush of embarrassment heated her cheeks when Mrs. Milton came into the drawing room and caught her talking to a portrait.

"I was just . . ."

"There, there, you don't need to explain anything to me," Mrs. Milton said, bending to clear the tea service. "But I do want to say that my son and I would like to help in any way we can during this difficult period. You just say the word, Mrs. DeWilde, tell us what we can do."

"Thank you." Grace glanced at the early afternoon light slanting in the windows. As always, work was the antidote, the only remedy she knew against pain. "I believe I'll change into slacks and begin tagging the items I want shipped to the U.S."

"Begging your pardon for intruding—" Mrs. Milton held the tea tray like an offering "—but is there any chance that you and Mr. DeWilde might . . ."

Grace thought of the latest bitter conversation. "None at all," she said softly, speaking around the sudden lump rising in her throat. "Well." She dusted her hands together in a brisk movement. "I'll start with the basement. Tomorrow we'll go through the first floor, then the second floor. I dread the attic. I can't remember when anyone was last up there."

Mrs. Milton departed, shaking her head and making tsking sounds under her breath.

As soon as the housekeeper passed from sight, Grace's shoulders collapsed and she covered her face with both hands.

She still loved him. And somewhere, underneath all the pride and defensiveness, Jeffrey still loved her. That was the greatest tragedy of all. Neither had been very lovable during this last year. Neither had displayed much of the charm and graciousness for which both were famed. They had flung verbal daggers across an ocean, had assembled private armies of attorneys and sent them on a mission to wound, conquer and accumulate. On the face of it, nothing remained of their deep love but cutting shards.

And yet…neither had spoken an unkind word about the other to their children. Neither had fought this very private battle in the press, despite myriad opportunities to do so. And for all their turbulent emotions, they had been sensible about decisions such as who would keep which belongings. Jeffrey worried if she had arrived safely; she worried if he was taking his vitamins, and she had tried to repair the damage to his ego caused by her own thoughtless remarks.

How had all of this happened? Why were two people who loved each other tearing apart their lives and their history together?

Eyes glistening with unshed tears, Grace looked helplessly at the smiling portrait of Anne Marie DeWilde.

"How did you bear it?"

CHAPTER THREE

BY THE FOURTH DAY at Kemberly, Grace's frustration had reached the point of explosion.

"I should have stayed in California!" Lifting a hand, she wiped her forehead and glared at an antique bureau in the master bedroom.

The bureau was one of her favorite pieces, one of the items memory insisted she must have. She had created a makeshift bed for infant Kate in the bottom drawer of the bureau when Kate arrived before the new nursery furniture did. Megan had carved her initials in the side of the bureau, earning a rare spanking for her artistry. Gabriel had climbed the drawers like a ladder. Since the bureau had been in the family for generations, additional history reverberated in the scarred top.

Unfortunately—and Grace recognized this clearly—the bureau belonged here at Kemberly, surrounded by matching pieces, not in her shiny, modern condominium in San Francisco.

"Damn it." Flinging herself into a chair, Grace stared at the bureau that she loved but could not bring herself to remove. It would simply be wrong to break the web of history that bound the antique to Kemberly.

She had reached the same frustrating conclusion about every item she had traveled halfway around the globe to claim. The heavy silver tea service that had been a gift from the president of France, the small rocker in the children's nursery, the cherrywood desk in the study, the porcelain collection in the library. They were all part of Kemberly's long history. And Kemberly was where these items belonged.

Grace could have spared herself the lengthy flight, the time away from her new store, the distress of knowing her son was within driving distance but didn't want to see her, the painfully nostalgic memories that waited in every nook and cranny to blindside her. She could have spared herself the ache of being this near Jeffrey without seeing him.

"I'm glad I'm leaving tomorrow." Muttering to herself, she climbed the staircase to the attic access.

An inch of dust furred the attic floor, disturbed only by the skittering tracks of mice. Grace stood, hands on slim hips, and slowly surveyed the castoffs of several generations. Her heart sank. For twenty years she had been promising herself that someday she would set aside a month and explore all the trunks and boxes piled willy-nilly in an attic three times the size of her San Francisco condominium.

A faint glow of late afternoon light illuminated decades of dust laid like a gray-brown coat over furniture, lamps, rugs, trunks and boxes long forgotten by Kemberly's previous owners. Following Baron Kemberly's family, three generations of DeWildes had added to the jumble of discarded odds and ends.

With a smile, Grace noted that someone, probably Jeffrey's practical and capricious mother, Mary, had sectioned off the attic areas. A handwritten scrawl indicated the west portion of the attic had been designated for items once belonging to Baron Kemberly and his forebears. Undoubtedly history buffs would someday discover a treasure trove among the old trunks and cartons. Another fading sign identified a section for Max and Genevieve. The smallest area was marked Charles and Mary.

Grace had never found time to sign off a section exclusively for her own family's use. Megan's first pair of skis was tossed in Max and Genevieve's area. She identified a box of her own girlhood mementos in Charles and Mary's section.

A sudden grin curved her lips. Finally she'd spotted something good about the impending divorce: never again would she feel guilty about not finding time to clean out Kemberly's attic. Smiling at the dust and jumbled items, Grace resolved to remember the attic every time her heart grieved for Kemberly.

It didn't take long to tag the items she wanted shipped. She left her children's outgrown toys and games for future DeWildes, admired castoff furniture but left the pieces to be rediscovered by other DeWilde wives. The boxes she tagged contained personal items, valentines composed in childish penmanship, a diary she had begun years ago then abandoned, old letters too precious to discard, her mother's photograph album.

As the light was fading, she resisted an urge to examine the contents of the boxes she'd tagged. That was a bittersweet task she would save for a rainy day in San Francisco. Or perhaps she would take a box or two with her to Nevada to occupy the time while she waited to fulfill the residency requirement. Yes, that was exactly what she would do.

"Mrs. DeWilde?" Mrs. Milton called up the attic stairs, her voice happily conspiratorial. "You have a visitor. Your husband is here."

Grace froze, then turned her head toward the stairs. "Jeffrey is here? At Kemberly?"

"He's waiting in the drawing room."

"Tell him..." Oh, my God. Was there a mirror in the attic? "Tell Jeffrey I'll be down directly."

There had to be a mirror. After searching frantically, Grace spied a cloudy cheval glass among Baron Kemberly's possessions. Stirring puffs of dust with every footstep, she hastened past the DeWilde sections and used her cuff to wipe clean a circle on the mirror large enough to examine her face.

"Oh, my," she murmured in dismay, hands flying to push and poke at her hair. Wisps had pulled free from a loosely woven French braid. Dust had irritated her eyes, her cheeks were flushed from the exertion of moving heavy boxes. Smuts and smudges made her loose shirt look like a candidate for the ragbag.

A twinkle of amused irritation flashed in her eyes. For thirty-two years she had told Jeffrey that she disliked being surprised, and for thirty-two years Jeffrey had not believed her.

For a long moment she considered letting him wait while she bathed, shampooed the grime from her hair and dressed in a skirt and heels. If she did, she would feel far less vulnerable, at far less of a disadvantage.

On the other hand, she decided, watching in the cloudy mirror as her chin steadied with resolve, it seemed faintly ridiculous to worry about how she looked to a man she was in the process of divorcing. Moreover, this would be a good opportunity to test their future relationship. If she could hold her own when her disheveled appearance made her feel apologetic and uncomfortable, that would be a positive sign.

After flexing her hands against the front of her slacks in an effort to press out the tremble in her fingers, she squared her shoulders and marched down the attic steps, down the staircase, and didn't stop until she reached the door of the drawing room.

There she paused to draw a deep breath and frown in irritation when she realized her heart was pounding and a cloud of butterflies fluttered in her stomach. No amount of flexing had chased the tremble from her fingers.

In a way, it was almost amusing. She, who had given speeches to an audience of a thousand, who had entertained royalty, who had hosted charity balls with numbers of international celebrities in attendance, and had done so without a flicker of nerves, was now experiencing stage fright at the idea of confronting the one man whom she knew better than anyone else in the world.

Shaking her head impatiently, Grace entered the drawing room, then stopped short. The sight of Jeffrey, after all these months, halted the breath in her chest. Her heart gave a hitch and she felt her cheeks grow hot.

Jeffrey stood before the fire in the grate, one elbow resting on the mantel, his other hand stretched before him. He was studying his unsteady fingers with a look of wry exasperation.

Grace had a moment to notice a similarity of features between her husband and the portrait of his great-grandmother, Anne Marie DeWilde. They shared the same clear gaze that faced the world directly with a hint of self-deprecating amusement. Anne Marie's features were delicate, whereas Jeffrey had inherited the handsome ruggedness of his male ancestors, but the aristocratic nose and cleanly sculpted jawline had followed Anne Marie to her great-grandson. They would have recognized each other.

"Jeffrey?"

Dropping his outstretched arm, he turned to face her. A frown of earnestness tugged his eyebrows. "I know you don't want to see me, but damn it, Grace. It just isn't right. God knows when we'll be in the same area again."

Having delivered his small outburst, Jeffrey made a helpless gesture with his hands, then simply looked at her, a dozen questions darkening his eyes.

They were both exquisitely aware that this was the first time in three decades that they had met after an absence without rushing to hold each other. The awkwardness of this realization created enough tension that Grace imagined she felt an invisible cord draw taut between them.

"You've lost weight," she whispered. His face was thinner than when she had last seen him. The gray at his temples now extended beyond his ears. He was still the handsomest man Grace had ever met. Her pulse accelerated and her breath shortened as she absorbed tiny changes that only made him more attractive.

Abruptly it occurred to her that women would be strongly attracted to her husband. He was handsome, wealthy, sophisticated and charming. Women drawn to powerful men would find him devastating.

Jealousy ate through her system like battery acid.

"I told myself that you couldn't possibly be as beautiful as I remembered," he said softly.

Nervous laughter rose in Grace's throat. "Then your eyesight must be failing. I mean, look at me." She couldn't help pushing at the wisps of hair floating around her face. "I've been in the attic, rearranging the dust."

He smiled. "You look exactly as you did ten years ago. Remember? You were wearing slacks and a loose shirt that day, too, one of my old shirts, if I remember correctly. You'd decided to tackle the attic, but a bathroom flooded downstairs or something, then Mrs. Milton's son broke his arm, and—"

"And Gabe was home, sick with the flu, and Megan tied up the phone for hours, talking to a new boyfriend, and I missed an important call from the Paris store." She smiled, remembering. "That was the day Kate wanted to adopt the mangiest dog I'd ever seen."

"Mr. Peabody," Jeffrey recalled, returning her smile. "A noble creature in a disreputable body."

"I was never so glad to see anyone as I was to see you that day." The memory was suddenly so fresh, the events might have happened yesterday. "You calmed everyone and settled each crisis."

"That didn't happen very often, Gracie. I can only recall a handful of times when you didn't handle a dozen catastrophes at once and make it look easy."

A powerful impulse to run to him and smother his face with kisses nearly overwhelmed her. They had built so many good memories, had accumulated so much history together. Their lives were stitched into one fabric by strong threads of joy and small sorrows, memory and shared experience.

For an instant Grace could not recall why on earth they were seeking a divorce. And then she did.

Turning toward the drink cart, she concealed an expression of pain and deep sadness. "Would you like a drink?"

"Please."

She poured Scotch for him and a glass of sherry for herself. When she handed him the tumbler, their fingers brushed and a warm thrill shot up her arm. Even after all these years, his commanding physical presence aroused her. She pressed her lips together and managed a wobbly smile.

"To our children," she said quickly, her voice husky. Their usual toast was "to us."

"To our children," Jeffrey echoed, gazing at her over the rim of his glass.

"Will you stay for dinner?" she asked impulsively. Flustered by almost instant regret, she added quickly, "It would please Mrs. Milton."

"Would it please you?" he asked quietly, kneeling to poke up the fire in the grate. Grace sensed he expected a rejection and didn't want her to see his expression when it happened.

"If we could agree not to talk about...certain things," she replied, speaking slowly. An hour ago, she would have sworn the last person she wanted to see was Jeffrey De-Wilde. Now that he stood before her, close enough that she could inhale the familiar intoxicating scent of his cologne, she didn't want him to leave. The resultant confusion spinning her thoughts threw her off balance, an uncharacteristic situation that made her acutely uncomfortable. "I don't want to argue or fight with you."

"Agreed," he said firmly, rising from the grate with a smile.

She laughed. Of course he would agree. Jeffrey loathed arguments and marital spats. It was she who believed a good, spirited argument cleared the air, not Jeffrey.

His grin told her that he knew what she was thinking.

Except their situation was different now. Their arguments didn't clear the air but only led to flares of bitterness.

Grace finished her sherry and returned the glass to the cart. "I'll inform Mrs. Milton that you'll stay." She started toward the door. "I need to shower and change clothes." She glanced back to find him watching her. "I'm glad you came," she said softly, surprised that it was true.

"I am, too." For a long moment their eyes held, then Jeffrey touched his tie and cleared his throat. "Well. I have some work to catch up on. I'll wait for you in the study."

As Grace showered and shampooed her hair, she thought about his last comment. She'd heard him say the same thing a thousand times, but this time his comment about working in his study reminded her that she was no longer mistress of Kemberly. This was Jeffrey's home, Jeffrey's study. It was no longer hers. She was here as Jeffrey's guest.

Wrapped in a towel, she stood in the center of the master bedroom and slowly looked around her. After tonight, she would never again sleep in the downy four-poster. Never again would she wake to an English country sky, or gaze out that window at dewy meadows dotted with sheep. When she drove away tomorrow, it would be for the last time. And she would leave a piece of her heart within these old stones.

"What's wrong with you?" she whispered, pressing the heels of her palms against her eyelids.

Grace DeWilde was not a weepy woman. She was not the type to indulge in a wallow of poor-me's. Early on she had adopted the English credo of maintaining a stiff upper lip. But since arriving at Kemberly, she had been awash in sentimentality, wandering in memories of past, happier times as she had never before done in her life.

But those had been safe and wonderful times. Now the future loomed with uncertainties that undercut her sense of control and confidence.

"Enough," she admonished herself sharply.

But then she confronted the nerve-racking decision of what to wear for dinner with her husband. The Chanel suit was too businesslike—out of the question. The Armani slacks were nice but too casual. Her new Valentino was lovely, but a cocktail dress might impart the wrong impression. After a bout of indecision that was as amusing as it was annoying, Grace chose a simple wool skirt and blue silk blouse. She wound her hair into a loose knot on her neck and added the lustrous pearl earrings and necklace that Jeffrey's mother had given her on her fortieth birthday.

At the foot of the staircase, Grace paused and sniffed in surprise. She followed the scent of cherry pipe tobacco to Jeffrey's study.

"You're smoking again?"

''Occasionally.'' Immediately, he tapped out the pipe's ashes into a heavy ashtray on his desk, then stood and smiled at her. ''You look lovely. That blouse matches your eyes.''

''Thank you.''

Sudden panic flared in Grace's chest. What would they talk about? Once they had run out of polite compliments and had covered the weather, what on earth would they say to each other? Every subject that jumped to mind was laden with potential pitfalls.

''I believe Mrs. Milton has freshened the drink cart in the drawing room,'' Jeffrey said, walking around his desk.

His study was a room that Grace had carefully avoided. This was Jeffrey's sanctuary, his personal retreat. Now she saw that he had made subtle alterations since her last visit. His desk chair was new, and he had installed a sofa long enough to accommodate his tall frame if he wished to stretch out. For years, he had kept a photograph of her on his desk. She noticed he had moved the photograph across the study to a bookshelf.

After glancing again at the pipe rack near his desk blotter, she turned wordlessly and led the way to the drawing room. They were both making changes, altering their environment to accommodate solitary tastes, so new to them both. Gingerly experimenting with a life that no longer included each other.

He hadn't hidden her photograph away in a drawer. But he had moved it from his line of sight. Gradually, inevitably, all reminders of their life together would disappear from Kemberly's rooms.

Sadness opened a hollow deep within her.

''So,'' Grace said brightly when they were settled in front of the drawing room fire with fresh drinks in their hands.

She drew a deep breath. "How is everything at the London store?"

How he answered would determine the tone for the remainder of the evening. Her question was weighty with the possibility for sharp or bitter recriminations, but she couldn't think of anything else to say. The DeWilde stores had played such a large role in their life together.

Jeffrey studied the contents of his glass, then lifted it to his lips. "We're considering some renovations." His tone and features were expressionless.

"Excellent. The store is a grand old dame, but she could use a bit of a face-lift." If their marriage had not crumbled, Grace would have been in the thick of the renovations, happily and busily involved with designers and fabricators, carpenters and lighting engineers.

"I understand Grace was an instant success," he said, raising another subject laden with potential disaster.

"The store's doing very well," Grace answered carefully. "The true test will come at the end of our first year. Competition is fierce in the States. There are more than seven thousand bridal-apparel shops. And according to the National Bridal Service, ten percent of new bridal gown businesses fail in the first year."

Jeffrey laughed and toasted her with his glass. "Trust you to have the statistics well in hand."

"Statistics are usually your department," she said, returning his smile. "But I did my research." Lowering her head, she gazed at the surface of her drink. "I want Grace to succeed, Jeffrey. I need something to do with the rest of my life." For a moment neither of them spoke. "Launching Grace has been an exciting experience. I've been frantically busy this last year. I've met a lot of new people. I haven't had time to feel sorry for myself."

"You were never the type to feel sorry for yourself."

Her head snapped up. "The two things an aging wife dreads and fears most have happened to me. My husband had an affair with a much younger woman, and I'm getting a divorce. When I think about living alone for the rest of my life, something freezes inside! I didn't plan to spend the last half of my life alone, it certainly isn't what I wanted. Believe me, there is indeed a temptation to feel sorry for myself."

Rising, Jeffrey moved to stand in front of the fireplace. "You don't look like an aging wife, as you put it. You're a beautiful woman, Grace. You look at least ten years younger than you are." He gazed into the flames leaping in the drawing room grate. "As for the rest...what do you want from me? Do you want me to say I'm sorry about Allison?" Lifting his head, he stared back at her. "I'm sorry. I wish it had never happened. I hurt you, I hurt Allison, and I hurt myself. All my life I've felt nothing but contempt for men who betray their wives. I would have sworn it could not, would not, ever happen to me. But it did. And I can't change that. Nothing I say or do is going to make anyone's pain go away."

"If you think I care about easing Allison Ames's pain, you're dead wrong," Grace said, her eyes flashing. She, too, stood, and they faced each other across the sofa table. "If she's suffering because she slept with a married man...fine. And if you're suffering because you threw away a good marriage and a loving wife...that's fine, too. You should suffer for what you did to us!"

They glared at each other.

"Is that what this divorce is about, Grace? Punishment?"

"People can't be married without trust! Happily married people don't have affairs. They don't live a continent apart. They don't fight the same unresolvable issues over and over! They don't try to hurt each other! *That's* what our divorce is about. You made it very clear that our marriage wasn't important to you, that *I* wasn't important to you!''

"That's ridiculous! You're the most important thing in my life. You always have been. I loved you from the moment I saw you. Your hair was longer then, but you look the same to me now as you did the day I met you. You were wearing a lemon-colored linen sheath that day. I looked at you and thought the sun had come to earth. When you smiled at me, I felt ten feet tall. To me, you were a young queen and I wanted to slay a dragon and lay it at your feet! I wanted to spend the rest of my life trying to be your hero!''

"Oh, Jeffrey.'' Abruptly the fury drained out of her system, and Grace gazed at him helplessly. "We were so young then. We aren't the same people now.''

She was trembling, and so was he. The emotion between them fizzed and crackled like heat lightning, electrifying them both. It suddenly occurred to Grace that anger stirred many of the same emotions as passion. Her pulse pounded, and every cell felt quiveringly alive. Jeffrey's eyes had darkened as they did when he gazed at her naked body. His shoulders squared and his jaw tightened. The power of his physical presence made her stomach flutter and her throat grow hot.

When she realized that this moment of anger, accusation and memory was intensely arousing, Grace gasped softly. She covered trembling lips with a hand that shook, and struggled to steady her knees.

Jeffrey watched with smoldering eyes. Then he crossed to her in three long strides and caught her around the waist, pulling her against his body. When she felt the power and strength of his erection, she knew he felt the same confusing arousal that she did.

His fingers were uncharacteristically rough on her chin when he lifted her mouth to his. And then he kissed her as he had not kissed her in years. Fiercely, hungrily, a kiss that punished as well as possessed. Theirs had always been a passionately physical relationship, but the intensity of their passion ebbed and flowed as it did in any marriage. The kiss they shared now was electrifying, and seared Grace to her toes.

When their lips finally parted, they moved back slightly to stare into each other's eyes. Both were breathless and trembling.

"My God, Gracie."

Before she could reply, he kissed her again, deeply, ardently, as if he had not kissed her a thousand times before. Hairpins scattered from the knot at the nape of Grace's neck. She twined her fingers into his hair, surprised by the silky-fine texture as if she had never before caressed him there.

Frenzied, their hunger for each other intense, they kissed again and again. Their hands flew over familiar terrain, making new discoveries. Grace probed his mouth with her tongue, exalting when he groaned. Her hands traveled over his jaw, the corners of his mouth, then to his shoulders and chest. His erection throbbed through layers of clothing, his and hers, and when she touched him, his hips stiffened and he groaned and crushed her in his arms.

"Grace," he whispered in her ear, his voice thick. "Would it be wrong to...?"

In other circumstances, she would have laughed. Even now, part of Jeffery's analytical mind struggled to place a label on what was happening between them. She knew him so well, and loved him so much.

After returning another deeply erotic kiss, and struggling for breath, Grace spoke against his lips. "I don't know. I can't think. I just know that I've never wanted you so much in my life!''

It was the answer he needed to hear. Wordlessly, he lifted her in his arms and strode out of the drawing room and up the staircase. Deliberately forcing the past and the future out of her thoughts, Grace surrendered to the present. Wrapping her arms around his neck, she nipped his throat with her teeth, then covered the spot in kisses. His arms around her body were like bands of fire, holding her close to the greater flame that was his need for her and her need for him.

He placed her carefully on the spread of the old four-poster; then, without taking his eyes from her, he threw off his jacket and tie and reached for the zipper on his pants.

"Let me," Grace said, her voice husky with emotion.

With a groan, he let her open his slacks and push them to the floor. When she tasted him, the breath rushed out of his body and he swayed above her. "Gracie! Oh, God, Gracie!"

Then he pulled her roughly to her feet and his mouth burned down on hers, sucking the breath from her body and replacing it with raw animal desire. She craved him, was on fire for him. Shudders of desire shook her body and she felt an answering vibration in his.

Panting, desperate for each other, they tore off their clothing and threw the discarded items into the bars of moonlight sliding past the windowpanes. Locked in a naked embrace, they fell on the bed, thrashing and rolling, trying to press into each other and melt together. Scalding kisses grazed Grace's shoulder, nipped lightly at her breasts, slid past hips and belly and found the electric pulse of her center.

Arching to the mastery of his lips and hands, she offered herself to his expertise, and cried out with release and a pleasure that rocked her, body and mind. And then she was pulling frantically at his shoulders, guiding him on top of her, needing him inside her.

Touching his face in the darkness, finding his demanding kiss, Grace surrendered to his powerful, hard thrusts and met them with her own power and need. Their lovemaking was wild and punishing, alternating the selfishness of mindless need with flashes of familiar generosity.

What might have been a waltz they had danced before was instead a wild and erotic tango, spinning them to thrillingly new heights of inspiration and acrobatics. When the crescendo came, they clutched each other in gasping ecstasy and let the shudders of sexual pleasure overwhelm them with surprise and a strange new fulfillment.

Afterward, spent and gasping, they lay wrapped around each other's damp bodies, inhaling the lovely scents of mingled perfume, after-shave and the musky reminder of their wild lovemaking.

When Grace could speak, she pressed her damp head against his shoulder and said, "Not since that time in Italy have I... and this was even...." Words failed her. "That was... simply spectacular!"

He chuckled softly, his lips tender against her hair. "You are amazing. The sexiest woman I've ever known."

And suddenly, chillingly, Allison Ames was in bed with them. Hadn't he thought Allison Ames was sexy? Who but the sexiest woman he had ever known could have tempted him from Grace's bed?

Destructive thoughts seeped through a tiny opening and swiftly enlarged a pinprick of doubt and acid jealousy to flood-tide proportions.

Had it been like this with Jeffrey and Allison? Had they been wild and hungry for each other? Had they torn their clothing in their passionate haste to blend two bodies? Had he touched Allison the same way he touched Grace? Or had

Allison plumbed new depths, inspired new techniques, new realms of emotion?

Corrosive and desperately unwanted images overwhelmed her. She pictured her husband in the arms of another, much younger woman. "No!" she whispered, her voice raw and agonized.

She did not want to imagine Jeffrey and Allison Ames together. She couldn't bear the thought of Jeffrey looking at Allison Ames with the same powerful desire as he had looked at her. It was agony to imagine him kissing, caressing another woman.

A younger woman.

Burning with self-consciousness, Grace reached for the sheet and drew it over her body. Her cheeks flamed in the darkness that she suddenly felt grateful for. She was slender and she tried to keep fit, but she was not thirty. Her breasts and thighs were those of a mature woman. She had borne three children, the evidence revealed in faint stretch marks that she usually viewed with pride. Now those same marks, and the old scar of a hysterectomy, seemed like pale arrows pointing to the difference between her age and that of Allison Ames's.

Rolling away from Jeffrey, she stared through the darkness at the high ceiling, struggling to swim against tides of pain and self-doubt and a high wave of anger that crested through her body. She was appalled that the marks of her pregnancies had been altered, even for a moment, into imperfections that embarrassed her. She loathed the feeling that she was competing with Jeffrey's memory of a firm-skinned woman twenty years her junior. It was a competition that she could not win. Age had fixed the result eons ago.

No, she was not the sexiest woman Jeffrey had ever known. Maybe she had been once... but now? The answer whirled through her mind like a sharp blade, drawing blood. If she were the sexiest woman her husband had ever known, then he would not have left her bed and sought the arms of Allison Ames.

"Grace?" Turning, Jeffrey gently brushed a tendril of damp blond hair away from her cheek. "Did I say something to upset you?"

It was what he had not said. Yes, he'd admitted he regretted the affair. But he had not asked her forgiveness. He had not said he wanted her to come home. He had not said anything to chase the torturous images from her thoughts. Maybe there was nothing he *could* say to make her stop imagining him with Allison. But he hadn't tried. Or maybe he had tried, but they had grown so far apart during the last year that she could no longer identify his efforts or take comfort from them.

"I thought...immediately after we made love, I hoped..." She swallowed hard. "But I was wrong."

She spoke in the shorthand of long-established marriages. A stranger might have mistaken her misery and her dangling sentences as an invitation for discussion. But Jeffrey understood.

He stiffened beside her and she felt him erect a protective wall around him. The silence lengthened, and although he didn't move, Grace felt him withdrawing.

"Gracie," he said, and his voice broke her heart. "Something wonderful happened here tonight."

She was wrong. He didn't understand. He didn't have an inkling.

"I know," she whispered. "That's what makes it so unbearably sad."

Say the words, she begged him silently. Ask forgiveness. Say something that will make everything like it was before. Make me believe that you love me still, make me forget Allison Ames. Make me forget the arguments and all the ugly words we've exchanged during this past terrible year. Say something that will crack that shell of pride. Please, Jeffrey. Find the words.

Instead, he rolled away from her and swung his long legs over the side of the bed. Silently, he found his clothing in the moonlight and stepped into his slacks.

Grace turned her face away, clenching her hands beneath the sheet that covered her body. The sounds of Jeffrey dressing were as familiar as her heartbeat. She knew he hadn't buttoned his waistcoat, didn't take time to knot his tie.

When he walked to the door, she turned for a last glimpse of the only man she had ever loved. But the moonlight didn't reach his face. He stood for a moment, framed in the door, looking back at the bed.

"Have a safe trip home, Gracie," he said in a low voice. "I . . . don't forget to take your vitamins."

Once upon a time they would have laughed at her reminder.

They looked toward each other for the span of a century. Stars exploded. New universes were born. After tonight the world would be a different place.

Then, like a shadow, Jeffrey slipped away.

IN THE MORNING, Grace loaded the rental car with the boxes of mementos she would take with her on the plane. Examining the contents would help fill the long, lonely days of waiting in Nevada for a divorce she didn't want.

"Will I ever see you again, Mrs. DeWilde?" Mrs. Milton asked, her eyes glistening in the morning sunlight. Tactfully, she hadn't mentioned the untouched dinner she had lovingly prepared, only to discover that Grace and Jeffrey had forgotten all about eating.

"I hope so," Grace whispered.

She embraced Mrs. Milton and shook the hand of Mrs. Milton's son, then she slid behind the wheel of the rental car.

At the end of the driveway, she braked and gazed back at Kemberly, her Kemberly. Sunshine bathed the old stones in gold and warmed the porch steps. She knew each fireplace the chimney stacks led to, could picture each room behind the polished windows. Her gaze lingered on the corner panes of the master suite.

"Don't be silly," she said aloud. "It's just a house."

And diamonds were just rocks.

Twenty hours later, Grace stood in the living room of her condominium in San Francisco, her luggage at her feet, staring at the clean, spare lines of contemporary furniture and the high-tech gadgetry so alien to her previous surroundings. Her condominium was elegant and beautiful; it had already been featured in two magazine layouts.

But right now, her new home impressed her as sterile and unlived-in. No small wheels had ever skated across these gleaming floors. No children had bounced on the furniture or invaded the kitchen. The air smelled neutral. It didn't resonate with the memory of birthday parties or holiday celebrations. There had been no children here, no teenage tantrums. No tradition, no cherished recollections. No arguments followed by glorious reconciliations. There had been no lovemaking here.

This was not a home. This was merely where she lived now. And she could not bear it.

As tired as she was, Grace walked directly to the telephone and dialed Rita at the store.

"You must be exhausted," Rita said after they had caught up on business matters. "We didn't expect to hear from you until at least tomorrow."

Juggling the telephone, Grace shrugged out of her jacket and tossed it toward the sofa. When the jacket fell on the floor, she nodded with grim satisfaction. She badly needed to mar the elegant perfection with a bit of clutter.

"Since things seem to be doing so well at the store, I'd like you to phone the attorney who's representing me in Nevada and tell him that I'll be arriving in Las Vegas on Tuesday. Instruct him to do whatever he must to document the beginning of the residency requirement."

Rita's surprise came through the phone line. "I thought you weren't leaving for Nevada for another week."

Grace closed her eyes and pushed a hand through her hair. "There's no point in waiting any longer. Unless you think there's something at the store . . . ?"

"Nothing we can't handle. The travel agency has vacated." Grace heard the rustle of turning pages. "We can put off your interview with the new designer, or possibly she could meet you in Las Vegas . . . hmm . . . there's nothing on your schedule that can't be rearranged."

"Good. I'll depend on you to clear my commitments."

"Grace? I'm sorry," Rita said quietly. "I guess everyone hoped that . . . well, we just assumed you would see Mr. DeWilde and . . ."

"Thank you for being concerned," Grace said, tactfully evading any discussion of herself and Jeffrey. Fatigue sapped her energy and she felt the effects of jet lag and too many conflicting emotions. "I'm going to sleep for ten hours. Then I'll check in at the store, clean off my desk and take care of any loose ends. And then . . ."

And then she would catch a flight to Las Vegas, Nevada, and begin the painful process of shedding thirty-two years of her own cherished history.

It was only now that she realized she and Jeffrey had not said goodbye to each other. Maybe people in their circumstances didn't say goodbye. She didn't know. She was new at divorcing a man she loved with all her heart.

CHAPTER FOUR

IN ONE OF THE MANY articles published about Grace De-Wilde, the writer had penned: "Grace DeWilde stands as the epitome of taste, style and elegance." The writer, Grace thought with a smile, would have been as surprised as Grace herself to learn that gaudy, glittery Las Vegas charmed and captivated her from the moment she stepped into Mc-Carran Airport.

Close to the boarding areas, multicolored slot machines beckoned seductively to those looking for a first chance or a last chance. And Grace laughed aloud when she spotted tall fake palm trees on her way to collect her luggage. In a region where it would have been relatively inexpensive and convenient to pot real palm trees, it seemed outrageous and strangely charming to erect silver metal trees instead.

"Your first trip to Vegas, ma'am?" her driver asked as he loaded her luggage onto a cart.

"Yes." Even in the baggage area, people lined up to slide quarters into banks of slot machines. The electricity of high hopes energized the air; noisy laughter and excitement created a delirious din around her.

Grace had imagined she would arrive in a broad desert valley, as sere and barren as her thoughts. In a low state of mind, she had anticipated feeling in perfect sync with the silent desert landscape she had expected to find.

Las Vegas, however, was anything but silent, and certainly not somber. It was impossible not to smile at the eagerness and excited anticipation reflected on the faces around her, impossible not to feel revitalized by the collective enthusiasm generated by arriving passengers.

Still smiling, she mentioned her impressions to the driver as her limo drove away from McCarran and headed southwest toward the Toiyabe National Forest.

"Believe me, the departure gates aren't nearly as noisy or buoyant," the driver commented, smiling at her in his rearview mirror. "Las Vegas is the most exciting city in the world, no doubt about it. Whatever you're looking for, you'll find it here. But the bright lights hide a darker side, that's true too."

Grace didn't encourage further conversation. She didn't care to hear about the city's somber side, not right now. Most especially, she didn't want to hear about the sad people who came to Las Vegas to wait out the dissolution of marriages that had begun with love and bright promises of forever.

Falling silent, she gazed out a tinted window at vast expanses of silvery sagebrush rolling toward the distant Spring Mountains. Gradually the terrain climbed, and clumps of low desert trees began to emerge from the ocean of sage. Here and there she spotted magnificent homes set back from the road, surrounded by palms and greenery as unexpected as an oasis.

When the driver entered the gates of Marsha and Bill Ingram's desert estate, Grace leaned forward to inspect what would be her home for the next six weeks.

Royal palms lined the drive that ended in a brick circle before a sprawling hacienda. A red-tiled roof overhung a long, inviting veranda that shaded the front of the house, crowded with terra-cotta planters bursting with riotous blooms. Reds and yellows, blues and pinks and purples glowed in the desert sunshine. Spring came early to the desert.

As the driver wheeled the limo around the brick circle, Grace caught a quick glimpse of the tennis court behind the house and a stable situated a discreet distance from two smaller guest houses.

Since Bill Ingram was a landscape architect, it didn't surprise Grace that lush vegetation flowed back from the house, offering tantalizing glimpses of shaded brick paths that beckoned one to follow and explore.

A tightness she hadn't previously let herself recognize relaxed inside her as she slid from the limo.

"Mrs. DeWilde?"

At the sound of her name, Grace turned a smile toward a plump woman emerging from heavy double doors. "You must be Señora Valdez." Señora Valdez was exactly as Marsha had described her. Dark eyes sparkled above beautiful light brown skin, and she must have parted her salt-and-pepper hair with the aid of a ruler. A spotless apron partially concealed a crisp white blouse and turquoise skirt. "Marsha promised that you're the best cook and housekeeper in Nevada."

Señora Valdez beamed, flashing teeth as bright as white satin. "*Sí*, that is true. Welcome to Casa Ingram. If there is anything I and my sons can do to make your stay more pleasant, you have only to mention that thing and it is done."

"Thank you. Your kindness is appreciated."

The gentle sympathy in Señora Valdez's dark eyes suggested that Marsha had explained Grace's stay in Nevada. Resolutely, Grace swallowed a sudden lump that sprang into her throat. She couldn't allow a kind face and sympathetic eyes to shatter her determination to be cheerful.

Señora Valdez issued a series of commands in rapid-fire
Spanish and at once two handsome young men in their late
teens appeared to carry Grace's luggage inside the hacienda. Almost immediately the one named Carlos dropped
a cardboard box, which broke open against the bricks,
spilling books and papers. Looking up with stricken eyes,
he apologized profusely.

"No harm done," Grace said lightly, watching the limo
glide away. Through the palms she glimpsed the towers of
the Las Vegas skyline, which, she suspected, would eclipse
the Milky Way at night. She turned to Carlos with a smile
and a shrug. "Those papers have withstood attic mice and
years of neglect. I imagine they'll withstand a bump or
two."

Bending, she caught a loose page pushed along the bricks
by a puff of dry, warm wind. She was about to hand the
page to Carlos, who was collecting other loose papers, but
hesitated. Frowning, she turned the page right side up and
tried to decipher what she was seeing. Even without her
reading glasses, she noticed the page was written in a language she didn't recognize. German? Dutch?

Puzzled, she studied a flowing feminine script in faded
brown ink.

"Carlos? Wait a minute." Walking forward, Grace knelt
beside the broken carton and examined the contents. Surprise lifted her eyebrows.

She had expected this box to contain items she had kept
and cherished from her children's childhoods. With no demands on her time, she had anticipated devoting several
days to the bittersweet pleasure of examining each item, remembering why she had saved this valentine or that school
report, recalling her days as a young mother of three energetic children.

But the box contained items she had never seen before. She didn't recognize the maroon leather books, the notebooks or the loose pages filling the broken carton. Curious, she selected one of the leather books and thumbed through it. At once she suspected she was peering into someone's diary or personal journal. The color of the ink changed from page to page, but here was the same feminine script she'd found on the loose page, written in the same unknown language.

Convinced an error had occurred at the airport, Grace checked the label on the box. But there was no mistake. This was one of the boxes she had tagged for shipment in Kemberly's attic. It was she who had erred; obviously, she had tagged a box that belonged to someone else.

The mysterious maroon diaries continued to niggle at her mind as Señora Valdez gave her a tour of the hacienda. Inside, the air was pleasantly spiced by the tantalizing scent of roasting chilies and freshly baked tortillas.

Bright Indian rugs contrasted beautifully with rust-colored tile floors. The furniture was heavy Spanish Colonial, perfect against white stuccoed walls and serving as counterpoint to the heavy beams exposed overhead. All the rooms were large and airy, bright with bold primary colors and bursts of beautifully arranged greenery.

Finally, Señora Valdez led Grace to a spacious guest suite occupying the north wing of the hacienda. She was greeted by fresh flowers and a welcoming note from Marsha Ingram.

Dearest Grace,
Señora Valdez is a sweetheart. She'll mother you to death if you let her, and everyone does. Don't be shy. Open drawers, explore all the nooks and crannies, treat Casa Ingram as your own. Relax. Play some tennis,

enjoy the pool, take a horse ride into the hills. We had the car serviced for you. Enjoy.

I hope you like your surprise. (Imagine me smiling here.)

Bill sends his love. We're sorry we missed you, and sorry about the whole mess between you and Jeffrey. When a marriage like yours fails, it scares all of us. On a cheerier note, I'll phone when we return from Europe. San Fran isn't that far away. I'll fly up and we'll have a long catch-up lunch.

Love,
Marsha

Surprise? Lifting her head, Grace scanned the room. An enormous oversized bed caught her attention. And there was a mirrored vanity, a bureau, a reclining lounge. One door led into an opulent bathroom, another to a generous closet. Glass sliders opened onto a flower-strewn deck with steps dropping to the pool.

The surprise must be something she would discover later. Perhaps a special welcoming meal from Señora Valdez's gleaming kitchen.

"Are you hungry, Señora DeWilde?" Señora Valdez asked. "What time would you like dinner served?"

"I'd like to change clothes and explore the grounds a little," Grace said, considering. "And I'd like to see the box Carlos dropped. Would you ask him to put it in the library, please?" She glanced at her wristwatch. "Let's have dinner at seven-thirty, if that's agreeable." Habit was a hard thing to break.

"*Con mucho gusto, señora.*" After asking Grace if she needed assistance unpacking, Señora Valdez withdrew.

Grace gazed after her with a fond smile. She had the feeling that Señora Valdez had had to restrain herself from patting Grace's hands and clucking over her.

After inspecting her quarters, Grace kicked off her high heels and changed into linen slacks, a silk blouse and sandals. As it was early, she took her time unpacking.

An hour later she accepted a call from Walter Kennedy, her Nevada attorney, and agreed to meet with him tomorrow. She phoned Rita at the store to give her her new number. Then finally she was at liberty to explore the grounds.

The hacienda, she discovered, was built in a U shape, enclosing a courtyard patio and an Olympic-sized pool. When she bent to test the temperature, she found the water was almost as warm as a bath, and Grace promised herself an evening swim very soon.

Deserted and heated by the afternoon sun, the tennis court had less appeal. It didn't matter, since Grace doubted she would pick up a racket during her stay. Tennis was a game for two.

The most delightful surprise was the landscaping. After a few steps along one of the brick paths, Grace imagined she had entered a tropical Eden. Another path led to a shaded grotto complete with water trickling down the face of a shallow cave and falling into a silvery pool.

She laughed aloud when she discovered the cave rocks were made of extraordinarily realistic plastic. She decided Bill Ingram used his own backyard to perfect the landscape designs he created for the huge hotels she could glimpse in the shimmering distance.

The path behind the pool wound through beds of exotic cactus and delicate spring flowers, and eventually opened near a brick courtyard shared by two guest houses that appeared to be smaller versions of the main hacienda. At present, the guest houses slumbered in the afternoon sun,

lulled by the lazy drone of insects. Only the faint sound of
a television broke the pleasant silence. The Valdez family
must occupy one of the guest houses, Grace surmised.

Late in the afternoon, she returned to the main house and
entered the library. A sweating pitcher of fresh lemonade
waited on a tray near the desk, a gesture of thoughtfulness
that made her smile. And Carlos had delivered the mystery
carton, placing it in the center of a long library table.

Eyeing the box curiously, Grace satisfied her thirst, then
carried a second glass of lemonade to the library table and
opened the carton wide.

The first task was to organize the jumble inside. She removed three thick leather books, the journals or whatever
they were, and laid them to one side. Next she took from the
box what she had originally thought was a notebook of
some sort, but now saw was a bound typewritten manuscript. The loose paper she sorted into two piles, one containing pages in the faded brown ink, and the other, pages
that had worked loose from the manuscript.

"Now then, what do we have here?"

Taking a seat, she examined one of the maroon leather
books. Yes, she decided, it was definitely a diary, as the entries were organized around dates. Her eyebrows lifted when
she located the first entry. It was dated 1870. Curious, she
inspected the other two books to find the date of the last
entry.

"Good heavens!" The diaries spanned seventy-two years.

Her mind raced. Could the diaries have been left behind
by a member of Baron Kemberly's family? A treasure forgotten in the vast attic spaces? She frowned, thinking it
through. No, the diaries couldn't belong to Baron Kemberly's family. Max and Genevieve DeWilde had purchased
Kemberly in the thirties; the owner of the diaries had writ-

ten her last entry in 1942, long after Baron Kemberly's family had faded into obscurity.

Engaged by the mystery, Grace pulled the heavy manuscript in front of her. Impatiently, she flipped past some introductory pages, then smothered a gasp as she read the first paragraph of text.

June 14, 1870. Today is my wedding day! At seven this evening, I will marry my handsome, my darling, my beloved Maximilien. The bells of the Nieuwe Kerk will ring out our joy!

"Good Lord!" Stunned, Grace fell backward in her chair, her eyes wide.

This was the diary of Anne Marie DeWilde, Jeffrey's great-grandmother. A private journal written by the woman whose engagement ring Grace now wore. She glanced at the sparkling sapphire surrounded by diamonds, then stared again at the books and papers before her.

She still hadn't recovered from her surprise when she read the letter tucked inside the manuscript's cover.

The letter was addressed to Mary DeWilde, Jeffrey's mother, and it confirmed that the manuscript was a translation of diaries written by Anne Marie DeWilde. In his letter, the translator agreed with Mary DeWilde that additional volumes must have existed and expressed his regret that only three of the diaries had survived.

Grace replaced the letter inside the manuscript cover and frowned again, puzzled. Rising, she poured another lemonade and wandered to the French doors that opened into the courtyard and pool area.

In three decades, she had never heard so much as a hint that Anne Marie had kept a diary, or that part of it still existed. She strongly suspected that Jeffrey had no idea that his great-grandmother had left a record of her life. He absolutely would have mentioned it if he'd known.

Why didn't he know? Why had Mary DeWilde kept such a rare treasure secret?

One of the first things Grace had learned upon marrying Jeffrey was that his was a proud and far-flung family who wore the DeWilde name like a crown. It was no accident that the attic at Kemberly was crowded. The DeWildes possessed a keen appreciation for their own history. They revered the family's past and present accomplishments, refused to part with items acquired by earlier DeWildes. Over the years, Grace too had absorbed the pride of being a member of the powerful, prominent DeWilde family.

As their father had before them, her children had grown up hearing, "That isn't the DeWilde way." "Remember...you're a DeWilde." "Retailing is in your genes." "DeWildes have an eye for fine gems." And so on.

Anne Marie's diary should have been the DeWildes' equivalent of the Bible. Copies should have been made and sent to DeWildes in every corner of the globe.

Grace turned to stare back at the papers covering the library table.

Why hadn't it happened that way? Why on earth would Jeffrey's mother have had the diaries translated, then conceal information every DeWilde would give the earth to read?

Her eyes widened and her long fingers tightened around the lemonade glass.

There was something in the diaries that Mary DeWilde did not want the family to learn. This was the only logical answer.

And now, Grace realized, she faced a dilemma. Slowly she returned to the library table and stood looking down at Anne Marie's diaries.

Of all the people who might have found these diaries, she had the least right to read them. She, who was leaving the family.

She should package everything up right now and mail the carton to Jeffrey. If anyone had the right to know the history of his forebears, it was Jeffrey, head of the family. Or she could send the carton to New York City, to Mary DeWilde.

But the portrait of young Anne Marie DeWilde that hung above the drawing room mantel at Kemberly rose in her memory, along with a rush of curiosity.

Grace absently turned Anne Marie's engagement ring on her finger and thought about the long, empty days stretching in front of her.

"Curiosity killed the cat," she murmured, lifting one of the diaries in her hands. Anne Marie had held this diary. She had recorded her wedding and her days as a young bride within these pages.

A long sigh lifted Grace's chest. "I'm a dead cat," she said with a humorless smile.

Her curiosity had been piqued, and she had six weeks of unaccustomed idleness opening before her. Unless something earthshaking occurred, she could begin reading the translation tonight after dinner.

She had forgotten Marsha Ingram's surprise.

SEÑORA VALDEZ SERVED dinner in a dining room the size of one of Grace's in-store boutiques. If there was anything worse than dining alone, Grace decided glumly, it was dining alone in a room designed to accommodate a large party. Unless she wanted to thoroughly depress herself every evening, she would have to consult with Señora Valdez on alternative arrangements.

After praising a meal genuinely fit for a queen, Grace pulled on a sweater and carried a fragrant cup of coffee outside to the courtyard chairs beside the pool.

Underwater lights made the pool glisten like polished turquoise. Hidden beams artfully illuminated palm fronds and ferns, creating a dense tropical illusion. It was hard to remember that a large, dry desert lay but a few hundred yards away.

A sigh whispered between Grace's lips.

Romantic settings were wasted on a woman trying to adjust to a solitary life. And not adjusting very well, she suspected, if she were honest with herself.

The past months had been frantically busy arranging the financing for Grace, scouting locations, meeting with contractors and designers, interviewing personnel, ordering merchandise, attending to the thousands of small details that would contribute to a successful launch.

But even in the midst of chaos, there had been small warning signs that eventually she would have to face her altered status.

The time of truth had arrived.

Grace stared up at the desert stars and realized she would dine alone most evenings from now on. It would be a long, long time, if ever, before she woke up with a head on the pillow beside her. And the thing she missed most, the thing that carved a hole in her psyche, was that there was no longer anyone in her life who truly cared about sharing the small events of her day. No one to tell her small triumphs to, no one with whom to share the ups and downs of daily life.

Her children, Kate and Megan especially, were interested in her life, of course. But only the broad strokes. They were involved in their own busy lives. Why would they want to hear about Grace closing the in-store travel agency or discuss other possible uses for that space? And she wouldn't dream of bothering them with personal concerns, wouldn't confess that she hated to dine alone or that she couldn't imagine taking a vacation by herself.

What did single people do when they wanted a vacation? Or when they wished to attend something as simple as a museum opening or a film? Or if they wished to sample a new restaurant? And how did single people handle couple events? Would she be expected to invite a man to escort her to a charity function, for instance?

Ask a man for a date? Grace shrank in her chair and shuddered. She couldn't conceive of doing such a thing. Even if she knew how one approached such a dismal task, her pride wouldn't allow her to ask a man to escort her.

Thank heaven for a sense of humor. It suddenly struck her as hilarious that here she sat, a mature woman cringing at the thought of telephoning a male, something teenage girls managed to do as a matter of course. Grace herself phoned men every day at the store and charmed them into doing exactly what she wanted them to do. It occurred to her that most of her friends would scoff at her dilemma. They would insist that if Grace DeWilde couldn't charm a man into thinking it was his idea to be her escort, then the man was hopeless.

She laughed aloud.

"I would recognize that laugh anywhere in the world."

Grace started, then sprang to her feet, straining to see into the dark foliage beyond the pool. "Ian?" she called uncertainly. It couldn't be. But even before he walked into the light, she recognized his thatch of silver hair and loose confident stride.

"Ian Stanley! It *is* you!"

Delighted, Grace ran around the pool and threw herself into Ian's outstretched arms. She embraced him and kissed both cheeks, then leaned back in his arms to return his grin with a radiant smile.

"Ian, I don't believe it! What are you doing here?"

Taking her arm, he pressed it against his side and led her back into the courtyard. "Didn't Marsha tell you that I'm using one of the guest houses?" Blue eyes twinkled down at her.

"She didn't say a word, not even a hint! Oh—wait a minute. You're the surprise!" Grace laughed. "Your sister left a note promising... but if you're staying in one of the guest houses, why didn't you appear earlier?"

"I wanted to give you a chance to settle in."

They took chairs facing the turquoise pool and smiled at Señora Valdez, who wheeled out a cocktail cart. "You were in on this," Grace said, still laughing.

"Señor Stanley, he say you two are old friends. He want to surprise you." Señora Valdez beamed at Grace's flushed cheeks and Ian's smile.

"Usually I don't care for surprises, but this is wonderful! I've known Marsha's rascally brother for... how long?"

Ian sucked in his cheeks and gazed up at the velvety night. "I don't know. I only remember that I met you on a Saturday night at eight-forty-six at a boring party hosted by Evelyn and Rad Cornish. You were pregnant with the twins at the time, wearing a green velvet maternity dress that made your skin look like porcelain. I first saw you standing beside Evelyn's Christmas tree, smiling like the Mona Lisa. I thought you were the blondest, most radiant, most beautiful woman I'd ever seen."

"The 'blondest'?" Grace repeated after a burst of laughter.

Light gleamed in his silver hair when he nodded. "Then I learned your name was Grace, and all I could think of was

Grace Kelly. You looked like her, carried yourself like her, at first I thought you were her.''

Grace softened a glare by affectionately squeezing his arm. ''You know I hate being compared to Grace Kelly. All my life people have told me that I look like Grace Kelly.'' She laughed again. ''And we did *not* meet at Evelyn and Rad Cornish's party during the Christmas I was pregnant. You were Jeffrey's best man at our wedding! Or have you forgotten about almost losing the ring?''

''Whoa.'' He blinked in mock astonishment. ''Are you telling me that *you* were that gorgeous blond princess who took pity on Jeffrey and married him? You'd think I'd remember that.''

Shaking his head and grinning, Ian rose to fix drinks, and Grace noticed that Señora Valdez had discreetly vanished. Ian gave her a Scotch and water, then bowed from the waist before he returned to his chair beside her.

''I'm sorry, darling, but you *do* look like Princess Grace.''

Grace tossed her hair with a gesture of exaggerated exasperation, then smiled. ''Enough of this nonsense. Tell me what you're doing here, how long you'll be staying, everything!''

''First—'' he touched his glass to hers ''—to the most beautiful woman in the civilized world.''

''To dear friends,'' Grace murmured. Grateful tears gathered behind her eyes. She was so glad to see a familiar face.

''God, I love your voice. If your store fails, you can always find work with one of those telephone porn lines. They'd pay real wages to get a sexy-voiced dish like you.''

Grace burst out laughing. ''You're as outrageous as ever!'' Fondness glistened in her eyes. ''Oh, Ian. You don't know how glad I am to see you. I can't remember the last time I really laughed.'' Reaching across the small table between them, she took his hand. "Now, are you going to tell me why you're here, or do I have to wheedle it out of you?"

"The bank is putting together a deal on a large gypsum mine about fifty miles east of here. I'm representing the buyer, a very careful Swiss." He shrugged. "It's standard stuff, actually. Verifying the books, checking management, taking a look at the operation. I'll be here another six weeks."

Grace studied his handsome face. "Standard stuff, huh? Then why is the CEO of Deuxville et Cie verifying books, checking management and so on? Why are you here instead of assigning this to some ambitious young turk who isn't light-years beyond this type of scut work?"

"Maybe I heard that a friend who needs a little support would be in the area...."

Grace stared and tears sprang into her eyes. "Oh, Ian," she whispered. How had he guessed that her supporters were few and far between, or that she had never felt this alone in her life? If ever she had needed the comfort of an old friend, now was the time.

"I'm sorry, Grace," he said softly, reaching again to take her hand. "Jeffrey treated you wrong."

Her body stiffened, and she withdrew her hand, gazing steadily at the pool. "You know about...?"

He tasted his drink and nodded. "It happened by accident. I ran into Jeffrey and Allison in Paris. Very awkward." He sighed. "Jeffrey and I had drinks the following night. He said he'd broken it off and planned to tell you about her."

"I found out from someone else. A friend who decided to tell me 'for my own good.'" She couldn't help a hint of bitterness. "I didn't believe it," she continued after a minute. "There are moments when I still don't believe all of this has happened to us." Lifting her head, she gazed up at the cool desert night. "I don't know exactly how I came to be here."

"If it's any comfort, very few people know about Jeffrey's affair. There are rumors, of course, but most are mere speculation in an effort to explain the collapse of a marriage everyone thought was solid and would endure forever."

"I thought so, too," Grace said quietly, blinking at the pool.

"How are the kids taking it?"

"Not well," she admitted after a pause. "Especially the twins. Megan is in Paris, busy with the store. Gabe..." Briefly she closed her eyes. "Gabe and Lianne are expecting their first child. They don't know about Jeffrey's affair, of course. They blame me for everything. Gabe more so than Megan. They're confused and angry. On the surface, it appears that I left their father for no reason."

"And Kate?"

"I thought I'd see more of Kate now that we're living in the same area. But the medical profession doesn't give her a minute to call her own. We frequently speak on the phone. She's trying to keep an open mind, but it's difficult for her." Grace touched her fingertips to her forehead. "It's difficult for all of us."

"It's just like you to protect Jeffrey and let everyone blame you," Ian said, gazing into his drink. "But is that wise? Don't your children deserve to know what happened?"

"I continue to struggle with that question," Grace finally admitted. "But as long as there's the smallest hope for a reconciliation, I'd rather our children didn't know their father had an affair."

Ian gazed at her. "Is there hope for a reconciliation?"

"There's always hope. But it's getting dimmer." Grace looked around her, then managed a small smile. "If I truly believed Jeffrey and I could patch up our marriage, I wouldn't be here."

They sat in companionable silence, listening to the sounds of Señora Valdez moving around the kitchen inside the house, and to the lulling thrum of frogs conversing beyond the pool area.

"An affair doesn't happen in a vacuum," Grace said, picking up the conversation as if there had been no pause. "Marriages break apart gradually, crumbling along the fault lines of small wounds."

Raising her head, she studied the lights shining on leathery palm fronds. "I'm as much to blame as Jeffrey. I didn't have an affair, but I'm guilty of complacency, of taking Jeffrey and our marriage for granted. I thought we were strong enough to be utterly truthful with each other. In retrospect, I'm not sure any marriage can withstand absolute truth."

"None of my marriages could, that's for certain."

Grace laughed, and her blue eyes sparkled mischievously. "You just haven't found the right woman, Ian. But I admire your optimism. You keep trying."

"I found the right woman thirty-three years ago," he said softly, looking into her eyes. "Unfortunately, my best friend married her."

CHAPTER FIVE

IT WAS POSSIBLE that Ian's lavish compliments were nothing more than an effort to cheer her, Grace decided as she washed her face and prepared for bed. But there had been a moment beside the pool when they had looked at each other and seen not old friends but an attractive man and a desirable woman. Such awareness of a man other than Jeffrey had not happened to Grace since she was nineteen, and she was not entirely comfortable seeing Ian as an attractive and stimulating man instead of ... well, just Ian, one of her dearest friends.

Because she equated physical stirrings solely with Jeffrey, she had excused herself shortly after a second drink, needing time alone to sort out unexpected and confusing feelings.

"Which you are not doing," she chided her image in the mirror above the vanity sink. "You're avoiding the issue, and that isn't like you."

Suddenly critical, she stared at her reflection, at a face scrubbed free of makeup.

Her skin was still good, she decided, trying to be harshly objective. The pores were tight, the color glowing and vibrant. Leaning forward, she studied her eyes. They were a clear, keen blue, fringed by thick blond lashes. But fine lines radiated from the corners. She conceded lines were to be expected at her age, but no woman welcomed the inevitable arrival of wrinkles.

She frowned, then immediately noticed the lines between her brows and smoothed her forehead. The frown lines were faint, thank heavens, as were the lines beginning to appear between her nose and mouth. But she could glimpse the future. Damn. Her lips were getting thinner, she thought. Or were they?

She sighed as she reached for her toothbrush.

A woman starting life over needed all the assets she could garner. But Grace was fifty-two. She couldn't hope to defy age forever. She had started to touch up her hair two years ago, and it required longer to apply makeup than it had ten years ago. Middle age tapped at the window.

All in all, she supposed she was holding her own, but how did one know?

Before her life shattered around her, she had never thought about aging, hadn't taken time to notice that it was happening to her. Oh, there was the annoyance of needing glasses to read fine print, and the appearance of a few gray hairs. But she exercised and ate properly. She was healthy and energetic. She still photographed well.

Since her self-confidence was not based on beauty, she had not expected to worry about aging. And she wouldn't have, if her marriage to Jeffrey had survived. They tended to see each other as they always had, as two vital energetic people with mutual physical appeal. They joked about the small changes that came with growing older.

But now she was starting life over, and that changed everything.

That tingling moment beside the pool with Ian brought forth an idea both disturbing and confusing. Possibly there could be another man in her life. Not just an escort to an opening or a ball, but a man who might be important in her life.

Grace paused with her toothbrush midway to her lips. The possibility stunned her. A man in her life who wasn't Jeffrey? A man whose habits she didn't know? Whose kiss and touch would be unfamiliar?

A flicker of panic widened her eyes, and she fled to the bed in the adjoining room. Immediately, she felt small and lost on the oversized mattress. Irritated, she moved to the very center of the bed. After five minutes of feeling foolish, she sighed and returned to her side. Her side, because thirty-two years ago Jeffrey DeWilde had mentioned that he preferred the left side of the bed.

What if she met a new man and things progressed and it developed that he preferred the right side of the bed? Could she change a thirty-two-year-old habit? Would they argue about it?

Groaning softly, Grace pressed her fingertips to her temples. This was not productive thinking. She didn't want to worry about other men or aging or sides of the bed or think about why she was sleeping in a strange house near Las Vegas, Nevada.

Flinging back the sheets, she slid out of bed and looked around, desperate for something to distract her thoughts. When she remembered Anne Marie's diaries, she sighed with relief, then pulled on a robe and retrieved the translation from the library.

After finding her reading glasses, which never seemed to be where she was, she punched up the pillows and settled in to read about someone else's life. Within minutes, she was totally absorbed in a story that had taken place almost one hundred and thirty years ago.

June 14, 1870. Today is my wedding day! At seven this evening, I will marry my handsome, my darling, my beloved Maximilien. The bells of the Nieuwe Kerk will ring out our joy!

Mama says I am too young at fifteen to choose a husband, but I knew from the first moment when Maximilien entered Papa's shop that I would never love another. Oh, Maximilien! I gazed into your blue eyes and I saw my future in your smile!

Poor Papa! If Papa had his way, I would be marrying his old friend, a jeweler named Jan de Graf. Papa says the DeWildes are new to diamonds, mere upstarts; they have been in the field only eighty years. Papa says De Graf is not as comfortably situated as the DeWildes (which means the DeWildes have more money), but De Graf is more settled (which means he is as old as Papa, forty years, at least) and he is an Alderman, which no DeWilde has yet been (which means De Graf speaks of boring things such as city politics).

Maximilien and I have such plans! Maximilien says DeWilde creations will be remembered long after De Graf's uninspired baubles have been forgotten! I am certain that Maximilien is correct! The ring we designed together flashes and twinkles as I write these words, the most beautiful ring ever created!

Now that Maximilien has completed his apprenticeship, we intend to open a shop of our own above the old Corn Exchange. We will combine my knowledge of cutting, learned at my dear papa's side, with Maximilien's skill in buying and selling. To think I shall work beside my husband! My husband! Maximilien says we shall found a DeWilde dynasty, a large family of powerful and influential diamond merchants. Someday, all of Europe will sparkle with DeWilde creations, and then Papa will not mutter in his ale about Jan de Graf. I think my dear Maximilien is jealous of old De Graf! They stare at each other and barely exchange nods

when they encounter each other at the Dam. It's so silly
and so amusing. As if I would ever, ever, ever, ever look
at another man!

Oh, Maximilien, my love, my heart. We will be so
happy together in our snug little home by the canal! I
must remember to thank your father again for giving
us such a fine house, and especially to praise the work-
manship on the gables. And you must remember to
thank Papa again for sending us to Italy on our wedding trip.

I dare to hope that we shall bring home a special re-
membrance of our time in Italy!

Grace smiled and adjusted her reading glasses. The first
entry was exuberant with exclamation points, vibrant with
the love between two young people enamored of each other
and filled with dreams for the future. Still smiling, she
touched a fingertip to the ring on her finger, Anne Marie's
ring. Grace had not known that Anne Marie and Maximilien designed it together. She wished Anne Marie could know
that her ring was still in the family, still worn by a DeWilde
bride. And she wished Maximilien could know that his prediction was correct. As far as Grace knew, the De Graf name
had faded to obscurity while the DeWilde name had climbed
to international fame.

August 20, 1870. Italy was beautiful and almost as
wonderful as my husband! We found inspiration
enough to last us a lifetime in Rome, were charmed by
Florence, and made sick for home in Venice. After
Venice we were happy to return to our own canals,
though most of our friends had departed for summer
homes on the Zuider Zee. Maximilien says we will have
a summer home someday, too, only ours will be on the

Amstel to the south of the city. Maximilien says the Amstel is more fashionable.

I am so happy to be in our new home! As the lots in Amsterdam are but twenty feet wide, our house is narrow but tall. We have three stories. The front is brick clad in sandstone, and our stoop is the whitest on our street! Our kitchen is at street level, convenient for throwing slops into the canal, and we sleep on the third floor where we might catch any cool breeze that comes our way.

We are both disappointed that a certain hoped-for event did not happen, but Mama laughed and said it is much, much too soon to feel discouraged. We are young, there is plenty of time.

Maximilien's dear friend, and now mine, Martin Vanderhaden, helped us set up our shop above the old Corn Exchange. It was a merry occasion! We drank bottles of Flemish wine and bought sausages from the noisy merchants downstairs, and I danced with Maximilien and Martin until my head was dizzy. Maximilien filled my lap with the diamonds that will begin our venture, and Martin sprinkled them in my hair. They declared I was the prettiest bride in the kingdom and continued such foolishness until my face was on fire with pleasure and I begged them to stop.

Afterward, we had supper at our house, then Martin played the piano for us. I have never heard anyone play as well! Maximilien says Martin's beautiful hazel eyes are so sad because he wished to make music his profession but his father insisted that he join his brothers at the family bank. Maximilien says that Martin has a wonderful head for figures and will be successful despite his preference for music. Maximilien says I draw Martin out as no one else does. He says he has never seen Martin so animated and happy as when he is with us for an evening.

Tomorrow we begin our first day at the new shop! Since Italy, my small head has been swimming with ideas for brooches, rings, bracelets, necklaces. But Maximilien says we must begin with what we know. He will buy the diamonds and I will cut them and then Maximilien will sell them again. First we establish ourselves as merchants. We build our name and a secure future, then we will venture into design. I came home from Italy with a half-dozen notebooks filled with ideas for that happy day!

Grace felt a ripple run up her spine. She was reading of the very beginnings of the DeWilde empire. Wishing she weren't so tired that the words had begun to blur on the page, she tried to imagine Anne Marie with diamonds filling her lap and sparkling in her dark hair, her eyes shining with dreams and happiness.

Grace fell asleep with a smile on her lips, wondering if, as a young bride, she had begun nearly every sentence by saying, "Jeffrey says..."

WALTER KENNEDY'S craggy good looks reminded Grace of the late Richard Burton. Although they had spoken on the telephone countless times, this was the first time she had actually met her Nevada attorney, the attorney who would present her divorce petition in court.

Walter escorted her to his office personally rather than delegate the duty to one of his secretaries, a gesture Grace appreciated. And he chose to conduct their first in-person interview across a coffee table instead of at his desk.

"You look like—"

Grace raised a hand. "If you say Grace Kelly..."

"Your photographs," he finished with a grin.

"Thank you." A smile touched her lips as she lifted a china teacup. "Is there anything new that I should be aware of?"

Leaning toward the coffee table, he opened a thick file. "A few items are still in negotiation, but the major points have been settled. At this time, I don't foresee any reason for a delay. Therefore, I've scheduled court time for the day after your residency requirement is fulfilled."

"Has Jeffrey withdrawn his insistence that I sell my block of DeWilde stock—if I decide to sell—only to a member of the family?"

Walter Kennedy laughed and gazed at her with a smile of admiration. "You were absolutely right on this one. The minute we came back with a demand for a seat on the board of directors, Mr. DeWilde backed off."

"I don't wish to have a seat on the board. It's cleaner if I sever all ties with the DeWilde Corporation."

"You and I know how you feel, but the other side doesn't. And the fact is, the size of your stock holding entitles you to a board seat." He glanced at his notes. "Mr. DeWilde would like a first option to buy if you decide to sell your DeWilde stock, but he's no longer attempting to place restrictions on any sale. In return, we will not insist on a board seat."

Grace considered. "That seems fair. I'll agree to a first option."

Walter leaned back against the sofa cushions and studied her, making Grace glad that she'd worn the slim Dior silk suit. "That stock gives you a lot of leverage. A block sale could affect the composition of the DeWilde board of directors, the price of the shares...." He shrugged. "How bloodthirsty are you?"

Grace's expression cooled. "I thought I'd made my position clear, Walter. This divorce is to be as amicable as circumstances allow."

"Many divorces begin with an intention to be gentle, but few end that way. My obligation is to protect your interests, not Mr. DeWilde's. In this instance, I wish to bring to your attention that as long as you hold a sizable portion of DeWilde stock, you have a whip to crack."

"I'm well aware of that."

"On another subject, I've received a fax stating that you've relinquished any claim to Kemberly. Is that correct?"

"Yes," she said, reaching out to place her teacup on the coffee table.

"There's no reason for you to do this. You've given Mr. DeWilde the flat in Chelsea. You've given him all furnishings." He spread his hands. "May I remind you that you're the injured party, Grace? Kemberly was your home. You're entitled to keep it."

Kemberly rose in her thoughts with painful clarity. It would be so easy to waver.

She drew a bracing breath. "I intend to make my home in San Francisco. My brother and niece are there. My daughter Kate is there. The new store is there." She shook her head. "It doesn't make sense for me to keep Kemberly. It's been in Jeffrey's family for three generations."

Frustration drew Walter Kennedy's brows together. "You're giving away the farm, Grace."

She met his eyes. "I don't want thirty-two years to end in quibbling over who gets the silverware or who gets the Chippendale in the library."

"A laudable attitude, but we're not talking about a penny-ante item. Kemberly represents a considerable amount of money. At least let me insist that Mr. DeWilde buy your share of the estate.''

''That wasn't my agreement with Jeffrey.'' Before he could express the exasperation she saw building in his expression, Grace continued. ''No amount of money will compensate for the loss of Kemberly,'' she said softly. ''But it will give me pleasure to know my children and future grandchildren will continue to use Kemberly on weekends and holidays.''

''As well as Mr. DeWilde.''

''It's his home, too, Walter. Please, I feel as if I'm fighting enough battles already. Let's not you and I argue. I ask that you respect my wishes on this issue.''

''You're a remarkable woman,'' Walter commented an hour later after they concluded their discussion. He walked with her to the door of his office. ''Mr. DeWilde is not going to be one of those men who can claim his wife took him to the cleaners. I don't understand everything you're doing, Grace, and I don't agree with much of it. But I greatly admire the way you're handling a difficult and painful time in your life.''

Walter's comments remained with her as Grace left his office building and emerged into the bright, crisp sunshine. It struck her as a sad commentary on society when fairness and dignity were so uncommon as to merit praise.

An insistent honking caught her attention, and she glanced toward the street, her glum expression relaxing into a smile as Ian Stanley leaned from the window of a rented Lincoln.

''I had a leggy show girl lined up as a lunch date, but she canceled, the cheeky wench. Care to save me from the embarrassment of eating a fancy lunch alone?''

Grace walked over and bent down to the car window. ''I drove Marsha's car.''

"We'll come back for it."

"Frankly, Ian, I'd better take a rain check. I'm not sure I'd be good company right now."

Ian covered her hand and spoke in a low tone. "Did it get rough?"

"I don't know how you've endured this three times. I suspect Jeffrey and I weren't nearly sympathetic enough."

"Have lunch with me, Grace. I'll regale you with tales from the divorce wars." Ian's blue eyes twinkled up at her. "Hear how Ian Stanley, that paragon of male virtue, was battered by female outrage. Learn how to outwit wily attorneys. Thrill to the excitement of court dates and alimony demands. The crab Louie is a fringe benefit, as is a great bottle of Montrachet. Get in this car, Grace DeWilde. You're blocking traffic. Plus, the sight of your delectable fanny bending toward this window has already nearly caused two car crashes."

Grace laughed, charmed by Ian's outrageous appeal. When confronted by the cool elegance she projected, most of the people in her world either found her unapproachable or treated her with varying degrees of formality. Ian, on the other hand, had always teased her on an earthy level that secretly delighted her.

Giving in, she slid into the passenger seat beside him, buckled the belt, then smiled. "I'm a poor substitute for a leggy show girl, but I'll do what I can to save you from the humiliation of lunching alone. Where are we going, by the way?"

Leaning over the steering wheel, he studied her legs. "Short, but not bad." Laughing, he pulled into traffic. "I'm taking you to Caesar's, out on the strip. There's a terrific restaurant upstairs. Great shopping, too, or so I'm told. And if you're in the mood, we can stop by a roulette table

and put a fiver on your date of emancipation. Do you know
when it will be?''

"April 17 is the court date.''

"Seventeen. One of my lucky numbers. I think we'll up
the ante, put ten dollars straight up. What do you think?''

He would have said the same thing no matter what date
Grace mentioned. She smoothed her palms over her skirt
and swallowed a lump in her throat. "Ian? Thank you. I'm
beginning to realize I was foolish to think I could get
through this alone.''

He gave her a look of alarm. "You aren't going to go
weepy on me, are you, darling? I've only seen you cry once,
when your mother died, but frankly, it was horrifying. Your
eyes got all puffy and red, your nose ran, you made awful
little sounds. You left a trail of soggy handkerchiefs all over
Kemberly.''

"Stop,'' Grace protested, laughing. "After that descrip-
tion, I'll never cry again!'' She studied his handsome profile. "I'd forgotten that you were at Kemberly when we
received the call about my mother.''

"Oh, great. Now you're telling me that I'm forgettable.''
He patted her hand. "The truth is, I've been there for most
of the big events in your life, Grace.''

She sat very still, considering his comment. Ian had been
Jeffrey's best man at their wedding. He had waited with
Jeffrey when the twins were born, and again when Kate
came into the world. He had visited the hospital when she
had the hysterectomy. And he'd appeared with champagne
to celebrate most of her business triumphs. He had thrown
her a party for every birthday with a zero in it. Now he was
here to support her through the end of the marriage he had
helped to launch.

And all she could think to say was, "You weren't at the
grand opening for Grace.''

"Only because I was in hospital."

Grace stiffened and turned sharply to face him. "Why didn't you tell me you were in the hospital?"

"I didn't tell you because, knowing you, you would have flown to Paris and delayed your grand opening."

"You're damned right I would have! Why were you in the hospital?"

Mammoth hotels rose from the desert floor on both sides of the traffic-clogged street. Amazing structures that replicated a castle and an Egyptian pyramid. But Grace didn't see them.

She stared at him. "Ian?"

"It turned out to be nothing, really. But the cheeky doctors insisted on doing tests immediately, and I had to miss your opening."

"You sent enough flowers to almost bury my office. If I'd known you were in the hospital, I would have sent a few back to you. Ian, I'm upset that you didn't let me know."

He braked at a stoplight and watched a crowd of pedestrians dash across the intersection.

"It was nothing, darling, really. Look at me. I'm in the pink, the very picture of health."

Eyes sharp, Grace studied his tanned face and lively gaze before she began to relax. "You do look exceptionally well."

And exceedingly handsome. Silver-white hair contrasted wonderfully with his sun-dark face and cobalt eyes. Laughter and a lot of living had carved fans at the corners of his eyes, had deepened the interesting lines that ran vertically down his cheeks. He still had the dimple that had made her laugh when she first met him. It added a mischievous quality to his smile.

"You've lost weight since I saw you last," Grace commented.

"Not an ounce of fat on this body," he said proudly, winking at her as he turned past the fountain bubbling in front of Caesar's Palace. "You're probably thinking, The man is an Adonis. How does he do it?"

Grace grinned at him. "That's exactly what I was thinking."

He placed a hand on his chest and gave her a look of choirboy innocence. "Righteous living, my dear. All things in moderation."

"Ian Stanley, you have never done anything with moderation in your entire life!"

Grace was still laughing when the valet opened her car door. Ian took her arm and escorted her into the largest, noisiest casino she had ever seen.

"A bit different from the casinos in Europe," Ian commented, leading her through flashing lanes of slot machines, rows and rows of card tables, roulette wheels, crowded craps tables.

"I've never understood this kind of gambling," Grace commented when they paused beside a roped-off section reserved for baccarat players. Her eyes followed a long-haired cocktail waitress dressed in a thigh-high silk toga and wearing sandals that laced up her shapely calves. "This is an amazing place!"

Statues of Roman gods towered over a splashing fountain. Grace felt positive that the eyes of the statues followed her.

"They come to life every hour," Ian explained, grinning at her expression. "We'll come back to watch."

Ian led her to the elevators, and five minutes later they were seated in a restaurant as opulent as any Grace had seen.

"Scotch and soda for me, Scotch and water for the lady, no ice," Ian said to the waiter.

"You don't forget a thing, do you," Grace said fondly.

"Not about you, darling." When their drinks arrived, he toasted her then took her hand. "Now. How are you bearing up, really?"

Grace thought about it. "I feel numb," she said finally. "Sometimes I'm so angry that I can't concentrate. Other times I feel as if I'm hollow inside, that pain and sadness have carved a hole in my chest. Then the numbness sets in, and it's as if someone else is talking to the lawyers and trying to tactfully evade the questions of confused friends. Does that make sense?"

Ian nodded, idly rubbing his thumb over Anne Marie's diamond-and-sapphire engagement ring. "It's always easier for the person who wants the divorce." He looked into her eyes. "You don't want this divorce, do you, Grace?"

"No," she whispered, gently withdrawing her hand. "Oddly, I don't really think Jeffrey wants it, either. We're just . . . caught in something that neither of us can stop. It's gone too far."

Ian stretched an arm along the back of the banquette, letting his fingertips rest lightly on her shoulder. "You know, I kept waiting for you to phone me after you left London for the States."

A flush brightened Grace's cheeks. "I decided to make my home in San Francisco for many reasons, Ian. I grew up there. . . ." She let her voice trail. "One of the reasons was the hope that if I left England, I wouldn't force our friends to choose sides. I've always hated that." She glanced at him. "I told myself that I wasn't going to lose touch with Caroline, Marla and Diane—I liked all of your ex-wives—but eventually, of course, I stopped inviting them to parties rather than cause any awkwardness for you."

"So you hoped to spare me the painful task of choosing between you and Jeffrey?"

"I'd like to think our friends can continue to accept us both without feeling they have to choose sides."

"I knew which side I was on the minute I saw Jeffrey head-to-head with a woman young enough to be his daughter," Ian said sharply.

Distress darkened Grace's eyes. "You and Jeffrey have been good friends for forty years. He couldn't be fonder of you if you were his brother. Please, Ian. Don't judge too harshly. You of all people must know that it takes two people to make a marriage successful, and it takes two people to destroy a marriage."

Ian might have been better able to understand if Grace could have explained her role in the drama that had led Jeffrey to betray their vows. But some things were too private to share even with the best of friends. If Jeffrey wished to confide the insecurity that Grace had triggered, that was his choice. A lifetime of loyalty prevented her from doing so.

"Grace—" Ian gently stroked his fingertips along the curve of her jawline "—occasionally even longtime friends do something that cannot be forgiven. I can't forgive Jeffrey for hurting you. He and I will never again be close."

Grace stared at him. "Oh, Ian. I'm sorry. That will be a great loss for Jeffrey. For both of you."

Suddenly it occurred to her that it would surprise and possibly wound Jeffrey if he knew that Ian was here with her now. He and Ian had attended school together, and university. Ian and Jeffrey had been close long before Grace met either of them.

Ian must have read something of what she was thinking when he looked into her eyes.

"Years ago I told myself that if Grace Powell DeWilde was ever single again, I would move the earth to make her mine." His gaze traveled over her wide-eyed expression.

"Grace...don't you know that I've been in love with you for more than thirty years?"

She hadn't known. She hadn't had even a suspicion. When he mentioned his affection, she had believed he was teasing her, heaping on compliments as a form of gallantry and friendship.

"I love you, Grace. I always have. I always will."

CHAPTER SIX

June 16, 1871. Martin gave us a party to celebrate our first anniversary. Martin's gift to Maximilien was a portrait of me. For weeks I had to invent excuses to make time for the sittings. I wore my wedding gown for the portrait and everyone praised the likeness.

Maximilien gave me a small, exquisite gold brooch! It's heart-shaped with a diamond at the point of the heart and also at the top. I was so thrilled and happy to receive this symbol of our love. I shall treasure it always!

For me, Martin composed a piano sonata, which he played for us. The piece is so beautiful, so tender, that I wept on Anika's shoulder.

Anika wears her apron high and blushes when she gazes at her husband, Claus. This will be their first child. How I envy her! There were many children at our party, several friends wearing aprons high.

Mama says it is good that I have no infant making demands on my time. Maximilien needs me at the shop. But the shop is succeeding beyond our dreams. We could afford to employ a nurse, or an employee to take my place at the cutting table.

Maximilien comforts me every month. Like Mama, he says we are young yet, there is time. But I see worry in his blue eyes. He teases that our dynasty awaits, and please, Mrs. DeWilde, let us begin.

I have no one in whom to confide my anxiety. My friends are busy with their own families. Only Martin seems to sense my sadness and Maximilien's growing disappointment.

On a happier subject, I find I am gifted with figures! Maximilien says I am a marvel with the household accounts. Next week I will begin keeping the accounts for the business. Maximilien says we will grow twice as fast if I manage our bookkeeping.

As I reflect over our first year of wedded life, I can say that I have never been happier. Maximilien is the sun in my heaven, the joy of my heart. Never has there been a handsomer, tenderer, more wonderful man. I gaze at him and I think how blessed I am that this splendid man is my husband. I wear his name with pride, and lift my head when the shopkeepers call, "Good morning, Mrs. DeWilde. Will you sample my ale, Mrs. DeWilde? Will you buy my coal, Mrs. DeWilde?"

Oh, Maximilien! I long to give you a son to carry your name into the future. Take heart, my love, my life. One day soon, I too shall wear my apron high!

GRACE STOOD AT THE FRONT window of the hacienda, hands in the pockets of Jeffrey's old bathrobe, and watched Ian's rented Lincoln glide down the lane of royal palms. Ian would be gone for a week, taking care of business at the gypsum mine east of Las Vegas. A mixture of regret and relief washed over her expression as she watched him go.

Almost two weeks had passed since Ian's stunning revelation in Caesar's finest restaurant, a whirlwind of sightseeing, dinner out, headline shows and casino hopping. Days of excitement, laughter and a few awkward moments when Grace had attempted to speak seriously. When a man declared his love, she felt the declaration merited a considered response.

But each time Grace attempted to address Ian's admission, Ian had gently placed a finger to her lips, silencing her. "Not yet, darling. It's too soon."

Perhaps he was right, she decided, turning from the window to a tray of hot coffee on the table behind her.

If she had responded immediately, she would have gently, tactfully turned aside his avowal. She would have emphasized the importance of their friendship, how she had relied on him over the years. As a friend. She would have stressed that she valued his friendship and did not want their status to change. Friends were all they would ever be to each other. She would have delivered this small speech diplomatically but firmly.

But almost two weeks later, her thoughts were not as simple or clear-cut. Ian had planted a seed that day in Caesar's restaurant. Never again would Grace regard him in quite the same way she had before he'd admitted his love for her. A woman could not set aside or ignore a statement so flattering and touching. A woman never forgot a declaration of love. Like a stone dropped into a pond, the ripples from Ian's admission continued to reverberate.

Grace sighed, sipped her coffee and again glanced at the window, but the Lincoln had passed from sight.

Hers was an analytical mind, capable of absorbing and analyzing complex rows of figures or merchandising information. But she was also mercurial and volatile on occasion. Everyone in the family teased her about occasionally going emotional and relying on instinct rather than hard fact. This duality in her nature was at least partially responsible for her business success. But occasionally it wreaked havoc with her personal decisions.

The analytical side of her nature warned that if she were ever to have a serious relationship with a new man, Ian Stanley could not be a worse choice.

First, Jeffrey would be doubly wounded by a relationship between his best friend and his ex-wife. The cordiality she and Jeffrey had struggled to maintain would vanish in a flash of bitterness and feelings of dual betrayal.

She couldn't guess how Gabe, Megan or Kate would accept any new relationship she might eventually have. But if the man were Ian... Like Jeffrey, it was probable that her children would view Ian's devotion as an additional betrayal of their father.

Frowning, Grace rubbed her temple. Friends would speculate and gossip as to how long Ian and Grace had been enamored of each other. Had the relationship begun years ago? During Grace's marriage to Jeffrey? Was Ian the reason for the DeWilde divorce?

Finally, she let herself think about Ian's three previous marriages. A man with three failed marriages was hardly a good candidate for an enduring relationship.

And yet... Instinct told Grace that Ian truly loved her. Now that the words had been spoken aloud, Grace recalled incidents from the past with an altered viewpoint. Ian *had* been there for her. Always. When Jeffrey was unavoidably out of town, it was Ian who escorted Grace to significant affairs. And Ian *had* been present for all the important events of her life. It was Ian whom Grace had phoned when Jeffrey fell ill in Italy and she needed assistance. Ian whom Grace had called when Kate broke her arm and she couldn't reach Jeffrey.

Jeffrey had been the first man in her life, always. What she now realized with a tiny jolt was that Ian had played a strong role as the second. If someone had inquired last week, she would have stated confidently that her son, Gabe, was the second man in her life. She would have erred.

Deep in thought, Grace carried her coffee cup out to the pool and stood looking at the water, watching sunlight sparkle like diamonds on the placid surface.

Ian was humorous, whereas Jeffrey was witty. Ian cast his personality like a net over all he met. In contrast, Jeffrey was a private man, reserving the best of himself for his wife and children. Ian was flamboyantly handsome; Jeffrey was quietly handsome. Ian was a banker; Jeffrey was a jeweler and retailer. Both were enormously successful men, powerful men, in the prime of their lives and careers. Both were charming and sophisticated, men who were undeniably exciting and attractive to women.

Grace's frown deepened. It wasn't fair to compare people.

After placing her empty coffee cup on one of the courtyard tables, she stretched, then pressed the wide collar of Jeffrey's old bathrobe around her cheeks. Although the bathrobe had been laundered innumerable times, she imagined the scent of Jeffrey's after-shave. He had worn the same fragrance for as long as she had known him.

Jeffrey was predictable; Ian was not.

This comparison made her smile. She, who had a signature perfume, could hardly scoff at Jeffrey's preference for the same cologne. And Jeffrey's affair had hardly been predictable.

Shrugging, she turned in a slow circle, faced with a quiet, empty day. She had already spoken to Rita in San Francisco. The store was running smoothly. Problems thus far had been small and easily solved.

Yesterday, before she and Ian had left for a picnic and a tour of Hoover Dam, she had tried to phone Gabe in London. He had been in a meeting. She had spoken to Megan and Kate shortly after arriving at Casa Ingram. She had talked to her brother and her niece after returning from Kemberly. There were no dangling loose ends, no phone calls she had to make, no places she had to be.

There was nothing she had to do. No appointments to keep, no speeches to make, no letters to write.

This was such an unusual state that Grace didn't quite know what to do with herself. For the first time in years, she had absolutely no demands on her time or energy.

Suddenly she missed Jeffrey. The strength of her yearning to be with him almost brought her to her knees. Throwing out a hand, she gripped the back of a wrought-iron chair and steadied herself with difficulty.

How long had they dreamed about a vacation where they had nothing at all to do but relax and delight in each other's company? How long had it been since they had enjoyed such a miracle of a vacation? She couldn't recall that they ever had. Business had played such a large role in their lives that even vacations were at least partly devoted to business matters.

Well, this was the vacation they had dreamed about. Here she was in one of the world's playgrounds with no demands on her time or thoughts. There was nothing to do but play and relax.

"Where are you?" Grace whispered angrily, her voice husky with emotion. "Why am I taking our vacation alone?"

Jeffrey should have been with her. It should have been Jeffrey placing a ten dollar chip on number seventeen. Jeffrey laughing beside her when she was struck speechless at the sight of Hoover Dam. Jeffrey should have been here now, standing beside her at the pool. Jeffrey would have known what to do with the long day stretching ahead. He

would have picked her up in his arms and carried her into
the cool dim bedroom and...

Grace covered her face with her hands and shook her
head.

What in the hell was she doing? What were *they* doing?

June 22, 1873. Last year Maximilien took me to Ger-
many for our anniversary, to take the waters at Baden-
Baden. There was much excitement, as the town is being revitalized as a medical spa. A grand new estab-
lishment called the Friedrichsbad is being built around
the mineral waters, but it was not open yet. We stayed
near the Trinkhalle.

I was assigned a *Kurarzt*, which is a spa doctor. My
doctor prescribed the exact amount of water to be
taken, and when, and what temperature it must be. I
was sent to the hottest springs in Europe, Friedrichs
Spring and Hell Spring, then to the coldest. I was immersed in mud baths and mineral baths and drank
more water than I have consumed in my life. The regi-
men was stringent.

When I became downcast and balked at drinking one
more glass of nasty-tasting water, dear Martin teased
me into following the spa doctor's orders. Playing
nursemaid surely did not make an interesting vacation
for poor, wonderful Martin.

While I was bathing and drinking, being poked and
prodded by the *Kurarzt*, Maximilien conducted business, showing our wares to barons and counts and their
fashionable ladies. In the evenings, Maximilien went to
the casino. Martin said Maximilien lost a hundred
florins at the tables the first night then did not play
again. However, he continued to visit the casino to
make business contacts. Martin said it was necessary

for Maximilien to spend the afternoons and evenings with Countess von Ebberling because the Von Ebberlings could be a large account for us.

The Von Ebberlings did order several diamonds this past year, but they did not develop into a significant account.

This year, Maximilien spent our anniversary in Paris on business. I passed the day at the shop, bringing the books to date, then, to cheer myself, I worked on my first real design. I have received a small commission to create a very special hat pin for Madame Cleo, who visits the De Groots from Toulouse. I should be more excited than I am, but I just—

Here, the translator noted that a watery ink blot had smeared the remainder of the sentence.

Martin took me to the Kalverstraat and I chose a café for my anniversary dinner. After dinner, we examined the windows of the luxury shops and Martin invited me to choose a gift, but I couldn't. I missed Maximilien so much. When Martin took me home, he played "my" sonata for me, the one he composed in my honor. The music was so sweet, so filled with love and tenderness that I wept for wanting Maximilien.

Anika is pregnant again. My envy pains and shames me.

Grace removed her reading glasses and rubbed the bridge of her nose. She sipped from a cup of tea that had cooled hours ago.

All afternoon she had been reading the translation of Anne Marie's diary, feeling a vague mounting anxiety as

Anne Marie's vivacity began to fade along with her exclamation points.

Caught up in the story, it worried Grace that Maximilien was spending considerable time away on business. And if she wished to speculate, there seemed a hint between the lines that Maximilien's interest in Countess von Ebberling had been more than business-related. Also, as the diary progressed, Martin Vanderhaden was appearing more and more frequently.

Now it was, "Martin says..."

Señora Valdez entered the room briskly, turning on lights, plumping pillows, removing invisible bits of lint from cushions. "Shall I bring a fresh pot of tea, *señora?*"

When Grace looked up from the pages in her lap, she half expected to see a woman dressed in a white apron and cap, with a windmill turning behind her.

She laughed and touched her fingertips to her forehead. Anne Marie's story had totally engrossed her concentration. Her head fairly spun with the figures from Anne Marie's household accounts, and the price of fish and eggs a hundred years ago. The business details captivated her, as did the homey remarks about laundry day and marketing day. The translation made fascinating reading.

She smiled at Señora Valdez. "Did you know it rained in Amsterdam—" she glanced at the page she had just laid down "—on August 1, 1873? The water in the canals rose a full inch."

"*Perdone?*"

"Never mind." Grace waved a hand and smiled at how real Anne Marie's world had become to her. A frown replaced her smile when she suddenly grasped a parallel to her own life. Anne Marie seemed no more aware that Martin Vanderhaden loved her than Grace had been aware of Ian Stanley's deeper affections. Yet Martin's love seemed so clear, particularly when viewed against Maximilien's growing coolness.

"We have marvelous new technology, but life itself changes very little," Grace murmured. "The human heart is ever the same."

Señora Valdez made a sound of assent, but she couldn't know what Grace was thinking. They both looked up at the sound of the telephone.

"I'll get it," Grace said, unfolding her legs from the deep chair in which she was sitting. Pushing her glasses on top of her head, she moved to a corner of the sofa and picked up the telephone.

"Grace? Jeffrey gave me your number in Nevada."

"Mary?" Astonishment widened Grace's blue eyes. "How lovely to hear from you!" Jeffrey's mother was one of her favorite people.

"You could have heard from me sooner if you'd picked up the telephone yourself," Mary DeWilde stated crisply.

A flush heated Grace's cheeks. "I've written...."

"Oh, yes. I was delighted to learn about the weather in San Francisco and your new furnishings and all the other boring items that you decided would not upset me." Mary's chuckle vibrated across the lines. "And not a word about any of the things I really want to know."

"I thought perhaps—"

"Now, listen to me, Grace DeWilde. I'm about to tell you the same thing I've told my stubborn son. You have been my daughter for thirty-two years and this foolishness between you and Jeffrey is not going to change our relationship. You are divorcing Jeffrey, not me. Is that abundantly clear?"

Grace laughed. Mary DeWilde was autocratic, opinionated and one of the most generous and unique women Grace had ever known. They had liked each other on sight, even though they were as different as the North and South poles; alike in many ways, a world apart in others.

"I didn't wish to place you in an awkward position," Grace explained. She drew a breath. "And I'm guilty of assuming that you would support Jeffrey."

"Of course I support Jeffrey. I support you, too. I'm not about to choose between two people I love. Now then, I'm phoning for three reasons. First, to thank you for remembering my birthday. I adore the scarf you sent. Second, to tell you that I'm coming to visit you."

Grace smiled through the window at the flowers on the porch. It was so like Mary to announce a visit rather than inquire if a visit would be convenient. Even at eighty-one, her mother-in-law was an indefatigable traveler. Mary thought nothing of hopping on an airplane and flying from her home in Manhattan to all parts of the globe.

"I'd be delighted to see you. When will you arrive?"

"I'm not as chipper as I used to be." The admission came in tones of impatience and brisk annoyance. "I'm leaving here this evening. Then I plan to spend a day or so in New York catching up on my beauty sleep and tending to my house and mail, and then I'll come to you."

Surprise lifted Grace's eyebrows. "Where are you now?"

"At Kemberly, of course."

"Oh."

"I've never liked this house. It's drafty and old. The best thing Charles and I ever did was to give this place to you and Jeffrey. Although I must say, Grace, I've never understood why you care so much for this pile of old stones. But then, I've noticed that Americans are unusually sentimental."

Grace pictured her mother-in-law waving a jeweled cigarette holder, seated in the drawing room beneath the portrait of Anne Marie DeWilde. Two such different DeWilde brides could not have been found. The thought made her smile.

"You said there was a third reason you phoned?"

"Ah, yes." An uncharacteristic hesitation entered Mary DeWilde's voice. "I happened to be in the attic yesterday."

Smiling, Grace rolled her eyes. She could not imagine under what circumstances Mary had ventured into the attic. To her recollection, Mary had shown no interest in the attic since moving out of Kemberly twenty-two years ago.

Suddenly, Grace sat up straight and blinked. Of course. She knew exactly where Mary was leading. In a flash, she understood why Mary had gone to Kemberly and why she would visit the attic.

"I noticed a box missing from our section," Mary said carefully. "And I wondered if perhaps..."

"The day I was tagging items in the attic, Jeffrey arrived unexpectedly," Grace explained. "Apparently I was more flustered than I realized, and I ended up tagging one of your boxes, thinking it contained mementos from the children's early years." She paused. "I have the box with me, here in Las Vegas."

A soft sigh sounded across the distance. "I guessed as much." A brief silence followed. "Well, what's done is done. How much of the translation have you read?"

Grace glanced at the pages beside her reading chair. "Enough that I'm captivated. And very curious as to why Anne Marie's diary has been kept a secret."

Mary did not volunteer the reason for secrecy. She let another silence develop as if she were thinking. "I suppose it would be useless to ask you not to read further?" she inquired in a hopeful tone that was almost a plea.

A puzzled frown tugged Grace's brow. She looked at the pages carefully stacked beside her chair. "The diary is a fascinating and historically important document." She considered a moment. "I'm sorry, Mary, the temptation is too great. Now that I've begun reading the translation, I feel compelled to continue to the end. I hope you won't ask me not to finish Anne Marie's story."

Mary sighed again. That made two more sighs than Grace had heard her utter in the last twenty years. "Yes, I thought you might say that. I doubt I could have resisted, either."

"May I ask why you haven't made this diary available to the family?"

Mary's response emerged in a dry tone. "You'll uncover the reason very shortly, my dear. In a way, your discovery of Anne Marie's diary is something of a relief. Yes, I believe it is. The knowledge of the diaries has been an uncomfortable burden for far too long." She interrupted Grace's exclamation. "We'll discuss it further when I see you. And then you can tell me how you are bearing up, and more about Grace, and what the children are doing."

Less than a minute later Mary was off the phone. Grace looked at the receiver for a moment, then replaced it in the telephone cradle. She had a sense that Anne Marie's diary had been the primary reason for Mary's call.

There was a secret buried within the pages of the diary. Perhaps a secret important to the family.

Standing, Grace lowered her glasses and approached the reading chair.

Would the secret be obvious? Would she recognize it when it appeared?

A long, quiet evening stretched in front of her as she settled into the chair, curled her legs up under her, and picked up the pages of Anne Marie's diary.

But before she began to read, she glanced toward the road in front of the hacienda and idly wondered what Ian was doing right now. Was he tramping around the gypsum mine? Preparing to go out to dinner? Was he thinking about her?

She shook her head in annoyance. There was nothing like a declaration of love to focus a woman's interest. In all the years Grace had known Ian Stanley, she doubted she had thought about him as intensely as she had since their lunch at Caesar's Palace.

She couldn't put him out of her mind.

The cut limes Señora Valdez served with dinner reminded her of Ian's cologne. Moonlight gleaming silver on the surface of the pool made her think of his hair. Earlier this morning, she had caught herself wondering if his eyes were blue like the sky or blue like the periwinkles that carpeted the ground in the grotto.

"Stop this," she whispered, her cheeks hot.

She read a sentence of Anne Marie's diary then lowered the page.

Ian would return shortly after Mary DeWilde arrived. A rush of guilt gripped Grace. Biting her lips, she stared unseeing at the shadows tiptoeing across the room. Her nerves fluttered to the surface of her skin.

Suddenly, she laughed out loud. What on earth was she doing? She had nothing whatsoever to feel guilty about; she and Ian had not so much as exchanged a kiss. They hadn't made any missteps, hadn't done anything to shame either of them. They were old friends who happened to be in the same place at the same time.

Except . . . that wasn't quite true. Ian had accepted a minion's assignment because Grace was here. And he loved her. Now that she understood, Grace saw Ian's love every time he looked at her.

Mary DeWilde would see it, too.

CHAPTER SEVEN

October 14, 1875. It has been weeks since I last put pen to page. I do so wish Mama were still alive. I long to sit in her big, warm kitchen and hear her good words of advice. There is no one else in whom I can confide. Pride stays my tongue.

My beloved Maximilien no longer makes a pretense of sleeping in the guest room. He has stopped telling the house girl that the stink of the canal drove him there. Last month he moved his things out of our bedroom. Every night I sob until I am exhausted, wanting him, longing for him. Our bed seems so large and cold and empty without my husband by my side.

After five barren years, Maximilien no longer believes I can conceive. I have seen him standing on the staircase, staring with deep sadness at the portraits of his DeWilde grandparents. It torments him to accept that he will be the last in his line. He believes he has failed his forebears by not producing a son to carry the DeWilde name into the future. He has failed by wedding a barren woman. I see his dream of founding a family of great jewelers grow colder with every passing day.

And it is my fault. Is there anything more useless, more worthy of pity than a barren woman? I have tried everything. I pray at the church every morning. I have taken the waters at the most famous healing spas in

Europe. I drink no ale or liquor. I have spent a month in my bed without rising. I visited the city surgeon at St. Anthonis Poort and begged that he help me. It is no use. The surgeon said I am a healthy young woman and he found no reason why I should not conceive. I embarrassed myself by bursting into tears and moaning, "Then why don't I?"

Oh, why don't I conceive?

I have even, God forgive me, paid a secret visit to a witch in the Polders. I paid her a small fortune in gilders, and in exchange, she gave me a disgusting potion to drink. The potion made me very, very ill, but I drank it all. It proved as useless as I am.

January 2, 1876. We don't speak of it. My darling Maximilien comes to the breakfast table and greets me with a kiss on my forehead, as if we still slept in the same bed. Then he sits before his breakfast and reads the newspaper. He forgets that I am present. If I speak, he glances up with a startled expression and a frown.

Last year we moved the shop to a larger location away from the smell of the fish market. There are three cutters now, and I am no longer needed. Maximilien says it is unseemly for the wife of a prosperous jewel merchant to labor alongside our employees. I am needed nowhere. I spend the days at my kitchen table, drawing designs which Maximilien takes to the shop if he approves them. When I inquire, he tells me that my designs are selling well. Martin says the DeWilde pieces, my pieces, are the talk of the season. He says I am gifted, that I find beauty and shapes in the gemstones. Martin cannot praise me enough. But I wish to hear this praise and enthusiasm from the lips of my Maximilien.

Where does he go in the evenings?

Dear Martin and I play chess, or he plays the piano to distract me. Sometimes we are quiet together. Martin praises Maximilien's dedication to the business. Such a one, Martin says, shaking his head in admiration, to work far into the night. I am a fortunate woman, he says, that my husband is so devoted to the business and to our future.

But Martin does not meet my eyes when he says these things. And I wonder if Maximilien is truly working, and I despise myself for such thoughts. Maximilien comes to my bed infrequently, but I remember the passion we shared when first we were married, when we dreamed of children and each other. Now he spends his passion in work. And I see my failure in his eyes.

March 11, 1876. It is agony. Since the night Martin and I saw them together, I have been in torment. I cannot eat, I cannot sleep. I picture them together in my mind and it tortures me. I cannot stop the pictures inside my head, terrible images of Maximilien and that woman. The pain of imagining her in Maximilien's arms is sometimes more than I can bear.

I thought she must be from the brothel quarter around the Pylsteeg. I told myself that Maximilien bought her company for one night. Why this thought would comfort me, I don't know, but I clung to it. I told myself it did not matter. Men sometimes do these things. It is not so much of a betrayal. Not so much.

And then yesterday... oh, yesterday! Anika came to me and insisted I must get out of my house, I must have air and diversion. She said I worked too much on my creations. How I longed to open my heart to her, but pride would not allow it. I let her persuade me to attend an afternoon theater performance.

It was good to dress and arrange my hair, good to walk in the crisp, fresh air. Anika made me laugh at the antics of her children and then told me about her cousin who did not conceive until ten years after marriage. She meant well, but her words did not comfort me; I am as resigned as Maximilien.

We arrived at the theater in gay spirits, laughing over schoolgirl memories. Then, inside the lobby, we saw posters advertising the afternoon's performance. Anika and I stopped and we both cried, "Oh, no."

The portrait of the leading actress showed the face of the woman who has tormented my mind. She is not from the Pylsteeg as I'd supposed. She is an actress, and very pretty.

Anika's distress and flaming cheeks told me that she knew everything. "They assured me that Mrs. van Alt would not perform today." This is what Anika whispered when she turned to me, wringing her hands together. At once I knew that all our friends are aware that Maximilien has taken a mistress and who she is. They know he has abandoned the bed of his barren wife.

I ran all the way home. Martin came to me after supper. He seems always to sense when I need him most. We sat together and I wept until I was ill. Martin held my hands and told me that I am more beautiful than Mrs. van Alt, but it gave me no comfort. He struck the wall and cried, "Damn Maximilien!" But I said, no, it is my fault. If I could give Maximilien a child, I know his love for me would again blossom.

If only. If only I could.

I did not know that one small person could suffer so much. It feels as if I am dying.

April 23, 1876. Martin begs me to go out with him now that the weather has turned mild. He suggests all things to tempt me. Coffee and shopping in the Kalverstraat, lectures, the band concerts on the Dam. But I fear seeing Maximilien with Mrs. van Alt. If I saw them together again, I would surely die. So I do not leave my house.

Anguish has made me ill. I lie on my bed and do not bother to dress or curl my hair. Nothing matters, not my house, not my designs. I wish I did not know her name. I wish I did not know her face. I remember her laughing up at my Maximilien, I see it so clearly in my memory. I remember his hand, possessive on her arm. I imagine them kissing and turning to each other on the pillow. I wonder what he says to her and her to him. I think I am losing my mind.

Yesterday, I again saw Maximilien standing on the staircase, gazing at the portraits of his DeWilde ancestors. Such sadness in his eyes. I stole away before he saw me watching, but I wonder if he heard the sound of a heart breaking.

He loves me. I must believe this. I do believe this. My Maximilien, the sun in my life, he loves me. He turns to her in his pain at having no son to bear his name. If I could be like Anika's cousin and only conceive! But that tiny hope dies. Maximilien comes to me but once a month, and I think he does so from duty rather than joy. Long ago our joy died in the ashes of monthly hopes and anxieties. Each time our disappointment deepened and became more difficult to bear.

Mama would advise me to look for the silver lining. I have tried so hard to do this. If there is silver in this darkness, it is that we no longer speak of children. Once a month Maximilien used to greet me with hope leaping in his eyes. And I would crush that hope with a shake of my head. We don't perform this terrible ritual anymore.

There are so many types and degrees of agony.

Last night Martin dried my tears and attempted to speak to me, but he could not. In great frustration, he ran to the piano and filled the house with a torrent of music, great crashing chords followed by melodies of such tenderness and pain that I wept for all of us. Poor, dear Martin. He suffers for Maximilien and for me and he can help neither of us.

Grace put down her glasses and pressed the heels of her hands against her eyelids. Her eyes were wet and her chest ached. Anne Marie's pain was as immediate as if it were her own.

Turning her head, she looked unseeing at the darkness pressing the windowpanes. The hacienda was silent now, the pool lights and outside spotlights extinguished.

How well she understood Anne Marie DeWilde's agony. She too knew the torture of imagining an adored husband in the arms of another woman. For one terrible instant, Jeffrey and Allison Ames rose into focus in front of her eyes. Unable to stop herself, she pictured them wild in their passion, hungry for each other's bodies.

Shaking her head, Grace struggled to banish the painful images. Angrily, she wiped at the tears stinging her eyes, then she struck the arm of the chair with her fist.

Did Jeffrey have any idea of the anguish he had caused? Had Maximilien DeWilde gazed into the eyes of his suffering wife and recognized her torment? Had either of the men experienced a moment's remorse?

Sitting alone in the silent hacienda, thinking of all she had read, Grace found it ironic that Jeffrey had followed the same slippery path as his great-grandfather, the esteemed founder of the DeWilde family. No wonder Mary didn't wish to share Anne Marie's diary with members of the family. Maximilien was revered and remembered proudly. His portrait was prominently displayed in the DeWilde corporate offices. Would he be so honored if it were known that he'd been a philanderer and had caused his wife such pain?

Standing, Grace shook the stiffness out of her limbs, then walked outside onto the front veranda and filled her lungs with dry, cool air. In the distance, the sparkling neon of Las Vegas lit the night sky. Beneath those glittering lights, throngs of people laughed or frowned or shouted with excitement or shrugged in disappointment.

Grace wished she was among them. She wished she was almost anywhere except standing alone in the darkness, aching with Anne Marie's pain and her own.

With all her heart, she suddenly longed for Martin and wished he could be here now to pay her extravagant compliments and make her laugh.

"Martin?" she said aloud, her eyebrows arching. She'd meant Ian, of course. The foolish slip made her aware of how tired she was. She had been reading for hours.

As Grace flipped off the light and walked to her bedroom, she covered a yawn and told herself that at least she had discovered the manuscript's secret. The esteemed Maximilien DeWilde had feet of clay. He wasn't the paragon time had made of him.

Or did the translator's manuscript contain other secrets yet to be revealed? The answer to that question would have to wait until morning.

September 4, 1877. I see by the last entry that it has
been over a year since I last put pen to page. So much
has happened; so little has changed.

The shop has expanded again. Last year I designed
a pearl-and-diamond headdress for the Kammel wedding. The piece was so successful that Maximilien
opened a special room in front of the cutters to display
jewelry and sample headdresses for brides. The response has been so positive and profitable that Maximilien hired a full-time designer. I put away my own
poor sketches. I still keep the books for our business,
but not for much longer. The business grows so rapidly and has become so complex that Maximilien is
seeking to hire a clerk and bookkeeper. Very soon, I
will have no involvement at all.

Our summer house on the Amstel is nearly finished,
and I occupy myself with furnishings and wall hang-
ings. Maximilien says we must find a grander house in
town, lest others doubt our prosperity. But I cannot
bear the thought of empty silent rooms, and I resist. I
look at my small, snug house and wish to remain here,
close to happy memories, though few are of recent
vintage.

Dear Martin is estranged from his father now. I hope
I have been able to offer some comfort as he has com-
forted me. Martin's father wished him to marry the
eldest Van Hooten daughter, Marianna. She is my age,
twenty-two. She is not a beauty, but quite pleasant to
look at nonetheless. Her cheeks are rosy and she cov-
ers her lips when she laughs. She orders her clothing
from Paris and is quite stylish. She is a widow with one
child.

As dear to me as Martin is, and as much as I would
miss his company, I believe he should have a home of

his own. In his music I hear his longing for a wife and family. Martin is such a good, dear man. No person could have a more devoted or loyal friend. He would make a fine husband and father.

But he insists that he cannot wed Marianna as it would be unfair to her. There were dreadful scenes with his father. Martin speaks of leaving the bank, as the situation there has become untenable. Employees have remarked on the coldness between Martin and his father. Hazel eyes can look so sad. I hope he can mend this rift with his family.

October 7, 1877. My hand shakes so badly, I can hardly keep ink on the nib. If Mama were alive, she would strongly advise me not to commit these words to paper. But if I do not organize my thoughts, even on these poor pages, I shall go mad with happiness, fear, anxiety, joy, regret, all the terrible and wonderful emotions that grip my mind and heart.

Last week, Maximilien departed to Italy on business. His carriage was scarcely out of sight before a well-meaning friend made it known to me that Mrs. van Alt accompanied him.

My anguish cannot be imagined. He took her to our Italy, the Italy of our beginnings, the Italy we swore would belong always to us alone. Maximilien asked me to go with him, but I could not bear to face the ghosts of our honeymoon happiness. What a fool I was to refuse him. But how could I know he would take her?

Martin came to me, but I could not be consoled. I wept in Martin's arms, wept as though my heart were breaking, as it surely was. Martin kissed the tears from my eyelids. And then—oh, God, forgive me—I turned and our lips met. We gazed at each other, then clung together.

On reflection, what happened between us that night was perhaps inevitable. Martin proclaimed that he loved me, he has always loved me. And I see it now where I did not before. And yet, it was there, Martin's love, as quiet and steady as the wind that turns the mills. His love is in the music he plays for me, it shines in his eyes, it follows me as I move through the room. My eyes have been blind but are no more.

And I love my dear Martin, also. My love for Maximilien is like a wild summer storm, raging and crashing, whipping my passions to frenzy. My love for Martin is more a gentle spring rain that calms the spirit and eases the heart. Truly it is possible to love two men at once, yet differently. This I recognized as I lay in Martin's arms, our bodies wound together.

When we regained our senses, Maximilien rose like a specter between us, and our shared love for him crushed us with guilt. We vowed to each other that we will never again seek each other's arms. Maximilien loves and trusts us both and we have betrayed him. Heaven help me, I have done the unthinkable, I have betrayed my beloved Maximilien. I weep and tear my hair. There are not enough prayers to wash this stain from our hearts and thoughts.

Riveted, Grace read with the translator's pages propped in front of her breakfast plate. Her eyes widened, and her eggs grew cold. A tiny kernel of anger grew in her chest.

Maximilien's affair with Mrs. van Alt was ongoing and common knowledge. Yet Anne Marie, the betrayed wife, suffered torments over one night with Martin, an honorable man who loved her. But Anne Marie's era had been the time of the double standard. The sad injustice was that Maximilien's affair was accepted, whereas if Anne Marie and Martin were discovered, Anne Marie would be condemned out of hand.

Was it so different today?

Her brow tight, Grace stood and carried her coffee toward the stables, then leaned against the rail of the corral and watched Carlos and Roberto curry the horses. She returned the boys' greetings, but her mind lay elsewhere.

If Jeffrey's affair became known, would anyone think less of him? Frankly, Grace doubted it. But if she and Ian Stanley...

Intuition warned that if she and Ian pursued their attraction, she would tumble in the eyes and esteem of friends and acquaintances. It wasn't fair, and it made her furious to think about it, but it would happen. A woman's transgressions were somehow more egregious than a man's, even in this day and age.

She considered this thought for several minutes, then her chin lifted and her blue eyes flashed. She had never run from the opinion of others, and she would not begin now.

If she and Ian ended up in bed as Anne Marie and Martin had done, Grace would not feel an instant of guilt. She swore this to herself.

At once, she mentally kicked herself for planting the idea in her thoughts. She did not want to speculate about Ian in bed.

Fleeing uncomfortable images, she hurried back to the hacienda and returned to Anne Marie's diary, taking the pages to the big reading chair in the library.

January 1878. By December I was certain. The euphoric joy of it! The terror of it! I told no one, I didn't know what to do.

On St. Nicholas Day, while Maximilien was in Paris, Martin took me to the wharves to watch the arrival of Sinterklaas. The crowds were heavy and it was very cold. I watched the excitement of the children, and I thought that next year I will place carrots and hay in my child's shoes as a gift for St. Nicholas's horse. And in the morning, there will be sweets and gifts for my baby. My baby. I watched Sinterklaas arrive with tears freezing on my cheeks.

When we returned home, I heated chocolate for us but I don't remember doing it. I told Martin before I told Maximilien. I had to do it thus. Because...I don't know. That is my anguish, I don't know! To my shame, it could be either of them.

Martin, dear Martin, believes that he does know. He pleaded with me to elope with him. Such mad plans he made that night. England, he said. We would live quietly and so happily in England. How often have I said I would like to visit England? Martin placed England at my feet and begged me to go with him and make him the happiest man on this earth.

And I broke his heart, to the despair of us both. Martin is so dear to me, and I love him, I truly do. But there has never been any husband for me but my adored Maximilien. I would rather die than turn away from Maximilien. I cannot bear the thought of never seeing him again. As gently as it is possible to wound someone, I told Martin I could not elope to England with him. My heart will always be with my husband, my beloved Maximilien. At the end, Martin and I both wept.

When I bid Martin good-night, I insisted the child is Maximilien's. We must believe this, we cannot believe otherwise. I begged Martin to be happy for our joy, Maxmilien's and mine.

February 1878. Last night I told Maximilien the glad
tidings. I waited another month to be very certain.
And, oh, my heart, my love, my Maximilien! He fell to
his knees and wept with joy, his head in my lap. We
laughed, we danced, we held each other so tightly, so
tenderly in our happiness.

We could not stop talking. Lost in each other, swimming in grand plans, we toasted the dawn with tears of
joy. My Maximilien has confessed Mrs. van Alt to me
and wrung my heart with his shame and regret. He
turned to her, as I guessed, from the pain of loving to
distraction a woman, myself, who could not give him
children. He begged forgiveness for blaming me. He
held my glad face between his hands and swore there
would never be anyone but me, the heart of his heart,
not ever again.

We are giddy with our news, intoxicated with each
other.

But I am not sure if... but no, I will not torment
myself.

March 1878. Maximilien showers me with gifts. Silly
things that make me laugh or diamonds that make me
gasp. Every day, he runs up the staircase, calling my
name, then making me guess what gift he has brought
me today! I must pat his pockets and find my gift, then
I must thank him with a hundred kisses.

Oh, how happy we are! The guest room is empty
now, and we wake with our heads close together on our
pillows. We cannot pass without touching, cannot
speak without laughing our joy. I find notes from my
beloved in the pockets of my dressing gown or tucked
inside the book I am reading. He supervises my diet
with the eyes of a surgeon, will not allow me to risk
riding in a carriage. My darling Maximilien is like a boy

again. He leaps to fetch a pillow for my back, inquires anxiously if I wish coffee or chocolate, cradles me in his arms as if I were made of the most precious porcelain.

We have bought a new house in the most fashionable area of Amsterdam, and sent to Paris and London for furnishings. The nursery is very grand. Maximilien says I must have servants now, I must not engage in strenuous housecleaning. I am the mother of the DeWilde dynasty, he says, and then we laugh and touch and gaze into each other's eyes. How tender he is, my love, my heart, my darling, darling Maximilien. I am the most fortunate of women.

June 1878. I am too far advanced to walk about. I keep to my house, wandering through the new rooms in dreaming admiration. How strange and sweet are these last days. I sit in the window and gaze across the rooftops, lost in dreams for the child who kicks beneath my heart.

He will be Maximilien if he is a boy, and Marie if she is a girl. We wish for a boy to continue the DeWilde name and our ever-expanding business.

Maximilien has been asked to run for election as an alderman. He makes my heart swell with pride as he is becoming a presence in the city. Every day, ladies leave cards in the tray by the door, requesting that I repay their calls when I am able. Maximilien is pleased and has ordered new clothing from Paris for the time when I can reenter society.

Anika is admitted at this late stage, and of course, our dear Martin.

There is a strain between myself and Martin. I fear that what I see so clearly in Martin's suffering eyes, Maximilien will see, also. But Maximilien's joy and high spirits blind him to the torment in Martin's face.

And the music. Oh, Martin's music. It speaks so clearly of his love and his pain. Sometimes he plays English airs that make me weep with a bittersweet loss that hurts my chest.

We do not speak privately, Martin and I. I try to tell him with looks alone that I believe the child is Maximilien's. I *must* believe this or I will go mad.

August 1878. Today the doctor let me get out of bed! It has been a month since our darling Marie came to us. Never has there been such an infant! She is so beautiful, so good! Nurse says she has never seen a child with such perfect features, and Maximilien and I must agree.

I sat in the rocker and held my darling for an hour today, examining each finger, each tiny eyelash. She has Maximilien's blue eyes, and that stubborn DeWilde chin. I see my own mouth and ears, and something more that will be her alone.

Maximilien gave me a fabulous diamond-and-ruby necklace and earrings as a birth gift. Martin sent an exquisite box made of English porcelain. Anika and other friends have showered me with small gifts for Marie and myself.

Never have I been happier! Never!

The only blot on my happiness is the sight of dear Martin's face. I wish I could ease his suffering. I wish I could be two women. For I see if it had not been Maximilien, it would have been Martin. But all men fade in Maximilien's light.

"HI, GOOD-LOOKING. Are you missing me?"

Grace laughed into the telephone. "As a matter of fact, I am. It's very quiet around here without you."

"What have you been doing without me to supervise your daily activities? Swimming, perhaps?" Ian's voice sank to a low, suggestive tone. "I'm imagining you lying beside the pool wearing a skimpy bikini. Tell me that I'm right."

"Sorry, you must be thinking about one of your leggy show girls. I've been inside all day reading. Wearing slacks and an oversized shirt." She smiled. "I'm afraid I don't own a skimpy bikini."

"What? Well, I'll remedy that oversight. I'll buy you a bikini. Hell, I'll buy a bikini store and give it to you as an emancipation gift!"

"I already own a store that carries bikinis," Grace reminded him, grinning. "But thankfully, I have the sense not to wear one myself."

"That is your only flaw, darling. You're burdened with good taste."

Grace laughed. "You sound in good spirits. Things must be going well at the gypsum mine."

"You could not be more mistaken. It's hot as Hades out here in the desert, and dusty. Something makes clunking noises at night, the bed is a marble slab, and I'm desperately missing a certain blond entrepreneur who looks like Grace Kelly."

Grace made a face. "Despite that remark, I've ordered a case of your favorite ale. Marley's in London swore they would ship it yesterday. Will you arrive before the ale does?"

To her embarrassment, Ian reacted as if she had agreed to marry him, thanking her effusively. "Please, it's just a case of ale." His profuse gratitude pleased her but also made her a little uncomfortable. Clearly, he regarded her simple act as encouragement. Had she intended it that way? She wasn't certain.

"It's been so damned long since anyone did anything so thoughtful. Grace, you are absolutely..." He sighed, and she imagined him raking a hand through the thatch of silver gray hair. "I wish I were there to express my appreciation properly. But one of the reasons I'm phoning is to tell you that I'm going to be delayed here till the day after tomorrow."

"Oh." Disappointment came swift and deep, surprising her.

He laughed. "You must know that I'm listening intently and trying to interpret every small sound you make. I'm reading all sorts of things into that one husky syllable."

"I'll make it easy for you," Grace said softly. "I'm missing you, too, and I'll be glad for your return."

A short silence unfolded over the phone. "There's something different in your voice, Grace. May I dare to hope that you've thought about..."

"We'll talk when you return," Grace said carefully. She made an effort to lighten her voice. "But it may have to wait for a time. Jeffrey's mother is coming for a visit. She'll probably arrive tomorrow."

"Damn. Mary's a grand old dame, but her timing could not be worse. Finally I get you all to myself, I've bared my heart to you, you're teetering on the verge of falling panting into my arms, and what happens? Mary DeWilde decides to visit! Now, if that isn't an Englishman's luck!"

Grace burst into laughter. "I'm teetering on the verge of falling into your arms?"

"Darling, laughter is not appropriate here. A little breathless panting would be appropriate. A bit of sighing would be nice. You could use that sexy voice to whisper vile suggestions in my eager ears. You could lie about what you're wearing. You could—"

"Stop!" Grace wiped her eyes. "Ian Stanley, you are the most outrageous man I know."

"Wait until you discover what I have in mind for your delectable self," he said in a deep baritone ripe with promise. "You're going to topple, luv, and when you do, I'll be there to catch you in my arms. I've waited a lifetime for you."

"Slow down, old friend. It's been a long time since I . . ." A beep sounded on the line, and then again. "That's call waiting. Can you hold a minute, Ian?"

"There you are," he said morosely. "In the midst of some inspired sweet-talking, an interruption. Well, whoever it is, tell him to go away. Tell him you have a man on this line who wants to say things to you that will make your toes tingle."

"I'll get back to you in a minute." Grace pressed the click-over button and answered breezily, laughter sparkling in her voice, "Hello?"

"Gracie? I have to talk to you."

It was Jeffrey.

CHAPTER EIGHT

SUDDEN IRRATIONAL GUILT made Grace's knees tremble. Abruptly, she sat on the end of the sofa, feeling ridiculously like an adolescent caught doing something wrong. If the feeling hadn't been so strong, she would have smiled at the foolishness of it.

"Jeffrey?"

He laughed. "You sound breathless. Has desert living turned you into a jogger?"

"No, I was just . . . I have someone on the other line. Can you hold a moment?"

"I'll wait for as long as it takes," he answered softly. His choice of words and the emotion underlying them sent a tiny thrill shooting along Grace's spine. She drew a quick breath and her heart almost jumped in her chest. "Gracie, I—" He stopped. "Finish your other call, then hurry back here."

"I will," she promised. Every instinct shouted jubilantly that this was the call she had waited a year to receive. Dazed by an overwhelming rush of sheer joy, she had to pause a minute to recall who was waiting on the other line. When she remembered it was Ian, relief sapped the strength from her limbs. She had come so close, so close to saying something to him that might have created a difficulty. Thank heavens she had held her tongue.

She pressed the click-over button. "Ian?"

"Finally! Now, where were we? Were we talking about you wearing a sexy bikini? Or about how I intend to express my immense gratitude for your thoughtful gift?"

"Ian, Jeffrey is on the other line. Calling from London," she added unnecessarily. Her nerves skittered on the surface of her skin.

"I see," Ian said slowly. "Well, I suppose that's a call you have to take." When she didn't contradict him, he sighed in her ear. "All right, darling, I'll call you tomorrow night. Dream about me, that's an order."

Grace laughed uneasily, then hastily said goodbye. For a moment, she held the receiver between both hands and closed her eyes. Jeffrey was going to tell her to stop this idiotic divorce. He was going to ask her to come home where she belonged. She knew the various nuances in his voice, knew this was the reason for his call. And her small frame vibrated with happiness.

"Jeffrey," she said, breathing his name into the phone.

To her surprise, he didn't immediately respond. A heartbeat of silence passed before he spoke, and when he did, he sounded like a different man.

"Grace, something happened on the phone line. I overheard your conversation with Ian."

Her heart stopped, and her mind raced to recall what she and Ian had said. Her thoughts had been so firmly focused on Jeffrey, she'd been in such a rush to get back to him that she wasn't certain if she recalled exactly what Ian had said. Something silly about a bikini, something about expressing his gratitude. He'd told her to dream about him.

At once she understood how Ian's comments would have sounded to Jeffrey.

Heartsick, Grace held her breath, and in the ensuing silence heard her heart crash toward her toes.

"Jeffrey..." No, this couldn't be happening. Not now. His voice had been so happy, so decided and confident when she answered his call.

"I should have realized that Ian wouldn't let any grass grow under his feet," Jeffrey remarked quietly, coolly. "He's been in love with you for years. Does he phone every night?"

Jealousy flowed through his voice like a dark current. The emotion lay subdued beneath a veneer of sophistication, but it was there.

Grace's shoulders slumped and she raised a shaking hand to her forehead. A short while ago, she would have denied Jeffrey's allegation, might have made a teasing joke about it. But she couldn't do so now or ever again.

Adding fuel to the flame, Mary DeWilde would arrive tomorrow, and Ian would return a day later. It was futile to hope that Jeffrey wouldn't learn that Ian was staying in Marsha and Bill's guest house. He would. And the jealousy thinning his voice told her how he would interpret that news.

She drew a deep breath and reluctantly informed him herself. "Ian is in Nevada on business. He's staying in the Ingrams' guest house."

Jeffrey's silence lengthened and became frosty.

"It's been wonderful to see a face from home," Grace said, rushing to fill the silence. "Ian's always good company, you know that. He's made me laugh...." Her voice trailed. "Jeffrey?" she said finally, miserably.

"I'm glad you're having a splendid time," he commented tersely.

"Jeffrey, don't do this. You know I'm not having a 'splendid' time. I'm upset, confused...you *know* I never wanted a divorce."

"I didn't realize how late it's getting. I'm due at a reception in twenty minutes. I'm sorry, Grace, I need to say goodbye."

"Jeffrey! Please. Please tell me what you called to say."

"Oh, that." In the following pause, Grace could almost hear his mind flying, seeking a reasonable explanation. "I wanted to mention that Mother is on her way to visit. I hope her stay won't inconvenience you."

Innuendo sizzled in every other word. And of course, Mary's visit was not what he had called to discuss. He knew that Mary wouldn't arrive unannounced, knew that she and Grace must have talked.

"Mary's visit is in no way an inconvenience," Grace whispered. "I love your mother, and I'm eager to see her." She felt sick with disappointment. Her stomach ached.

"Well, then..."

She pictured him studying his watch, closing off his emotions one by one, protecting himself.

"Jeffrey, there is nothing between Ian and me. Ian's our friend, yours and mine. Our present situation has placed him in an awkward position."

"I doubt that, Grace. I think I've always known on which side of the fence Ian would land if you and I ever had irreconcilable differences."

"Damn it, Jeffrey! You are so wrong about what you're thinking!"

"Nothing irritates me quite so much as when someone presumes to know what I or anyone else is thinking."

She knew what was happening. Jeffrey's shock at overhearing her conversation with Ian was causing him to retreat into anger and snappishness. She was doing the same thing. And she didn't know how to stop it. Her disappointment over what had happened was intense enough to approach despair. In her heart, she sensed that Jeffrey felt the same sudden hopelessness.

"You didn't call to tell me about Mary's visit," she said, fighting to maintain a level tone. "And you didn't call to discuss Ian. Please, Jeffrey. Can we begin again?"

It wasn't like her to plead, and Jeffrey knew that. He would also know that she had guessed the reason for his call. After so many years of living as two halves of one whole, they knew each other well.

And because they knew each other so well, Grace abruptly understood that pride would not permit him to say what they both wanted to hear. When he placed the call, he had been sure of her, sure that he understood what she wanted. Now he wasn't certain. Jealousy had sunk its poisonous shaft into him, accompanied by the venom of pride, anger and a barb of insecurity.

"Grace, I really am running late." He hesitated. "I'm sorry I disturbed you and interrupted your previous call."

"Oh, Jeffrey." She covered her eyes with a shaking hand. "We used to know each other's thoughts, and it didn't annoy you. Not so long ago, we would have laughed at a situation like this. We used to trust each other." In the stiff silence, she drew a shaky breath of bewilderment. "When did all that change? Why can't we talk to each other anymore?"

They were sad questions that neither of them could answer.

"Good night, Grace."

He spoke quietly, his voice rough with regret. Long after the connection was broken, Grace sat doubled over, holding the phone to her breast, rocking back and forth as if her pain were physical.

GRACE READ FAR INTO the night, choosing to immerse herself in Anne Marie DeWilde's life rather than examine her own. Her thoughts settled and eased as she read about Anne Marie's shining joy in her daughter, Marie, and the happiness that surrounded Anne Marie and her beloved Maximilien. For a while, the diary entries glowed with reports of Marie's growth and every small delightful thing the baby did. Then the gaps between entries lengthened, reflecting a young mother's busy life and a lack of time to jot frequent notes.

Then, as Grace had dreaded, the series of entries she had secretly expected but hoped she would not find appeared. Although it was late, she could not stop reading. Biting her lip in mounting trepidation, she lifted another section of the translation and tilted the pages to the light.

May 1880. My hand shakes as I write this. All week I have taken to my bed, feverish with alternating spasms of despair and happiness I don't deserve. My head reels, bouncing from one thought to the other. This morning I awoke with my hands cupping my stomach, filled with radiance and such joy that I wondered how I could contain this miracle. But this afternoon, I am sunk in blackness so thick I think of flinging myself into the canals. I have wept a pail of tears.

Martin and I . . . we did not mean for it to happen again. I don't know how it came about that it did. We have been so careful never to be alone together, so different from the way it was with us for so many years. This change was not awkward or much noticed as my circumstances altered with the arrival of my darling Marie. And since Maximilien rushes home to be with us, I have few evenings alone, and Martin does not call as often as he once did.

But Maximilien had to go to Brussels, and I could not accompany him, as I needed to remain here with Marie. Martin came to me, and we talked privately as we have not done in so very long.

His anguish pains me. Oh, how it wounds. He sees that the color of Marie's eyes has changed from the blue of birth to his own hazel. She has his chin and sensitive mouth. There is no longer any doubt that Marie is Martin's daughter. We cannot deny this between ourselves. Martin and I looked in at our sleeping daughter and we wept.

My poor heart is cleaved in two parts. I love Martin, he is my dearest and most cherished friend. He has been companion, confidant, ally, and his love and loyalty have never wavered. But Maximilien is the soul of my soul, the missing half that makes me whole. There can never be another for me, only Maximilien. My Maximilien. There is nothing Maximilien could ever do or say that would cause my love to falter.

How could I betray my heart again? How could I have done this thing? I flog myself a hundred times a day, but no answer comes.

Martin and I are united in our love for Marie, this child we made in shame. We are filled with happiness for her being and sorrow for a future that can never be. My love for Maximilien wounds Martin so; he does not understand it and I cannot explain. His love for me has become his private purgatory. My heart flew out in sympathy for my dear friend's distress, and I shared his pain while I shared his passion. We could not look at each other afterward, so great was our despair. I turned my face away and wept into my pillow. Martin sank on the side of the bed and covered his face in his hands. I did not hear him leave.

Now I am pregnant again. And again, I do not know which of these dear and good men fathered my child.

But I think the unthinkable. I think perhaps it was Maximilien who could not make a child, when all the while we believed the fault was mine. Now I wonder if I am not the most fertile of gardens. Martin has planted seed twice, and twice his seed has taken root.

Maximilien must never know, must never suspect. To learn that he is to blame for our barren years would nearly destroy him. To learn of our betrayal would most certainly destroy him.

In both Maximilien and Martin, there is a hard center that finds it difficult, nay, impossible to forget, hard to forgive. They are alike in many ways, but in this above all.

I am thrilled and joyous about the child who grows inside me. I am devastated and frightened for my unworthy soul. I fear I shall surely be punished for loving two men.

December 1880. We have a son! Maximilien Martin DeWilde has come to us. Maximilien's joy is indescribable. He covered my blankets with rubies and diamonds, and he promised to make from them a crown for my head. I laughed and told him a necklace and earrings would do nicely. Every day he brings me gifts, and gifts for Marie and baby Max. His jubilation knows no bounds.

Such plans he makes for this small boy. He holds Max to the portraits in the gallery and says to him, "This is your heritage, but you will eclipse them all, my son. You are the beginning of the future, the House of DeWilde."

Martin gave me a potted English rose. He composed a brilliant symphony for the children. I cannot look into his eyes. His music has become too painful to bear. His music rends the heart.

Grace lowered the pages shaking in her hands and stared at them in disbelieving shock.

There had not been a single drop of DeWilde blood in any DeWilde descendant since Maximilien. The DeWildes were not DeWildes.

Good Lord. The secret stunned her.

Jeffrey, her children . . . they descended from the Vander-haden line, not the DeWildes. Jeffrey's beautiful hazel eyes came from Martin Vanderhaden. The family's musical talents sprang from Martin Vanderhaden. Anne Marie focused on Martin's gift for music, but he had also been a banker. Perhaps the family's business acumen also descended from the Vanderhaden line.

"Oh my God."

Grace stared at a point in space for several minutes. Suddenly, she felt very glad that Mary DeWilde would arrive tomorrow afternoon. The shocking secret revealed in Anne Marie's diaries was too great a burden to carry alone.

DUE TO GOOD GENES and numerous cosmetic procedures, Mary DeWilde appeared fifteen years younger than her eighty-one years. As a young woman, Mary had not been a beauty, but then, as now, she had been attractive and energetic. Her many friends valued her highly and considered Mary an interesting and complex personality who mixed opposing characteristics without seeming to be aware of her own contrasts.

Mary was capable of being briskly no-nonsense one minute, and delightfully frivolous the next. She encouraged family members to dream and stretch toward the stars, while cautioning them not to neglect practical matters. She took pride in her modern outlook, but fiercely defended family traditions. Her trademark had become her preference for blunt speaking, but she could also be the most tactful and gracious of women.

Grace adored her.

After Mary's arrival, Grace waited impatiently while her mother-in-law unpacked and then refreshed herself with a long nap. While Mary rested, Grace caught up on her phone calls, then immersed herself in Anne Marie's diary.

Again, the gaps between entries lengthened. When Anne Marie found time to write, she spoke constantly of her growing children and seldom remembered to mention business concerns except to note that the shop had opened branches in Antwerp and Brussels. Maximilien wished to combine the shops into a large concern in Paris and move his family to France, but Anne Marie resisted and her adoring husband acquiesced to her wishes.

With one exception, these were happy years for Anne Marie and Maximilien DeWilde.

March 4, 1885. All of our friends joined us at the wharf to bid dear Martin bon voyage and wish him well in the future he has chosen. Martin has decided to make his home in America. It is doubtful that we shall see him again, although we have promised to write.

Maximilien surprised me by his silence. He did not urge Martin to remain in Amsterdam as I believed he would. A chill gripped my heart when I considered Maximilien's silence, and I wondered suddenly, horribly, if he had guessed the truth. For nearly a year, I have lived in growing fear that Maximilien would see what others apparently notice so readily.

Martin treated us all to ice cream on Marie's birthday. We arrived before Maximilien did, and the waiter remarked how much Marie and Max resembled their doting father. He assumed Martin headed our little family. Suddenly, I saw what I have not allowed myself to admit. The hazel eyes, the hair, their little mouths, so like their father's. I looked at Martin in great fear. My agitation was so distressing that I could not speak when Maximilien joined us.

Now Martin forsakes all that is known and dear to him and is taking himself far, far from family, friends and homeland. And I know that he does this for me. And for Maximilien. He loves us both as much as he loves the children, loves us enough to accept exile rather than destroy us all.

Oh, Martin, beloved and cherished friend, I shall miss you all the days of my life.

Lowering the pages, Grace rested her head on the cushion of the chair and wondered if Anne Marie and Martin had said their goodbyes in private, or if they had avoided what surely would have been a painful parting.

"He must have loved her very, very much."

"So did Maximilien," Mary said, walking toward the cocktail cart. After examining the bottles, she expertly mixed two martinis and handed a glass to Grace. "I know you don't particularly care for martinis, but you're living in America now and everyone drinks them here."

"Thank you." The drink was dry and tart, perfect, as she had guessed it would be. "I didn't realize I spoke aloud. Once I begin reading Anne Marie's story, it takes over my mind. I find myself pondering the diaries at odd moments, wondering what will happen next." Standing, Grace shrugged the stiffness from her shoulders. Anne Marie's distress had created a tension in her back. "Are you up for a short walk before dinner? There's a lovely grotto not far from here."

Although the sun had dipped near the horizon, the air was still warm. Inside the leafy lushness of the grotto, the desert air was cooler, and the splash of water falling into the pond soothed jangled senses.

Mary and Grace seated themselves on a wooden bench and sipped their martinis in companionable silence, enjoying the sylvan ambience and each other's company.

"There are a few things we need to talk about," Mary said finally. "Once these items are disposed of, we can relax and enjoy ourselves."

Grace nodded, watching the water trickle over a tumble of realistic-looking rocks. That Mary had not offered one of her acerbic comments condemning plastic signaled the seriousness of the discussion to follow.

"Long-standing marriages generally dissolve because one of the partners has had an affair." Having crisply delivered this opinion, Mary shifted on the bench to study Grace's profile. "Therefore . . . even though I know it's none of my business . . . which one of you was idiotic enough to have an affair?"

Grace smiled. The blunt question was so like Mary. "I'd like to explain everything, but I think this is a question better put to Jeffrey. It should be his decision whether or not to answer."

"I see. My son was the idiot who had the affair."

A splash of martini spilled on Grace's linen slacks. Stricken, she turned to Mary. "I didn't say that."

Mary's smile was grim. "I've known you for thirty-three years, Grace DeWilde. And I've never known you to back away from the truth. If you'd had an affair, you would have said so. I'm sure the admission would have embarrassed you, possibly shamed you. But you wouldn't have hidden behind an evasion. Therefore, the culprit must be my pig-headed son."

Grace's resolve broke. The entire unhappy story poured from her heart. At first it surprised her that it was Jeffrey's mother in whom she finally confided everything. But after a moment's reflection, her surprise diminished. Of all the people she knew, Mary DeWilde was the most likely to take an objective viewpoint.

Mary nodded when Grace stopped speaking. A sigh lifted her chest as she fitted a cigarette into her jeweled holder, lit it, and exhaled a thin stream of smoke. "Regardless of the provocation, Jeffrey was wrong to take up with that girl. But now at least I understand this whole mess." She smoked and considered. "Jeffrey was always quick to find rejection in a situation," she said finally. "And perhaps with good reason.

"When it became apparent in 1939 that the world was destined to explode, my husband, Charles, wanted to join the war effort, but his father, Max ... yes, Max, Anne Marie's son ... refused to grant permission. Dirk and Henry had already announced their intention to enlist, and Max couldn't bear to give all of his sons to the war. He insisted that Charles leave at once for the emerald fields in Brazil. Max argued that he needed Charles to oversee the family's business interests."

"But Charles objected?"

"Oh my, yes. All the young men of that era burned to serve in the war effort. Charles and Max argued violently, but in the end Charles did as his father demanded. The two of us sailed off to Brazil so Charles could develop an emerald mine for the DeWildes. I guess you've heard this story. I'm sure you know that eventually Charles defied his father and enlisted with the Free French Army. His defiance resulted in a painful estrangement between the two of them.''

"It must have been a difficult time for everyone," Grace said gently.

"Lord, yes. Before the war ended, I'd had a baby, I'd buried Max and Genevieve and Anne Marie. I'd grown up." Mary watched the water falling over the rocks, but her eyes gazed into the past. "When I was pregnant, Charles was shipped out to North Africa on some secret mission. Jeffrey was five years old before he met his father. People came and went in Jeffrey's life, and he didn't understand why. He adored his grandfather, Max, then Max and Genevieve were killed in the blitz. My brother stayed with us for a time, then he flew off on a mission and never returned. I couldn't keep a nanny in those dreadful times. How does one explain something as monstrous as war to a child?''

"Did Jeffrey know Anne Marie, his great-grandmother?"

"He was still a toddler when she died. Moreover, she left London shortly after Jeffrey's birth. Family history insists that Anne Marie died with Max and Genevieve during a bombing raid on London. But that's not true. Anne Marie died in Amsterdam.''

"In Amsterdam?" Grace sat up straight and blinked.

Mary nodded. "Anne Marie purchased the small house that she and Maximilien had owned when they were first married. She lived there for almost a year before her death. After the war, Charles had her remains returned to England, and he brought Maximilien's remains from Paris. As you know, they are buried side by side in the DeWilde family plot. Neither Charles nor Henry ever corrected the general assumption that Anne Marie died in the same blitz that killed Max and Genevieve. In fact, they altered the date of her death on her stone to enhance the misconception.''

"Another secret."

"Every generation has its secrets, Grace. The DeWildes are proud people. Charles and Henry hoped to impart the impression that Maximilien and Anne Marie had reconciled what seemed to be a puzzling estrangement. But they never did." She gave Grace a questioning lift of the eyebrows, then nodded. "I see you haven't reached the section of the diaries that reveals the secret of Anne Marie's estrangement from her son, Max. This, too, is a family mystery. You'll discover the reason for it when you read that part of the diaries."

Grace was thoughtful as she watched the water falling into the pond. "I'm not certain that I agree with your contention that every generation has its secrets."

"Don't you?" Mary inquired, gazing into her empty martini glass. She removed the cigarette from the holder and crushed it beneath her heel. "Will future generations understand why you and Jeffrey are divorcing? Will your parting make sense to your descendants?"

A flush of color heated Grace's cheeks. "I hope not," she conceded in a low voice. "I'd like to think our pain will remain private."

"There you are." Mary shrugged, and let a small silence develop. "I knew, of course, that you didn't love Jeffrey when you married him. But I understood why you married him, anyway." She raised a hand and smiled. "Before you say anything, wait, because I've decided to tell you my own secret. I didn't love Charles DeWilde when I married him. I thought Charles was weak, too firmly under his father's thumb. Like Martin Vanderhaden, Charles had a self-sacrificing nature, and I didn't much like it."

Grace stared at her. "I had no idea. If you didn't love him, why did you marry Charles DeWilde?"

"I assume I married Charles for many of the same reasons that you married our son. I was dazzled by the De-

Wilde name and fortune. Like you, I came from a family that was socially prominent but lacked the fortune to support their position. And, also like you, my dear, I eventually fell in love with the man I married." She paused and her tone turned brusque. "But unlike you, I never told Charles that I hadn't really fallen in love with him until he defied his father."

Grace closed her eyes and swayed on the wooden bench. "You will never know how deeply I regret telling Jeffrey."

"Darling, I can guess. I also know how deeply it must have wounded Jeffrey to learn the truth." Mary looked at the cigarette holder she turned between her fingers. "He used to break my heart," she said, so softly that Grace had to strain to hear. "He tried so hard to be a good little boy. Somehow he'd gotten it into his head that if he were good enough, his father would come home. He didn't understand about the war, he was too young. Somehow, he decided it was his fault that I was sad and his father was away." She tossed back her head and gazed into the trees overhead. "Then, when Charles finally did come home, Max's death had left the business in shambles. From Jeffrey's viewpoint, it must have seemed that Charles returned only to disappear again. His child's mind decided that Charles had returned not for Jeffrey's sake or mine, but because the business needed him. DeWilde's came before anything else."

A lump blocked Grace's throat. "So Jeffrey grew up believing that the business was more important than he was."

Mary nodded. "Jeffrey has always wanted the world to see him and the business as separate entities. But of course it doesn't work that way. The lines blur. A DeWilde is first and foremost a DeWilde, with all the associations that accompany the name. One can't carve the stores away from the people. But deep inside, Jeffrey is still that little boy trying to compete with the DeWilde holdings for attention and love. Even those who know him well don't often recognize that small kernel of insecurity. But it exists, and it's entrenched.'' Sympathy softened Mary's gaze. She took Grace's hand. "When you revealed that you married Jeffrey before you fell in love with him, your admission would have unleashed insecurities that reach far into the past. Regardless of how you phrased the revelation, Jeffrey would have heard you say that you chose the business instead of him.''

Grace let a silence develop while she considered all that Mary had revealed. "Jeffrey fears abandonment,'' she said softly. On some level she had always known this but had refused to examine it.

"I would say so. Yes.''

"Then why is he agreeing to a divorce neither of us really wants?'' Her blue eyes snapped with sudden bright anger. "All he must do is ask my forgiveness! He's told me that he regrets Allison. He's told me that he still loves me. Why can't he simply take the next step and ask my forgiveness? Why can't he say the damned words?''

Standing, Mary took Grace's arm and they walked slowly back to the hacienda, following a tempting aroma of baking tortillas and mole sauce.

"Understand this, Grace dear. The affair meant nothing. I'd wager my favorite diamond earrings that Jeffrey wouldn't recognize that silly girl if she sat across a table from him.''

"It was important to me,'' Grace objected hotly. "His affair with Allison destroyed our marriage and changed our lives!''

"No,'' Mary corrected her gently. "Jeffrey learning that you married the business instead of a man you loved is what changed your lives.''

Grace touched her fingertips to her forehead. "What can I do?" she whispered. "I can't go back and alter the truth. I can't unsay the words. I can forgive Jeffrey for his affair, I really believe I can do that. But it won't stop this divorce." She frowned and looked inside herself. "In fact, I've already forgiven him, although I'm still hurt and angry."

"Time heals all wounds," Mary promised, patting her hand as they entered the hacienda.

"Will time erase Jeffery's hurt?" Grace asked. "Will he someday focus on the good years and the love, instead of concentrating on that brief span when I respected and admired him but didn't yet love him?"

Mary turned and clasped her hands. She gazed directly into Grace's eyes. "Yes," she said firmly. "Eventually, Jeffrey will come to his senses. I am utterly confident of that."

Grace recalled his phone call and suppressed the weepy feeling rising in her. "When?" she whispered.

"I wish I could answer that, but you know I can't."

"We've been apart for almost a year."

"I can only tell you that one day my son will wake up alone and curse himself for a fool. And then he's going to show up on your doorstep begging your forgiveness and praying it isn't too late to win you back."

"It will never be too late!"

Mary kissed her cheek. "You feel that way now, but . . . Grace, remember one thing. The DeWilde men do not forgive easily, and they never forget."

"So I'm discovering."

"I'm not referring only to the present circumstances. I'm offering a warning for the future. Darling, what I'm about to say isn't fair, but it's true. Divorce isn't necessarily the end. You and Jeffrey may still work this out. But that will never happen if *you* have an affair.''

''I...''

Mary interrupted hastily. ''I'm not saying that you will. But you're a beautiful woman and you'll be single and available, perhaps lonely. But the DeWilde men never forget—or forgive—an indiscretion from their women.''

''You're right,'' Grace said briskly, her eyes snapping. ''That isn't fair.''

Mary laughed and they went in to dinner. ''I couldn't agree more. But it's true.''

''Mary,'' Grace said after they were seated at the table. ''Surely Jeffrey won't expect me to conduct myself as if we were still married.''

''But of course he will,'' Mary said, smiling with pleasure at the dishes Señora Valdez had set before them. ''Right now, he's feeling hurt and unloved, abandoned. What you do from now on will validate either his fears or his hopes.''

Grace stared down at her plate, her appetite gone. ''What you're saying is that I must condemn myself to loneliness and live as a nun. Frankly, that makes me angry as hell.''

Mary hesitated before she replied. ''I could be mistaken, Grace. I have a tendency to speak dogmatically and to sound very certain. But I could be wrong.''

''However, you don't think so.'' Grace sighed. ''And in my heart...I have to concede that you're probably correct.''

Señora Valdez appeared in the archway, her gaze sweeping the table before she smiled at Grace. ''*Perdone, señora. Señor* Stanley is on the phone for you.''

Ian. Grace had forgotten him.

She cast a swift glance toward Mary's carefully averted eyes and understood at once that Mary also knew what it seemed that everyone had known but her.

"Please take Mr. Stanley's number and inform him that I'll return his call later."

"Ian," Mary murmured when Señora Valdez had withdrawn. "I haven't seen him in an age."

Grace's heart sank. In view of the previous conversation, she wished it wasn't necessary to inform Mary that Ian was staying in the guest house, not a hundred yards away.

When she heard the news, Mary nodded slowly and reached for her glass of wine. She gave Grace an unreadable look. "Ian is a good man," she said evenly. "I don't always care for his humor, it's a bit earthy for my taste. And I don't approve of all his marriages. But Ian has a good heart . . . and he's loved you for years."

Silently Grace thanked her mother-in-law for the reversal to tact. Mary didn't ask questions. There was no hint of judgment in her voice, not the smallest nuance of curiosity. It must have been difficult, but she made the moment as easy as possible for Grace.

Two hours later, after Mary had excused herself and retired to her room, Grace slipped on a pair of sneakers and took an evening walk, striding down the lane of royal palms, thinking about all that she and Mary had discussed.

Anger energized her steps. Jeffrey had no right to object to Ian. Not after his affair with Allison. And he had no right to expect Grace to remain faithful after they were divorced. Such an expectation was unjust, unfair.

Remembering his iciness on the phone and the way he had instantly retreated, she kicked at a pebble on the road.

Mary was right.

If Grace had an affair, even after she was single again, any and all hope for a reconciliation would be forever lost.

She stopped at the end of the royal palms and frowned across the desert toward the glittering towers of the Las Vegas skyline.

Grace had come to the desert to obtain a divorce, believing that her marriage had crumbled like the sand at her feet, believing that she and Jeffrey had no hope at all for a future together.

But after Jeffrey's phone call, and after talking to Mary, she was no longer certain that she and Jeffrey were finished with each other. Perhaps their divorce would be as unique as they had always believed their marriage was. Perhaps divorce was not an ending, as Grace had expected, but a new type of beginning.

If so, it appeared that the burden of any new beginning would fall squarely on her shoulders. Whether or not they could find a way to begin again would depend on her actions and decisions.

Was that what she wanted?

Was she willing to continue to wait for Jeffrey, especially when it might be a very long wait with no guarantee that waiting would end happily? Was she willing—and able—to forget about Allison Ames and truly forgive and forget? Could she accept a lonely future based on Jeffrey's terms, knowing that Jeffrey might not even be aware of his own deeper motivations?

Grace wasn't ready to analyze these questions or consider answers. For the moment, she burned with the unfairness underlying them.

Whirling, she strode toward the lights shining along the hacienda veranda. If it hadn't been so early in London, she would have phoned Jeffrey and... Her shoulders slumped. She didn't know what she would have said. She only knew she was shaking with the need to say *something*.

But it was barely dawn in London. So she didn't telephone her husband.

Instead, she returned Ian's call.

CHAPTER NINE

"MARY DEWILDE IS ONE of my favorite people," Ian commented. "I look forward to seeing her again." He paused. "Or would discretion suggest that I make myself scarce for a few more days?"

"Not at all," Grace answered firmly, feeling a warm flush rise in her neck. She gripped the telephone tightly in her hand. "Nothing has occurred between you and me that wouldn't bear scrutiny. And nothing *will* happen while I'm married to Jeffrey, which I am until my divorce is final."

Ian laughed. "Very tactfully done, darling. In other words, slow down, old boy."

Grace gazed out the window at a cactus garden illuminated by moonlight. Moonlit nights were the loneliest nights of all. "You've been through this, Ian. You know what a confusing time it is." She drew a breath. "Last night, if Jeffrey had asked me to stop the divorce and go home, I would have caught the next airplane to London. This afternoon, I was so angry at him that my hands were shaking. I feel as if forces beyond my control are playing kickball with my emotions. The point is, I'm in no fit state to make decisions about the future or to enter into an important relationship."

In another confusing flip-flop, Grace felt herself responding to Ian's warm, deep voice. She could picture him clearly, the thatch of silver gray hair, twinkling blue eyes, an intriguing dimple, that sexy mouth....

"Knowing you, you hate to admit to a lack of control."

A tired smile curved her mouth. "Truer words were never spoken." Few things upset her more than to feel that she was not in control of herself and her emotions.

And she wasn't. Yesterday, she had yearned for Jeffrey. Now she was missing Ian dreadfully. The emotional tug-of-war irritated and confused her.

"I understand perfectly," Ian said in a reassuring tone. "If I've rushed you, I apologize. I should have waited before mentioning how I feel about you. But I have a hunch that a dozen men are going to beat a path to your door the instant your divorce is final. I wanted to be at the head of the line."

"Ian, you will always be at the head of the line. I'm very grateful for everything you're doing to make a difficult time easier for me."

"I'll try to be a good boy, Grace. I'll try to wait until the seventeenth before I press you further. May I hope that you'll be willing to talk then about where we go from here?"

She hesitated before answering. It wouldn't be fair to promise something she couldn't deliver. Yet she was strongly drawn to him. "I've always believed in hope," she said finally.

"I'll accept that evasion as encouragement whether or not you mean it as such. Tell Mary that I plan to take you ladies to dinner tomorrow and then to a party at the MGM penthouse, unless you have other plans."

"That sounds lovely."

"Good. Wear something slinky and outrageous."

They talked for another twenty minutes, then Grace washed her face and pulled on the loose T-shirt she wore to bed. The emotionalism of the day had fatigued her, but she didn't feel sleepy. After fifteen minutes of staring at the ceiling, she tossed back the sheets, sighed, then slipped out

of bed and padded into the library. Until she finished reading Anne Marie's diaries, she suspected the pages would
continue to draw her like a moth to a flame.

Tonight she was due for a disappointment. The last page
she read had been dated March 1885. The next entry carried a date in February 1904. Nineteen years had passed. As
the translator had stated in his covering letter, several volumes of the diary were missing.

Before Grace settled into a deep library chair, she worked
out the dates in her mind. Anne Marie would be forty-nine
in 1904, a few years younger than Grace was now. Marie
would be grown, twenty-six years old, and Max would be a
young man of twenty-four.

February 3, 1904. Max is bringing a young woman to
meet us! We know very little about her except that she
is the most beautiful creature in the world, the gen-
tlest, the wisest, the wittiest. Listening to Max speak of
her brings joy to my heart. And if her name must remain a mystery, well, we shall meet her soon and enjoy
the surprise Max promises when her identity is revealed.

I am prepared to love this young woman and welcome her into our family and my heart. For I have
gazed into my son's eyes and I see the depth of his love
for her. Max is like Maximilien and myself. He may
love many people in his lifetime, but he will give his true
heart only once.

I suspect our Marie is the same. How I miss her! I
worry constantly that she is alone in a city as large as
Paris. Maximilien says we must set aside old-fashioned
ideas. He says it is not that unusual these days for a
twenty-six-year-old woman to have a career and a home
of her own. A career! For a woman! But our Marie

thrives at Cartier and assures us she has a splendid future as a designer. I am not so modern as my Maximilien. I pray Marie will find a man to love her as she deserves. At her age, I had been married for nearly eleven years and had two babies.

I've asked Marie to send me a length of bottle green mohair. If I pay extra, I'm sure I can have a new skirt made before Max brings his young lady to us.

Anika called this morning to assist me in selecting new draperies for the parlor. Now that her children are grown and gone, Anika sighs. I did not say so, but I pity all women who are not married to a man like my beloved Maximilien.

Far from regretting our empty nest, we find this is the happiest time of our lives. We look at each other over our breakfast fish and eggs and we laugh and blow kisses to each other. Our love has only grown and become stronger. Since we feel as if we are still on our honeymoon, we plan a visit to Italy, our Italy, as soon as Maximilien can arrange the time away from business.

There are five shops now, all thriving, the largest of which is in Paris. Max oversees all watch repair and custom designs. Maximilien heads finance and sales. The quality of DeWilde gems is lauded throughout all of Europe. For more than twenty years, Maximilien has spoken of consolidating in Paris, and I have resisted. Recently, the idea begins to appeal, and we have commissioned blueprints for a grand home in Faubourg Saint-Germaine. It will be good to live closer to our Marie.

Today I went to the old church and thanked God for the blessings and the happiness He has given us.

March 10, 1904. My life is over; all happiness lies behind me. I shall never be happy again. The sins of the past have returned to destroy us. For days I have lain in my bed with the shutters drawn, too ill to rise, too heartsick to take food.

Max brought his young woman home to us. She is lovely, as beautiful and as gentle a young woman as I have seen. She is quiet and gracious, her manners impeccable. And she loves Max as deeply and as totally as he loves her.

Her name is Catherine Vanderhaden. The surprise that Max guarded so carefully is that Catherine is Martin's daughter. I fainted when I learned her identity.

It was a dreadful scene, so terrible I can scarce bring myself to recount it. I came to my senses distraught and frantic, weeping and pleading with them not to marry. They *must* not marry! They looked at me as if I had gone mad. I told them I could never give my blessings to this marriage. Never!

Catherine fell silent and wept in her hands. Max argued and shouted. They didn't understand the horror in my expression.

But Maximilien did. When I appealed to him, I found him staring at me, his face ashen. Our eyes met, and I knew all. He has suspected, but refused to believe his suspicions. Time has blurred Martin's features in memory, and Maximilien has seen his children's faces in his ancestors' portraits because he wanted it so desperately. But now the truth is confirmed for him. We deceived him, and he has deceived himself. Now he despises me.

Max, too, appealed to his father, but Maximilien said that Max must demand from me the reasons why he

cannot, must not wed Catherine. White-faced and
shaking, he left the drawing room, unable to bear witness to what I must confess to them. But I could not
speak the words. I could not. I ran from the room, as
distraught as those I left behind, and I stumbled up the
stairs after Maximilien.

He stood in the gallery before the eyes of his De-
Wilde ancestors and he was sick before them. When I
flung myself around his knees, he threw me away from
him.

I know not where he is. A week has passed, and he
has not returned. Nor do I know where Max is. I have
heard nothing from husband or son.

If I had the courage, I would kill myself for causing
the ones I most love so much anguish and pain.

April 14, 1904. The doctor says I must walk and eat and
do those things I once did. I have not slept since he took
away the laudanum. Now I have the courage to end a
life that is no longer endurable, but there are no imple-
ments in this sterile place.

Max defied us. He and Catherine eloped. The horror is so immense that I could not commit these words
to paper except the doctor has ordered me to resume my
diary. He mistakenly believes that recording my
thoughts about all that has happened will aid my re-
covery.

Max married his half sister. The tragedy of this act
and what followed has destroyed me as it has destroyed my son and that lovely young woman, as it has
destroyed Maximilien and Martin.

Max and Catherine wired us from Paris, their words
full of jubilant defiance and shining with their love for
each other and their happiness. They admitted that

Catherine carries their child and begged us to relent and share their joy in each other, the future, and the child they had made together.

Maximilien wired them to return to Amsterdam at once. He also wired Martin and informed him that his daughter had married Max. But Max and Catherine had notified Catherine's parents at the same time as they wired us, and as Max and Catherine ignored Maximilien's demand for their immediate return, Martin arrived in Amsterdam the day before they did.

I cannot speak of this.

April 20, 1904. I wept as Martin told them; I could not utter a word. Max and Catherine were standing in the parlor, his arm protectively around her. In their shock they turned to the mirror. And we all saw it. God help us, we saw the same hazel eyes and brown hair. The same mouth and tilt of chin. They gazed at each other in horror, then they looked at Maximilien who sat on a chair with his face in his hands, at Martin, who suffered as none has before or since, and at me, who wept with shame.

My son cried out, and I have never heard such anguish in a voice, nor have I observed such pain as that which wounded Catherine's small face. But that is only because I myself did not face the mirror.

We shall have the marriage annulled, Maximilien said. He would not look at Martin or me. Then Martin reminded us that Catherine was pregnant with Max's child. What of the child if the marriage was annulled?

Maximilien and Martin fell to blows. Maximilien would surely have killed him if Max had not intervened.

And then we heard the shot. Oh, God. I shall never forget the sound of that shot. We ran into Maximilien's study, and Catherine lay dead on the floor. That beautiful young woman and her unborn child were dead. Because Martin and I, because we . . .

Profoundly shaken, Grace read the translator's note. "The remainder of the paragraph is too water-blurred to decipher." She read on.

. . . He hated me. He held her head in his lap and sobbed and screamed his hatred for me. He said he would never again speak to me or utter my name. He would never look at me. He said he had no mother, his mother died tonight with his wife and child. He told me that I killed Catherine as surely as if I had held the gun to her head. He would have joined her in death if Maximilien had not hastily removed the rest of the guns from his study.

No more. I cannot think of this now or I will go insane.

May 2, 1904. They found Martin's body in one of the canals the next morning. Martin left a letter for me, but Maximilien took it from me before I could read Martin's last words.

Max vanished after Catherine's service. Maximilien sent her body home to her mother, to be buried in the Vanderhaden plot in New York City.

He placed me in hospital for fear I would kill myself otherwise. Truly, I have been mad these last weeks.

I have not seen or spoken to Maximilien since the day after Catherine's service. He wrote that he is moving the family to Paris, but I am not to join them. He has

commissioned an agent in London to locate a home for
me. My punishment will be exile from family and
home.

My beloved Maximilien wrote that he could not bring
himself to divorce me, but neither could he bear to look
at me or speak to me. He vowed that Max and Marie
would always be his children, but they are no longer
mine.

My love, my only heart, my Maximilien. I pray that
you will one day forgive me. But how can you, when I
cannot forgive myself? Please don't send me away.
How can I live without you? How will I know if you are
wearing your scarf when bitter winds blow? How will
I know who I am if I cannot see myself reflected in your
gaze?

Oh, Martin. What tragedy we set in motion. How
could we have hoped for even a moment that our sin
would go unpunished? I miss you, my dearest friend. I
pray for you. May you find peace and forgiveness in
God's understanding.

Maximilien, soul of my soul, hear me. I will wait. I
cannot believe we will never again be together. Not you
and I. I will wait and I will pray each day for that moment when we hold each other again. Please, Maximilien. Please, my love. Let me come home to you.
Please.

Tears running down her face, Grace dropped the pages on
the library floor and stumbled to her bed, shaking with quiet
sobs.

"IT'S THE MOST heartbreaking thing I've ever read," Grace
stated the next morning, adjusting her dark glasses against
the glare glancing off the shimmering surface of the pool.

She and Mary took their coffee in the courtyard beneath the shade of palms and spreading junipers. "I couldn't sleep. I kept thinking about Anne Marie and Maximilien and Martin and Max. And poor Catherine."

Mary nodded, waving her cigarette holder. "It destroyed them all." She refilled her coffee cup. "Max was true to his word, he never spoke to his mother again. Even after the family moved to England, he refused to be in the same room with her."

"But he did marry again...."

"If it had not been for Genevieve Delmas DeWilde, Anne Marie would never have seen her grandchildren or known anything about her son's life. When Max met Genevieve, she was a seamstress working in one of the Paris couture shops, far beneath Max socially. Nevertheless, they appeared to have a comfortable marriage, if not a passionate one, though they managed to produce four children. But there wasn't any fire between them, if you know what I mean.

"As nearly as I could observe, the only items they shared in common were business and their children. Genevieve may not have enjoyed an impressive pedigree, but she was intelligent and accustomed to hard work. She and Max were the first to shape the DeWilde stores into the form they have today. After the First World War, they transformed the Paris shop into an exclusive department store that incorporated all the elements of the present DeWilde stores."

Grace gazed into her coffee cup. "But Max never loved Genevieve as he had loved Catherine."

"I didn't know about Catherine until I read Anne Marie's diary. Catherine Vanderhaden doesn't appear in any of the family records. I doubt there were a handful of people who knew Max had been married before he married Genevieve. It's possible that even Genevieve didn't know about Catherine. I was certainly aware that Charles's father was deeply estranged from his mother, but I didn't know why and neither did Charles. Max would never speak of it. Once I asked Genevieve why Max would not permit his mother to attend family holidays or gatherings. Genevieve could offer no explanation. She said that Anne Marie's plight broke her heart, and that she had been trying to effect a reconciliation for years, but Max refused. I do know that Genevieve was kind to Anne Marie. She defied her husband to make certain that Anne Marie had access to her grandchildren. Otherwise, my husband would never have known his grandmother."

"And Maximilien? What happened to him?"

"Maximilien was not the same man in Paris as he had been in Amsterdam. He traveled extensively, promoting DeWilde's, but it seems generally accepted that something had caused him to lose interest in business, even in life itself. Of course, until the diaries surfaced, there was no explanation for Maximilien's altered behavior. When he was in Paris, he usually stayed with his daughter, Marie. The grand house Anne Marie spoke of was never built. Maximilien died of tuberculosis in 1919, at the age of sixty-eight."

"Did he and Anne Marie—"

"They never again saw each other after Catherine's funeral service." Mary turned her head toward the cactus garden. "There was never another man in Anne Marie's life, and I could find no whisper that Maximilien showed any interest in another woman. Family legend insists he died calling for Anne Marie. But she waited in vain. Maximilien could not forgive her." Mary paused. "They seemed to genuinely love each other to the end of their respective lives. But they couldn't move beyond the tragedy that tore them apart."

Lost in solitary thought, Grace and Mary sat together in silence.

"I see now why you didn't want me to read the diaries," Grace admitted. "And I understand why you chose not to share them with the family."

"I've never been certain that I made the correct decision." Standing, Mary walked to the pool and bent to test the temperature of the water. "I found the diaries in Anne Marie's Amsterdam house when I went there to attend to her affairs after her death. I've always suspected that she intended to read through the record of her long life and then destroy all the volumes. I'm guessing she read the diaries from her middle years first, as that was probably the happiest period in her life, when her children were growing and she and Maximilien found such joy with each other. Perhaps my theory is wrong, because the diaries that would have recorded her life in England are also missing, and that was certainly not a happy period in her life."

"Part of me feels privileged at having this opportunity to know Jeffrey's great-grandmother on an intimate basis," Grace commented. "Another part shrinks from the burden and responsibility of keeping Anne Marie's secrets."

Mary rose from the pool and nodded, shaking water from her fingers. "After I spoke to you about finding the diaries, I realized how great a relief it was that someone other than myself now knew about them. Frankly, I've wanted to discuss this information with someone for a very long time." She smiled. "And now I pass the burden to you, darling. The diaries are yours, to do with what you will."

"My first impulse is to destroy them. What good would it serve to reveal this information? But I'm not sure I could do it. Or that it would be right to destroy historical documents."

"I've struggled with the same dilemma for years, along with berating my interest in genealogy and wishing I had never found Anne Marie's diaries in the first place."

"Clearly, the diaries were intended to be strictly private. They weren't written for the eyes of others."

"The decision is now yours, Grace. You can preserve the documents for future generations of DeWildes, or you can destroy them. Whatever you decide...I'll probably regret your choice. So, please, don't tell me your decision."

As horses were one of Mary's many interests, they followed a brick path to the stables and watched beside the corral rails as Carlos and Roberto exercised the Ingrams' Arabians.

Mary studied the horses and riders with an expert eye. "Has it occurred to you that there are similarities between Anne Marie's story and your own situation?" she asked mildly, her gaze fixed on the horses.

"Good heavens." Grace blinked in the hot sunlight.

"Like Anne Marie, you married at a young age. You have contributed enormously to your husband's success and to the evolution of the DeWilde stores. After a long, happy marriage, you are seeking to obtain a divorce. It's possible that you and Jeffrey will never again be alone together. A widening distance has opened between you and Gabriel. And finally, Jeffrey's closest friend is in love with you."

Grace stared at her mother-in-law. On an emotional level, she suddenly realized that she had grasped the parallels in Anne Marie's story and her own and had responded strongly to the similarities. Anne Marie's story affected her to a deep and profound degree. But consciously, she had refused to concede any similarity.

"Jeffrey and I will see each other shortly after the divorce. At Ryder's wedding in Australia," she whispered huskily. "But after that...I can't bear the thought of never seeing him again."

"Neither can I, darling. The two of you are so right for each other. I can't imagine either of you with anyone else."

On the return walk to the hacienda, Grace slid Mary a sidelong glance. "Was that a reference to Ian?"

Mary laughed. "Perhaps. I must be slipping. I didn't used to be so obvious."

Frowning, Grace kept her eyes on the brick path. "Apparently everyone but me has been aware that Ian's affection goes beyond friendship." She hesitated. "I don't know where our relationship will lead, Mary. I only know I'm very glad that Ian's here. His..." She couldn't bring herself to say love. "His attention is flattering and I need that right now. Jeffrey's affair rocked my self-esteem and my confidence in myself as a desirable woman. Ian's interest is helping to repair those cracks."

"All I'm suggesting is that you make no hasty decisions. Try not to do anything that cannot be undone unless you're very certain that it's what you want."

At the hacienda, they turned to face each other beneath the shade of the veranda roof. The perfume of potted flowers surrounded them.

"Could you love Ian, Grace?"

"I love him already," she answered promptly. "Ian has always been more than a friend to both Jeffrey and me. But could I accept him as a lover?" She considered Mary's question as if she had not asked herself the same thing a dozen times. "I will never love another man as I love Jeffrey," she said after a long pause. "A person loves that deeply and that completely but once in her life." Her chin came up and she met Mary's steady gaze. "But I'm not Anne Marie. I don't want to live the next thirty years alone. I'm too young to give up..."

"Sex," Mary supplied crisply.

"Yes," Grace said, her cheeks hot. This was not a subject one usually discussed with one's mother-in-law. "And companionship, and the pleasures of marriage. I imagine Jeffrey feels the same way. I doubt he wants to spend the rest of his life alone. *He* could fall in love with someone else."

"I doubt that, but I suppose it's possible. However, Jeffrey doesn't have a woman currently living in the guest house who has been pining for him for years." Mary's wry comment made them both smile.

"I don't know yet what I'm going to do about Ian," Grace admitted in a less defensive tone. "We won't decide the next step, or even if there will be a next step, until after my divorce is final."

Mary studied her face. "Your divorce will be final in less than three weeks."

Sudden panic swelled in Grace's throat. When she first arrived in Nevada, six weeks had seemed an almost endless span of time. But the days were zipping past.

"Well," Mary said brightly, ending a conversation that had become uncomfortable. "I know you have a meeting with your attorney this morning, and a dozen phone calls to make before you leave. I think I'll have a swim, then indulge myself with a nice, long nap. I look forward to seeing Ian again, but he's an exhausting chap, isn't he really? And I must decide what to wear to dinner and the party. Sequins, do you think? Or the beaded dress?"

Grace stopped and arched an amused eyebrow. "Sequins?"

"Well, it is Las Vegas, dear."

Before they parted for their morning activities, Grace hugged her mother-in-law. Leaning back, she smiled. "Please tell me there are no more stunning secrets in Anne Marie's diaries."

Mary returned her embrace and her smile. "Nothing that will shock you." She tucked a shining strand of blond hair behind Grace's ear. "The family seems to believe that Max and Genevieve purchased Kemberly in the thirties when they moved from France to England. In fact, Maximilien bought Kemberly two decades earlier, after he and Anne Marie had separated, as a home for her. She lived at Kemberly because she thought that was what Maximilien wanted, but it's much too large for one person. She gave the estate to Max and Genevieve when they moved their family to England. Anne Marie chose a modest house in the village. The truth about Kemberly isn't known, but it's hardly a secret. Anyone who wishes can discover the record of Kemberly's sale among public documents. But, aside from myself, I don't believe anyone has ever bothered to check."

"And that's all? No more secrets?"

Mary's eyes twinkled. "Marie, Anne Marie's daughter, may have had a child out of wedlock, whom she later adopted. That is what Anne Marie believed. And she believed the father of Marie's daughter was possibly Jean-Luc DuPlessis, who later married my husband's sister, Marie-Claire."

"So many Maries," Grace murmured, shaking her head.

Mary laughed. "Now you understand why I was so happy that you named your daughters Megan and Kate."

Grace telephoned Rita Mulholland at the store in San Francisco. They talked for an hour about minor problems and Grace instructed Rita to hire the new designer if Rita judged her qualified and approved of the initial set of designs.

"She could fly to you in Nevada," Rita said after a minute. But it was obvious that she was pleased by Grace's confidence in her judgment.

"I've considered that option, but I don't really think it's necessary," Grace said, setting aside the notes she had taken during their conversation. San Francisco and the store seemed very far away, part of a life that existed outside her current state of limbo. "I'm certain you'll make the right decision."

Next she phoned Kate and touched base briefly, and then Megan, enjoying a long chatty conversation with her eldest daughter. She let her hand rest on the phone for a minute before deciding to telephone Gabriel later. It saddened her to realize how much she dreaded the pain his coolness would cause her. Surely there was some way to close the distance between them. But the answer had not yet come to her.

After completing a list of business calls, she phoned Walter Kennedy's office to inform his secretary that she was running a few minutes late.

The instant she heard Miss Halliday's voice, it sprang to the tip of Grace's tongue to instruct the secretary to tell Walter to cancel the divorce. The urge was so powerful that she had to pause a moment and bite her tongue.

"Please tell Walter that I've reviewed the papers he sent by messenger and have only a few changes to suggest," she said in a low voice.

While she dressed for her appointment with her attorney, Grace considered what she would wear to dinner with Ian.

Suddenly she missed him more than she would have thought possible.

CHAPTER TEN

IAN TOOK GRACE AND MARY to dinner atop the MGM Grand. Mary's beaded Dior winked and twinkled in the candlelight; Grace had chosen a black silk cocktail suit that trimmed her slender, elegant figure to perfection.

"I am the envy of every man in the room," Ian complimented them when they had been seated. "A beauty on each side."

"You always were full of nonsense, Ian Stanley," Mary said tartly. But she patted her chignon and looked pleased.

Instead of consulting the menu, Grace gazed across the table at Ian. He had returned from the gypsum mine darkened by the desert sun and brimming with vitality. His blue eyes danced above a tan that made his hair appear more silver than gray. Though it was impossible, the dimple beside his mouth seemed deeper, his teeth whiter than she remembered.

He was devastatingly handsome.

And every time he looked at her, his teasing blue eyes made love to her.

Over poolside drinks at the Ingrams' hacienda, Ian's obvious devotion and infatuation had caused Grace no small discomfort. She had been acutely aware that her mother-in-law's keen gaze missed none of Ian's lingering glances or brief touches, all of which had made Grace very uncomfortable. In her efforts to be utterly circumspect and to discourage Ian, she had ended by creating a degree of formal awkwardness among the three of them.

As if he had read her thoughts, Ian blatantly winked at her and smiled. Sighing silently, Grace lowered her gaze to the menu, but her mind remained firmly focused on the far side of the table.

It was useless to pretend that she didn't respond to Ian's attention and sexual energy. She saw him differently now, and she reacted differently. His long, deliberate glances created a recognizable tension in her stomach. Her body had forgotten that she was supposed to feel these stirrings only with Jeffrey.

After the waiter had taken their order and withdrawn, Ian raised his cocktail glass. "A toast," he said, smiling. "To my two favorite women in the world." When they lowered their drinks, he smiled at Mary. "There are some things that need to be said."

At once Grace anticipated what was about to happen, and her chest tightened in alarm. "Ian, please," she said. "Don't."

Reaching for her hand, he clasped it firmly on top of the table. Fire kindled in Grace's cheeks, but he would not allow her to withdraw her hand even when he noticed the irritated warning chilling her gaze.

"We'll all be more comfortable if we're open with one another. So... Mary, I love Grace. I've loved her since the day I met her."

Mary pursed her lips in disapproval. "I know," she said sharply. "Apparently the only person who didn't know was Grace."

"At present Grace is holding me at arm's length." He cast Grace a glance of impatience and amusement. "She's staying maddeningly noncommittal. But the instant her divorce is final, I intend to pursue her in earnest."

Embarrassment and anger flamed on Grace's cheeks. Mary was Jeffrey's mother, for heaven's sake. And Grace was deeply moved by Mary's efforts to remain neutral regarding the serious difficulties Grace and Jeffrey were experiencing. If Ian jeopardized Mary's goodwill, Grace would never forgive him.

He sensed the tension in her hand. "Grace, darling, don't look at me like that. Mary has known you for thirty-some years, and she's known me even longer. I doubt either of us could hide our feelings from her if we tried."

"I have nothing to hide," Grace informed him coolly. She removed her hand from his and placed it in her lap. "As for my feelings, I believe I've made it clear that I wish to hell this divorce were not happening. In the best of all worlds, Jeffrey and I would still be together."

He smiled. "It's a good thing I'm not the type who is easily discouraged." Undaunted by Grace's frosty expression, he spoke to Mary. "For more than thirty years I've been trying to conceal the fact that I'm in love with my best friend's wife. Now circumstances have changed. I don't want to spend the next week tiptoeing around, worrying that I'm going to embarrass Grace or offend you. We may as well put the subject on the table, discuss it if we need to, and end this awkwardness."

Mary tilted her head to one side and narrowed her gaze. "If you're asking my blessing on your pursuit of my daughter-in-law . . ." she began in a dry, crisp voice.

"I'm not asking anything, Mary," Ian interrupted. "I'm merely stating how things stand. If Jeffrey hadn't behaved like an ass and thrown his marriage away, I would never have approached Grace. I believe you know that."

Mary frowned. It was one thing for her to acknowledge that Jeffrey had behaved badly, it was another thing entirely to hear someone else level the accusation.

"Grace is an adult," she said at length. "And so are you. Neither of you wants advice, but I'll offer my opinion. My hope, even at this late date, is that Jeffrey and Grace will find a way back to each other. I don't want this divorce to happen." She paused while the waiter served their salads. "You always did rush ahead, Ian, even as a child. I think your timing is precipitous and a bit disgraceful. You have no business being here with Grace."

Ian grinned at her.

"But I also believe that you're an honorable man. And I know Grace is an honorable woman. I doubt either of you will do anything to be regretted later."

Ian's laughter was so genuinely amused that Grace also smiled. She couldn't help herself.

"In other words, don't create a scandal, honor the agreement I've made with Grace and don't rush into anything. Mary, I adore you." He blew her a kiss across the table. "I think we've cleared the air, at least. I'm going to chase Grace regardless of your disapproval, and regardless of Grace's hesitation."

One corner of Mary's mouth tilted in a smile she could not completely hide. "You're a scoundrel, Ian. You always have been. You'll understand that I'm not cheering for you." She folded her fingers together under her chin and studied him. "I won't conspire against my son. I expect you not to place me in a more difficult position than you already have. I think you know what I'm saying."

"There's no hanky-panky going on, if that's what you mean. You have my word on that, Mary." He smiled. "Do people still use that expression? Hanky-panky?"

Grace didn't answer. She stared at him with cool anger, mortified that he'd raised these issues with Jeffrey's mother.

Pretending not to notice her stiff shoulders and set jaw, he turned back to Mary. "I've promised Grace not to place any pressure on her until the divorce is final. I certainly don't want to create additional stress for her."

Mary nodded doubtfully, as if his last statement rang as false to her as it did to Grace. "I'm sure you believe that, Ian, but this kind of talk is certain to be stressful for Grace."

"Yes," Grace murmured emphatically. She was rigid with the strain caused by this conversation.

"But before we leave this subject," Mary said, speaking to Ian, "I want to say that I don't think you would make a good replacement for Jeffrey."

Mary's choice of words was intended to make Grace wince, and she did, lowering her head in fresh embarrassment.

"I'm fond of you," Mary continued, "and I wish you every happiness. But not with Grace," she added bluntly. "Your track record with wives is dismal. I'd hate to see Grace added to your list of failures. I don't want her hurt more than she has been already."

"The last thing I want to do is hurt Grace."

"I'm sure that's true. Regardless, it could happen. And it pains me that your presence here is certain to end your friendship with Jeffrey. I'm sorry to see the end of a good friendship that began when the two of you were in short pants."

Ian nodded. For once, there was no sparkle of amusement dancing in his gaze. "Losing Jeffrey's friendship pains me, too. More than you can possibly guess. What concerns me at the moment is whether I'll lose your friendship, as well."

Mary studied him thoughtfully. Finally she sighed. "No, Ian, you and I will continue to be friends."

"I'm glad," he said softly. "I think we understand each other."

"I have always understood you, you rascal."

"And I've hated that since I was a small boy trying to pull the wool over your eyes." They both laughed before Ian turned to Grace. "You've gotten very quiet."

"Have I?" she said, leveling a glare at him that promised they would have a long discussion later.

"Now, don't be angry. These things had to be addressed."

"I don't agree."

"Well," Mary said, breaking a chilly silence. "I've been in Las Vegas for days and I have yet to gamble a single cent. Will we have time between dinner and the party to stop by a roulette table?"

Grace and Ian stared at her, then both laughed, easing the tension between them.

"Mary, I had no idea you enjoyed gambling," Grace said.

"Oh my, yes. I adore Monte Carlo." Throughout dinner, Mary regaled them with tales of her gambling exploits. Mary's efforts to break the bank at Monte Carlo made Grace laugh. She began to relax for the first time since Ian had returned from the desert. Still, the conversation had disturbed her.

After dinner they returned to the floor of the casino, but before Mary found a seat at a roulette table, Grace drew her aside with an apology.

"I'm sorry that Ian spoke so bluntly. I wish he hadn't."

Mary patted her hands. "Ian said nothing I didn't already know or suspect." A smile curved her lips as she withdrew her cigarette holder from a small beaded bag. "Of course, I'm going to do whatever I can to thwart the rascal. Ian is a wonderful friend, darling, but he isn't my first choice for you as a husband. I'm going to remind you both of that opinion every chance I get."

Ian moved past Grace to place a pile of chips on number seventeen, the date of Grace's court appearance. "My lucky number," he said, giving her a wink.

The reference did not escape Mary, who smiled when the winning number came up twenty. "Perhaps it's not as lucky as you'd like it to be," she commented cheerfully, leaning forward to place her next wager.

Briefly Grace closed her eyes. She felt as if she had just become the prize in a tug-of-war between her mother-in-law and Ian.

THE MGM PENTHOUSE OFFERED a stunning panoramic view of the strip and the city lights fading into the blackness of the desert. "I don't see the mountains," Grace said, raising her voice to be heard over the music from a live combo and the noise of a hundred conversations rising at once.

Here and there she recognized famous faces. Several film stars were present, and headliners from nearby hotel shows. She'd spoken briefly with several people she'd met in Europe at various functions and social affairs. Others had recognized her from photo layouts and chatted a minute before swirling away. To her surprise, the party was not peopled entirely by strangers, as she had expected it would be. Mary had discovered the same happy circumstance, and had vanished almost at once to visit with friends.

"Would you like to dance?" Ian asked, leaning near her ear.

Before Grace could refuse, he'd led her to the dance floor and taken her into his arms.

Instantly, her stomach tightened and a tingle raced through her body. She had danced with Ian countless times before, but never when she was so acutely aware of him as a man. Now his musky cologne reeled through her senses.

Now she felt the easy strength in his arms, was aware of his lean, hard body pressed to hers. It surprised her how well they fit together, and she wondered that she had not noticed this years ago.

Would they fit as perfectly and as comfortably in bed?

The thought sent heat rushing through her legs and thighs and she stumbled. An excellent dancer, Ian covered for her and pulled her closer to the hard heat of his hips and torso.

"Still angry?" he asked, his breath warm in her ear.

"Very," she said, struggling to keep her voice level. "Did you really think that Mary DeWilde would sanction the pursuit of her son's wife?"

"Her son's soon-to-be divorced wife," Ian corrected her, rubbing his thumb across her palm in a slow, sensuous caress. "I apologize if I embarrassed you, but I refuse to spend the remainder of Mary's visit pretending that I'm not crazy about you. Mary would have seen through the ruse, anyway."

Grace drew back to look into his eyes. The movement aligned their hips, and she felt a thrill of electricity rock through her. For an instant it was difficult to remember that she was angry at him, or even what they were discussing. Blond hair swung toward her cheek when she frowned and gave her head a shake. "I'm afraid I was a little slow on the uptake regarding this party."

"I don't follow," he said innocently, his blue eyes dancing with amusement.

"Oh, yes you do." Her own gaze was cool, in direct contrast to what was happening within her traitorous body. "This is our first public appearance as a couple. I didn't figure that out until a few minutes ago. You engineered this, Ian. You're not playing fair."

"I've escorted you to a hundred affairs in the past. I doubt the gossips will make much of our being together.

Besides, we have Jeffrey's mother as a chaperon. That should certainly deflect wagging tongues.''

"But you don't care if it does or not, do you?"

"The truth? No, I don't." His gaze dropped to her mouth, and Grace felt a tremor shiver down her body as his eyes lazily traced the contour of her lips.

"Ian, this isn't the same as escorting me to a ball when Jeffrey was unavoidably out of town. Circumstances have changed. We know people at this party. They're aware of my situation, and they're going to talk about us.''

"What's the old saying? All's fair in love and war. I'm waging an all-out campaign, Grace. You may as well get used to the idea of us as a couple, because that's how it's going to be.''

There were undoubtedly women who reacted positively to men who attempted to sweep them off their feet with such statements. But Grace was not one of them. Ian's certainty that he would prevail in the face of her hesitation almost challenged her to prove him wrong.

"There's another old saying," she countered, forcing her voice to remain light. "Don't count your chickens until they're hatched."

He laughed and twirled her around the floor.

Gradually her anger dissolved in the flow of music and the pleasure of floating in the arms of an accomplished dancer. Enjoying themselves, they moved easily from slow dancing into hip-teasing Latin rhythms and then, laughing, stepped apart to twist and gyrate to rock music that made the heart race and blood pound. When the music ended, Grace lifted a hand to her flushed face.

"That was wonderful, but I need to sit out the next dance and catch my breath," she protested when Ian reached for her again as the music returned to a more sedate selection.

"I can't risk that, darling. I don't want any other man to notice you on the sidelines and rush over to whisk you away from me. Besides, I learned to dance to this piece. 'Stardust.' It's one of my favorite pieces of music."

He drew her into his arms, and Grace inhaled sharply as she felt the heat of prior exertion mingle with the heat of Ian's desire. And her own. The signals flowing from within were powerful enough that she didn't protest when Ian held her a moment, then molded her along the length of his taut body. For a long moment they didn't move. They held each other, eyes locked in a speculative gaze, before Ian stepped forward and led her into a slow, sensual dance, guiding her with his hips. They moved fluidly, as if the heat between them had melted and reformed them into one person, one body. When Grace felt his lips against her forehead, she closed her eyes and sighed helplessly. His hand on the small of her back held her firmly against his body, and felt as if it rested on her bare skin instead of on her jacket. Her heart pounded against his chest.

When the sweet strains of the music ended, they stood together, holding hands and unwilling to step apart, waiting for the music to begin again. But the combo announced a break, and the dancers around them moved off the floor.

Feeling dazed, her breath quickened in her breast, Grace eased backward and gazed into Ian's eyes. Desire had darkened them to a midnight blue that was so intense she smothered a gasp. His expression made her legs go weak.

Suddenly self-conscious, Grace cleared her throat, then darted a quick look around the penthouse. She had lost herself in Ian's arms to the extent that she had forgotten the gossips. Had they noticed how closely Ian held her? Had the rumormongers observed the way their hands clung and their bodies meshed? Had they seen his mouth pressed to her forehead?

Grace wet her lips in a gesture of uncharacteristic nervousness. "I think we should leave," she suggested, her voice huskier than usual. "It's getting late."

Ian's glance lifted from her mouth to the flush heating her cheeks. "Yes," he said simply.

Again their eyes held as if they could not look away from each other, then Grace made herself turn and walk off the dance floor toward the group surrounding Mary. After a covert glance to see if her fingers were trembling, she touched Mary's beaded shoulder.

"Ah, there you are," Mary said, noticing them. "I saw the two of you dancing earlier, then lost you in the crowd."

During the drive back to the hacienda, Mary chatted about this and that, relating mild gossip she'd overheard at the party, expressing her pleasure at finding people she knew.

"I hope you don't mind, Grace dear, but I'm lunching with Gladys Frazier and her niece tomorrow. And I hope to see Marcella before I leave."

Grace turned in the passenger seat to better hear the chatter flowing from the back seat of Ian's rented Lincoln. As she did so, her gaze focused directly on Ian's profile. In the light from the dashboard, she observed a small knot rising and falling along his jaw, knew he was clenching his teeth as a man occasionally did when he waged a battle with himself.

She could guess what he was fighting. The same war between desire and honor, passion and principle, raged in her own heart and mind.

At the hacienda, Ian parked the Lincoln and assisted Mary and Grace out of the car. "Anyone interested in a nightcap?" he asked lightly, looking at Grace.

"Not for me." Mary politely smothered a yawn. "Parties make me feel my age, damn it." Lifting herself on tiptoe, she kissed Ian's cheek. "Thank you for a lovely evening." Then she bent to hug Grace, murmuring in a low voice, "Beware of moonlight and flattery, my dear."

Grace smiled and affectionately returned her mother-in-law's embrace. "I wish you'd join us."

"I'd like to, but . . . perhaps another time."

Señora Valdez had left the pool lit, and a fully stocked cocktail cart waited in the courtyard. While Ian mixed drinks, Grace studied the pool light reflecting on the palm fronds overhead. The lighting and landscaping created the illusion of a tropical paradise.

"It's cool, but a beautiful night," she remarked. The immediate setting might appear tropical, but a chilly desert night surrounded them. Stars spangled the sky, and each breath was perfumed with the scent of tiny night-blooming flowers. Smiling, Grace decided their hosts, Marsha and Bill Ingram, were romantics.

"Care for a midnight swim?" Ian asked, coming up behind her. "The pool's heated."

"Now, that would definitely be playing with fire," Grace said, turning with a smile.

Her smile wavered when she realized how close he stood, when she saw the intensity of the gaze he fastened on her lips. He had left their drinks on the table between two chairs, and his hands were free to circle her waist and gently draw her body close to his.

Grace's pulse accelerated swiftly and her breath became uneven. He was going to kiss her.

Intellectually she knew she should step away from him. But emotionally and physically, she understood that the entire evening had been leading to this moment. Perhaps the last thirty-three years had led inevitably to this moment.

As if suspended in a circle of evening enchantment, they stood quietly, hip to hip, their arms loosely holding each other. They gazed into speculative eyes, curious, questioning this new step in their relationship.

Then Ian glanced at her parted lips and a low sound rose from his chest. Grace closed her eyes and swayed against him, inhaling sharply as she felt his powerful arousal.

When his lips touched hers, she stiffened momentarily, before gradually relaxing as his kiss explored her mouth, tenderly, deliberately, and without haste. After a brief hesitation, she slid her palms up his arms and shoulders and twined her hands around his neck, returning his kisses with building ardor, making discoveries of her own.

They were not teenagers, not driven by uncontrollable urgency. With age had come the wisdom to recognize the pleasure of delayed gratification and to savor each moment of discovery and draw it out. They understood the value of prolonging desire, of allowing passion to build kiss upon deepening kiss, touch upon exploring touch.

But neither were they immune to the flames they fanned in each other's bodies. Their breath heated and emerged in gasps, their hearts pounded. Grace buried her fingers in Ian's thick, heavy hair. His hands slipped inside the jacket of her silk suit.

When she felt the scald of his palms against the sides of her breasts, she drew a sharp fainting breath and would have stumbled if she hadn't steadied herself against him.

"Oh, Jeffrey!"

They both froze. Jeffrey's name hung between them like a sudden barrier, shocking in its effect.

Grace felt as if she'd been abruptly drenched in icy water. She clenched her teeth then forced her jaw to relax. "I'm sorry," she apologized in a low voice. The error utterly mortified her.

Ian's hands dropped to her waist, tightened, then fell to his sides. "Don't apologize," he said evenly. "It's perfectly all right, perfectly understandable."

She opened her palms against his jacket, feeling the heat of his body radiating against her hands. "I just...it's habit, of course. I wasn't thinking, I..."

He interrupted her apology with a gentle kiss that forgave her blunder. But clearly, the mood between them had altered. There was nothing like calling one man by another man's name to cool his passion, Grace thought wryly. And perhaps that was best. Ian's kisses had swept her to the edge of control. She didn't want to think they might have done something she would deeply regret had they continued further.

Ian tilted her chin up and placed a kiss on the tip of her nose. "Well," he said, smiling down at her with an expression that mixed disappointment with an effort to smooth over the moment. "Shall we have that nightcap now?"

They seated themselves facing the pool and the liquid shadows flickering in the palms, a small table safely between them.

"I feel so foolish," Grace murmured huskily, not looking at him. "But perhaps... Jeffrey is the only other man I've kissed like that."

"Grace, it's all right. I understand." Reaching across the table, he gently touched her shoulder. "This kind of thing happens. I called Marla 'Caroline' and Diane 'Marla.' It's awkward, yes, but a common error when you've been with someone for a long time."

Ian might insist the mistake was common, but calling him by Jeffrey's name had shocked Grace. She stared at the surface of the pool and struggled to collect her thoughts.

"What we did just now was as much my fault as yours," she said in a low voice. "But, Ian, please. This can't happen again. I know I sound old-fashioned—I *am* old-fashioned—but until my divorce is final, I'm married.'' Guilt and embarrassment burned on her cheeks. She certainly hadn't behaved like a married woman tonight. "I suspect saying a few words in court isn't going to change the fact that I still feel married to Jeffrey. I think it's going to require some time before I stop feeling married."

"I think you wanted me as much as I wanted you."

She turned to look at him then, but his face was in shadow. "Wanting a man who isn't Jeffrey makes me feel guilty, as if I'm doing something very wrong…it makes me feel strange inside."

"Jeffrey was unfaithful to you. You're divorcing him, Grace. You're free to be with whomever you choose, free to do whatever you like."

"I think you must know it isn't that simple. Until last year, my world revolved around Jeffrey DeWilde. I thought it always would, and that's what I wanted. Then my safe life exploded and everything changed. In the span of a year, I've moved halfway around the world, set up housekeeping alone, begun a new business in the face of discouraging statistics, and now I'm divorcing a man with whom I expected to spend the rest of my life. My children don't understand what I'm doing, nor do our friends. Sometimes I'm not certain that I understand how this happened."

Frowning, she turned a pleading look toward his shadowy face. "A lot has happened in a short period, and I haven't assimilated it yet. I need time, Ian. I'll make the adjustments I need to make, and I'll eventually land on my feet. I always do. But I need time to sort out my feelings, time to work through the confusion, and time to stop thinking of myself as married. I need time to adjust to a new life that I'm not sure I welcome or want."

It was a long speech, and she paused to take a sip of her drink. "I'm attracted to you," she continued quietly. "I think tonight proved there's electricity between us. And I've loved you as a friend for more than thirty years. I can't predict the future, but...if I were ever to fall in love and marry again... I think the man involved would be you. But I'm a long way from being ready for anything like a new love and marriage. I need time, Ian."

The faint hum of the pool pump and the buzz of insects seemed overloud in the silence. Finally Ian reached across the table for her hand and Grace hesitated only briefly before she clasped his fingers.

"I understand everything you've said, Grace," he said quietly. "And I agree with most of it. I wish I could tell you that I'll go away and return in a year when you're ready. I know that would be the sensible and considerate approach, the best thing for you. But I can't risk a delay. I don't have much time to give you."

Something in his voice made Grace's chest tighten in alarm. "Ian, what are you saying?"

He stood then and guided her to her feet, placing his hands gently on her shoulders. "When you asked why I'd been in hospital, I told you I went there for routine tests and I assured you I was healthy. I lied to you."

"Ian?" Unconsciously she gripped his lapels with hands that had begun to shake. Frantically, she searched his face, seeking a hint of amusement, wanting this to be one of his jokes, even as every instinct warned that he was deadly serious. "Ian?" she said again when he appeared to hesitate and regret that he'd admitted what he had.

"I'm dying, Grace. This time next year I'll be dead."

CHAPTER ELEVEN

THE SKY HAD SPLINTERED into streaks of pink and indigo before they parted. Feeling ill, Grace performed the routine of washing her tear-stained face and preparing for an hour or two of sleep, but she did so clumsily and with frequent pauses to blot the tears that continued to brim in her eyes.

Ian was fortunate in one way. His cancer had taken one of the forms that caused little pain; there would be no intense discomfort until near the end. When the end might come was impossible to predict, but his doctors were not optimistic.

"One suggested six months, the specialist gave me a year," Ian had informed her. He had shrugged and smiled. "One of the doctors said I could outlive everyone in the room. Who can say?"

But Grace understood that his instincts leaned toward the specialist's prediction. Ian did not expect to enjoy another spring. He believed he had entered his last year, moving toward an eventuality that Grace could not bear to contemplate.

The news was so difficult to accept. If ever a man had appeared invincible, impervious to mortal disease, it was Ian Stanley. For as long as Grace had known him, Ian had sparkled with vitality and impish good humor. His energy seemed inexhaustible. He skied, yachted, played tennis and squash. He was first to arrive at his Paris bank and last to leave. Travel was one of his passions, and Ian liberally sprinkled his life with long and short jaunts to every corner of the globe.

How could a man this active, this energetic be dying at age fifty-five? How could such a thing happen?

Sinking to the edge of the bed, Grace dropped forward and buried her face in her hands. She knew Ian well enough to understand that pity would have appalled and embarrassed him, so after an initial burst of tears, she had exercised the iron control for which she was famous and had not permitted herself to cry while they talked. But now the tears came in a flood... angry, furious tears.

This was so unfair, so impossible to understand. Ian was in the prime of his life, at the pinnacle of his career. He was a good, decent man, and she loved him.

An hour later, Grace still stared at the ceiling, still sleepless. After she had cried her eyes dry for Ian's sake, her thoughts finally, perhaps selfishly, turned to herself.

Ian's death would open an enormous hole in her life. She had always relied on him. But until now, she hadn't quite realized the extent of her reliance, or how greatly she depended on Ian to be there. Just to be there.

Ian was the person she called when Jeffrey wasn't available. The person she instinctively turned to in an emergency. She relied on Ian to remind Jeffrey about her birthday and their anniversary, depended on him to cheer Jeffrey when she couldn't. When a husband's assurances were not enough, she had looked in Ian's eyes to judge the effect of her appearance or the value of her accomplishments. Ian's pride and approval had been almost as critical and important to her as Jeffrey's.

Ian was correct. He *had* been there for all the milestones in Grace's life. Naively, she had assumed that he always would be. How could an event be significant if Ian were not there to share it? Somehow, over the years, Ian had become the audience Grace played to. His beaming applause was as crucial to her sense of well-being as Jeffrey's.

Tears streamed down her cheeks and dampened the pillow. The shock of Ian's revelation and the grief of knowing she would lose him felt like an enormous thumb pressing down on her heart.

When the telephone jangled on the side table, she started, then sat up in bed and glanced at the clock. It was six-thirty.

"Grace?"

The instant she heard Rita Mulholland's voice, she knew something was badly wrong at the store.

"I'm sorry if I woke you."

"What's happened?"

"There was a fire last night in the accessories storeroom. The firemen believe it was probably started by someone sneaking a cigarette back there, then tossing the butt in a waste can before it was fully extinguished."

"How bad is the damage?" Grace asked, her mind racing, recalling the storeroom in full detail, seeing it packed with boxes and cartons.

"Not as devastating as it might have been, thank God. Someone called in an alarm right away. The fire destroyed the storeroom and some of the second-floor corridor. But we have a considerable amount of smoke and water damage. Most worrisome, there's a question about structural integrity, particularly in regard to the ceiling beneath the burned section."

Groping for her glasses, Grace pushed them on her nose and began compiling a list on the pad beside the phone. "We'll need to notify the insurance company and hire a cleanup crew. Block off the affected area. Were any of the gowns damaged?"

"Billows of smoke and soot reached the main floor, so I expect at least some of the gowns will require cleaning. The veils took the worst hit. We probably lost fifty thousand dollars' worth of veils to the flames, possibly more. I don't know yet which areas or what items were damaged by water, but we may be looking at several thousand dollars' worth of cleanup. The firemen aren't allowing anyone into the burn area, but as soon as I have a minute, I'll pull up the inventory records. We'll know more later today."

Frustration seared Grace's thoughts. Her eyes strayed toward the closet and her clothes and luggage. Her impulse was to leave at once. She could be in San Francisco before lunch.

"Grace? One of the firemen is standing beside me. Would you like to speak to him?"

"Please."

If she left Nevada, the divorce proceedings would halt. Everything would revert as if she had never filed for residency. To obtain a divorce, she would have to begin the six-week residency program again from the beginning. Which meant she would have spent the last three-and-a-half weeks away from the store to no purpose. Frustration closed her throat.

Making an effort to calm herself, she spoke at length to the fireman.

"I see," she said, tapping her fingernails on the table surface. "How soon can someone arrive to inspect for structural damage?" She listened, then struck the edge of the bed with a clenched fist. "Several days?"

In person she might have charmed him into persuading the inspector to check the structure today. But on the phone, Grace could not hasten the procedure; the fireman was obdurate. Speaking to his superior also failed to meet with success. A long sigh issued from her lips, doing nothing to alleviate her tension.

"Well," she said when Rita returned to the phone, "there doesn't seem to be anything we can do to speed the process. We'll have to close the store until after the inspection and the completion of any necessary repairs."

They spoke for another twenty minutes, then Rita asked in a tired voice, "How are you, Grace?"

"Right now? My stomach's churning and I'm frustrated half out of my mind. I want to be there. I want to see the extent of the damage myself. I want..." Her voice trailed and she thrust a hand through her hair. "Please don't misunderstand. I know you'll handle this situation as well as I would. I know there's nothing I could do if I *were* there."

"Surely the authorities wouldn't object if you just flew in for the day, would they?"

The instant she hung up from Rita, Grace dialed Walter Kennedy at his home and asked him the same question.

"Grace, we've discussed this previously. You can't leave the state, not if you want this divorce. I'd even discourage you from leaving the county."

"I wouldn't stay the night," Grace insisted stubbornly, staring at the list she had compiled, distracted by all that needed to be done.

"The fire is certain to make the news. All we need is for one photographer to catch you on film and then have that photograph appear in the media. We'd have to start over. You would have to begin the residency period again from day one, and we'd have to file for a new court date. Is that what you want?"

Standing, she paced as far as the phone cord would allow, clenching her jaw in frustration. "I need to think about this."

"Keep in mind that you're two-and-a-half weeks from your court date."

Grace slammed down the telephone and glared at it as if Walter were to blame for her sudden conviction that she was being held prisoner in the state of Nevada. Almost instantly, she regretted the rude gesture and jotted a note on her list to telephone Walter later and apologize. Thrusting a hand through her tousled hair, she sighed heavily.

It was useless to suppose that she might catch an hour of sleep. Not with the fire occupying her thoughts, and Ian. Frowning, she padded through the house to the kitchen, wearing only the long T-shirt that she used as a nightshirt. The coffee was already made, thank goodness, and she carried a large mug out into the sunshine bathing the courtyard.

"Good morning."

"Ian!" Shading her eyes against the bright sunlight, Grace blinked toward a chair facing the pool. He wore the same clothing he'd worn last night. A shadow of stubble shaded his jaw. "Didn't you sleep?"

"It was so close to sunrise that there didn't seem any point in going to bed." He, too, had found the coffee and raised his mug in a salute. "You look beautiful."

A rush of self-consciousness warmed Grace's cheeks. She hadn't combed her hair, she wore no makeup. The T-shirt covered her thighs, but not her bare legs or feet. She was unaccustomed to being seen when she wasn't looking her best, and the urge to flee was almost irresistible. But this was Ian, a man who claimed to love her. Perhaps it was good for him to see her tousled and unadorned, feeling a bit vulnerable and at a definite disadvantage.

Hesitantly, she approached the chair beside him and sat down, tugging the edges of the T-shirt as close to her knees as possible. "If our friendship can survive the sight of me in the morning, we can survive just about anything," she said wryly. No woman her age welcomed the morning sunlight.

Ian laughed and ran a hand across the whiskers sprouting on his jaw. "I'm not exactly at my best, either, darling."

"There was a fire at Grace last night." Drawing a deep breath, she told him as much as she knew.

"Poor darling. You're straining at the bit because you want to be there," Ian commented with a smile of understanding.

"Dealing with chaotic situations is one of my skills," Grace stated firmly. "Knowing I'll have to handle everything by phone or through Rita makes me feel wild inside!"

Ian watched her attempt to settle her nerves. "If you decide to inspect the store personally, won't that mean that you'll have to begin the residency requirement again from the beginning?"

Grace nodded. The tension behind her chest felt like a ticking bomb. "And that would mean I've wasted almost a month." At once, she realized how the statement might sound to him, and she reached to touch his wrist. "I don't mean the time with you has been wasted. I—"

"I know what you mean," he said, laughing softly. "And I understand. I resent wasting time, too. Selfishly, I'd hate to see you have to restart the residency requirement from the beginning. Speaking of selfish concerns...Grace, I had some time to think after you went inside."

He studied the surface of his coffee, then turned his head to look at her. For the first time, Grace saw his weariness, saw that it must be an effort for him to continually maintain an illusion of energetic good humor.

"I love you. I'd like nothing more than to spend the time I have left with you." His eyes searched her face. "But I want our relationship to be for the right reasons, not because you pity or feel sorry for me. I didn't intend to tell you about the cancer until after your divorce, until we had a clearer idea where you and I stand. But it troubles me to deceive you. I think that's why I ended up telling you sooner than I wished.'' He paused and glanced away from her steady gaze. "By telling you, I've created an additional pressure that you don't need at this time in your life. I'm sorry, Grace. I apologize for causing you additional strain."

"Oh, Ian," she said softly, tears welling between her lashes. "What you're going through isn't something you withhold from your friends. I'm glad you told me. I only wish you'd permit me to tell Mary and Jeffrey and your other good friends."

"I'd prefer that you didn't. People would try not to treat me differently, but they would. That's simply human nature." Reaching, he took her hand and clasped it on the table between them. "What I'm trying to say, Grace, and doing it clumsily, is that I don't want my situation to dictate your decisions."

"Ian—"

"Please, let me finish. I've been thinking about this for several hours." He paused to organize his thoughts. "I know you, Grace. Beneath that cool, elegant exterior is a warm, caring woman who puts those she loves before herself. Without much effort, I can imagine you marrying me out of pity, or from some well-intentioned idea that you'll make my last year happy and comfortable."

A blush of guilt stained her cheeks, and she shifted her gaze to their clasped hands. Those very thoughts had crossed her mind.

He sighed softly. "Exactly as I feared. Well, darling, do us both a favor and push that idea right out of your beautiful head. I don't want a marriage based on pity and neither do you. Most particularly, I don't want you to eventually resent me because my dying caused you to do something you didn't genuinely want to do.

"If you come to me, I want it to be because you love me. No other reason, Grace. But if you feel you must go to San Francisco, and you're hesitating because my illness casts a different light on the time required to wait out another residency period, well...go to San Francisco. You can't let my circumstances make your decisions."

"I'll try to be as honest as you've been," Grace whispered. "My instinct is to leave at once for San Francisco. But I'm not sure of my motivation."

Ian closed his eyes and drew a breath. "I know you don't require a reminder...but Jeffrey treated you wrong and that's why you're divorcing him. Nothing can change what he did."

"The reason for our divorce is more complicated than that."

"It always is. But Jeffrey's affair brought things to a head and you left him. Still, however much it pains me to admit this, I know you're conflicted about a divorce." A light shrug twitched his shoulders. "Maybe you're looking for reasons outside yourself to halt the process. Perhaps that's part of why you feel compelled to go to San Francisco."

He was such a dear friend, Grace thought, examining his face through a haze of moisture. He loved her enough to attempt to help her understand herself, enough to let her go, even though that was not what he wanted.

"Ian," she began, then looked up when Señora Valdez leaned out of the French doors.

"You have a telephone call, Señora DeWilde."

"That must be Rita with more news," Grace said, silently cursing the interruption. She touched Ian's shoulder. "Wait for me."

"Haven't I always?" he said softly, managing to place a kiss on her hand before she whirled away.

Hurrying inside, Grace took the call in the living room. She snatched up the receiver. "Rita?"

"It's Jeffrey."

Sitting hard on the edge of the sofa, Grace shook her head. Jeffrey would call now, when her heart was full of Ian. Guilt tensed her muscles as she recalled feverish kisses in the moonlight, the frantic touches and ragged breathing. Regardless of the impending divorce, at this moment she was still married. It didn't matter that her passion for Ian had been a pallid thing compared to the passion she experienced in Jeffrey's arms; it had been Jeffrey's wife exchanging passionate kisses with another man last night.

"Good morning," she said cautiously, instantly feeling foolish. It was not morning in London.

"I'll come directly to the point. I'm deeply disturbed that Ian is staying with you. Surely you're aware of the potential for scandal. If Ian lacks the sensibility to recognize that his presence at the Ingrams' places you in a compromising position, I'd have thought that certainly you would. Moreover, it is particularly offensive and distasteful on both your parts to use mother as a beard. That's unforgivable."

Grace stiffened and sat up straight. "I beg your pardon?"

"Possibly Mother is unaware of what's transpiring directly under her nose, but others are not. I've heard from two people who insist that you and Ian were carrying on like lovers at a party last night. Apparently you believed Mother's unwitting presence would paste a veneer of decency on your behavior. Or perhaps you hoped to convey the impression that Mother condoned your actions." Cold, tight fury shook his voice.

"That...you...those charges are utterly untrue!" She was so furious she was stammering.

"Ian must leave the Ingrams' at once, Grace. Now that the two of you have made a spectacle of yourselves, people will be watching and waiting for further indiscretions. You're inviting a scandal, fairly begging the tabloids to take notice. Furthermore, I insist that Mother leave immediately. You're making a fool of her, and I will not stand for that!"

Grace sprang to her feet, shaking all over, sputtering with fury and indignation. "Listen to me, Jeffrey DeWilde! Ian and I are not having an affair. That's *your* forte, not mine! Besides, Ian is Marsha and Bill Ingram's guest—I have no right to ask him to leave even if that's what I wanted, and it isn't. As for your mother...no one is making a fool of her, and we are *not* using her as a beard to disguise whatever you think is going on here. How dare you make these despicable charges? How *dare* you!"

"Even if you no longer value your reputation, I urge you to consider our children. Remember our children? How the hell are they going to feel when they learn that their mother, who as of this moment at least is still married to their father, has been seen in public with another man, hanging all over him like a lovesick teenager?"

"A lovesick...?" Grace was shaking so badly she could hardly grip the telephone. "I've attended a hundred functions with Ian because *you* were too damned busy with business to be bothered to escort me!" She knew that statement would hit home hard. It would remind him of his father and his own feelings of abandonment, and she didn't care. "Our friends are accustomed to seeing Ian as my escort and usually at your request! I doubt our children will give it a second thought if they learn I went dancing with Ian Stanley, but if they do, I hope they'll be glad I went to a party instead of sitting here alone and miserable. And I hope they would be happy that Ian cared enough to be here to offer a little support! Unlike you, I don't think Kate, Megan or even Gabriel would leap to the conclusion that Ian and I are sleeping together or using your mother! That is unforgivable, Jeffrey!''

''Please inform Mother that I will be calling later to assist with her arrangements for departure.''

Grace slammed down the telephone, and this time she did not regret it. Her hands quivered and tremors of fury shook her body. She felt as if she were choking. After a few minutes of furious pacing, she whirled and returned to the courtyard.

''Good morning, dear,'' Mary said. One carefully drawn eyebrow lifted when she noted Grace's disheveled appearance and the skimpy T-shirt. ''Did you just awaken?'' Then she noticed Grace's expression and she gripped the arms of her chair and leaned forward. ''Oh, my.''

Grace's blazing eyes focused on Ian. ''You were dead wrong. I *do* want this divorce! I wouldn't take Jeffrey DeWilde if he were the last bastard on earth!''

Ian and Mary stared at her.

''He'll be calling you later today,'' she said to Mary between gritted teeth. ''Now, if you'll both excuse me, I need to shower and dress, then I have a hundred phone calls to make.'' Spinning on her toes, she stormed through the hacienda like a small blond tornado. Rita Mulholland would have to handle the situation at the store. There was no way under the sun that Grace would delay obtaining her divorce in two weeks. She wanted it *now*. How *dare* Jeffrey say those things to her?

It was midafternoon before she finished her list of phone calls. Ian had driven in to town. Mary had gone to and returned from lunch with friends. Señora Valdez was making homey sounds in the kitchen, preparing for dinner.

Grace pushed her glasses to the top of her head and leaned back from the library desk. The situation at Grace had been contained to the extent that she and Rita could manage. All had been done that could be done for the moment. She had spoken to each of her children and mentioned that Ian was with her in Nevada, listening carefully to their response. None had indicated that Ian's presence was scandalous or unusual enough to merit a comment, not even Gabriel. Ian had been part of their lives from the time of their birth; they didn't question that he would visit Grace. Next, she had phoned Walter to apologize. And finally, she had completed the lengthy list of calls that Rita had passed along to her.

Now, feeling tired and drained, Grace leaned back in the desk chair and rubbed her ear where she'd held the telephone for most of the day.

And then it came to her, as suddenly as all insights arrive, abruptly and without warning.

Jeffrey DeWilde was wildly, crazily jealous.

Sitting up straight, she blinked hard. Not until very recently had Jeffrey displayed even a hint of jealousy. Throughout their marriage, his usual lack of jealousy had, in fact, annoyed her on more than one occasion. During most of their years together, it would have pleased her if he had demonstrated a little more possessiveness. Once or twice Grace had only half jokingly accused him of taking her for granted.

"Ah, there you are," Mary said, leaning around the library door. "May I come in?"

"Of course." Grace waved a hand toward the chair facing the desk. Mary still wore the Mary McFadden afternoon dress that she'd worn to lunch with her friends. She looked especially handsome and energetic. By comparison, Grace felt tired, pressured and on edge. It had been one hell of a day.

"I just hung up from Jeffrey," Mary announced, studying Grace's face. "He's very angry and upset. He's demanding that I return to London, without even stopping at my home in Manhattan."

"I'm sure he dislikes your being here. Your presence might be construed as support for me." Fresh anger forced some color into Grace's pale cheeks. "Jeffrey accused me of having an affair with Ian right under your nose."

Mary laughed. "He said the same thing to me."

"Well, we're not having an affair!" Grace protested hotly, resenting Mary's laughter.

"Of course you're not, and I told Jeffrey as much. But he's worked himself into a fit." A slow smile curved her lips. "It was Diane and Marcella who called and told him about the party last night."

Grace blinked. "Diane and Marcella? I've known them both for years and neither are gossips. Why on earth would they do something like that?"

"Because I asked them to."

"*What?*" Grace sat up straight and stared at her mother-in-law. A stab of betrayal pierced her fatigue, and she suddenly felt like weeping. "Oh, Mary. Why?"

"Now, darling, hear me out. I couldn't sleep last night for thinking about our dinner conversation and how frank I was in expressing my disapproval of Ian's pursuit. Eventually, it occurred to me that perhaps I was wrong. Perhaps I was letting my feelings obscure reality. It occurred to me that the marriage between you and my son may indeed be utterly finished, and a divorce is what you both truly want. In that regrettable case, you should each move on with your lives. You're much too young not to consider another man, there are too many lonely years ahead. If that's how things stand, then I should have kept silent last evening and been glad that Ian is waiting for you."

Grace fell backward in her chair with a feeling of helplessness. "I can guess where this is leading," she whispered. "You decided to test Jeffrey's feelings."

"Quite successfully, I would say." Mary smiled. "If he had no feelings left for you, Grace, if he didn't still love you, he wouldn't have cared a jot that Ian is staying at the hacienda or that the two of you danced at a party." She shrugged apologetically. "Instead, he's stewing himself into a boil. My son still loves you."

Leaning forward, Grace propped her aching head in her hands. "How could you do this?"

"Because I love you both. And you love each other. The two of you are about to make the biggest mistake of your lives. You belong together, not apart." She paused before continuing. "You assured me that you can forgive Jeffrey's foolishness with that girl. Have you told him?"

"No," Grace admitted after a minute. "And there's a big difference between forgiving and forgetting. I certainly haven't forgotten Jeffrey's affair." The painful image of Allison Ames intruding on the aftermath of their lovemaking rose in her memory. A light shudder trailed down her spine.

Mary waved a hand of dismissal. "As I've said before, time will solve that problem."

"If you asked Jeffrey the reason for our divorce, he wouldn't tell you it was because he betrayed our marriage vows. He would insist that he can't live with a woman who married him because he was a DeWilde instead of a man she would have loved regardless of family name and fortune. Will time solve that problem? It hasn't yet. A year has passed and Jeffrey is no closer to coming to terms with that issue than he was the night he signed into a hotel with Allison Ames."

Mary winced. "I have to believe that Jeffrey will find a way to accept a truth that ceased to matter thirty or so years ago."

"I doubt that he will. Jeffrey is angry that I focused on his affair instead of blaming myself for confiding the truth. He's furious that I can't or won't see his position. He's focused tightly on a period of less than a year, before I truly did come to love him, and he doesn't understand why I choose to concentrate on the thirty-two years of happiness that followed." Grace met her mother-in-law's troubled gaze. "I don't think Jeffrey will find a solution, Mary. I'm not sure he can. Jeffrey is going to let this divorce proceed because he can't forgive me for marrying him before I loved him. There may not be a drop of DeWilde blood in Jeffrey, but he's as stubborn and unforgiving as Maximilien De-Wilde was toward Anne Marie."

Mary stood and gripped the back of the chair. "Is there anything I can do to help either of you?" she asked quietly.

With difficulty, Grace squelched the urge to ask her mother-in-law not to interfere again.

"Jeffrey has to find his own way out of this mess," she said instead. "And he may not want to or be able to. Events have swept past the original problems. Things have been said that cannot be unsaid." Because Mary's expression wrenched her heart, Grace reached deep and found what she needed to manufacture a small smile. "But at least we know he's jealous. That has to mean something."

One of the things it meant was that she had been foolish to wish for even a moment that her husband was the jealous type. Jealousy was a destructive emotion. She doubted she would ever forget the distasteful things Jeffrey had said and implied.

AFTER DINNER, GRACE and Ian drove into Las Vegas to attend the opening of a comedy production. Afterward, Grace couldn't have repeated a single humorous line, didn't recall if she had laughed in the right places or even smiled.

"I'm sorry," she apologized as they exited the showroom. "I shouldn't have agreed to come. A nap late this afternoon didn't help much—I'm still tired and not very good company."

"It's my fault," Ian said, taking her arm as the crowd flowed past them. "I should have insisted that you turn in early instead of suggesting that we go out. I hoped the performance would cheer you a little."

"I'm as exhausted as I've been in years, but I doubt I would have slept. My mind is whirling. Since this time last night, I've discovered that one of my dearest friends is dying, my new store has been damaged by fire and water, and Jeffrey has accused *me* of having an affair!"

As they moved toward an exit, Grace caught sight of their image in a wall of mirrors. Ian was tall and handsome; he didn't look like a man who was dying. She appeared cool and stylishly elegant; she didn't look like a woman reeling with fatigue and frustration.

In the car, Ian shifted on the seat to look at her. "Jeffrey believes that you and I are having an affair?"

"Apparently," Grace said wearily.

The Lincoln shot forward into the street. "That's an insult to us both!"

Until now, Grace hadn't taken time to think about Jeffrey's accusation from Ian's viewpoint. But of course the affront was as much an assault on Ian's honor as her own.

"I shouldn't have told you." If she hadn't been so exhausted, she would have thought first and held her tongue.

"I'm glad you did. Even after seeing Jeffrey with that girl, even knowing how much pain he's caused you, I felt guilty about coming here, guilty about declaring myself, guilty about loving you." His hands tightened on the steering wheel. "I don't feel guilty anymore. Jeffrey should know that regardless of how I feel about you, I'm not going to push you into something before you're ready. And neither of us is going to be ready until you're no longer married to Jeffrey."

"Last night—"

"Last night got out of hand, and I apologize for that." He gave her a humorless grin. "I can't say I regret kissing you—I've fantasized about it for years. But I didn't intend things to go as far as they did. I meant what I said, Grace. I've waited thirty-some years for you, I can certainly wait another two weeks until your divorce is final. And goddamn it, Jeffrey knows both of us well enough to know that neither of us is going to do anything dishonorable or anything that might cause him embarrassment!"

"Ian, it can't be good for you to get this angry," Grace said. Concerned, she placed her fingers on his arm.

"Does he really think we'd have a flaming affair while his *mother* is visiting?" Anger blazed in his eyes. "Well, does he?"

There was no way she could refuse to answer. Deeply regretting that she'd mentioned the conversation with Jeffrey, Grace withdrew her hand and leaned back in the seat. "Jeffrey seems to believe we're using Mary to cover our affair," she said dully.

"Then he's insulted Mary, too!"

They didn't speak again until Ian had parked the car in front of the hacienda. For a moment they sat in the darkness, not moving.

"It isn't like Jeffrey to make these kinds of accusations," Grace said finally. "We both know that."

"You've forgiven him already?"

"No. I'm very angry, Ian. But I'm also trying to be fair."

Ian stretched his arm along the back of the seat, letting his fingertips rest lightly against the nape of her neck. Grace closed her eyes as a warm, liquid feeling flowed through her body. She yearned for him to hold her, caress her and tell her that everything was going to be all right. It didn't happen often, but occasionally, when she was very tired, she wished she were the type of woman to hand her problems to a man to solve. Even Jeffrey and Ian, the two people who knew her best, would have been astonished to learn she had occasionally harbored such thoughts.

"Since we're being blamed for the deed, we may as well have an affair," Ian said gruffly. "The more I think about this, the more I fail to see any reason to wait. Jeffrey doesn't deserve our consideration."

The timbre of his voice reached her on a primitive, raw level. For an instant his suggestion almost seemed reasonable. Desirable, even.

Grace pressed her hands together and looked at the lights shining along the hacienda veranda. "It's only about two weeks, Ian." She paused. "At the moment, everything is confused. A decision now might be taken for the wrong reasons." Peering through deep shadow, she tried to see his expression. "I'm angry enough that I'd like to hit back at Jeffrey, too. But *if* you and I decide to pursue a relationship, I don't want it to begin because we were reacting to something Jeffrey said. And I don't want to feel guilty about being with another man while I'm still married. Plus, I don't want you to feel that you've betrayed a man whom you've loved longer than I have."

"If there was any hope that Jeffrey and I might restore our friendship, he threw that hope away when he spoke to you on the phone today."

"I'm sorry."

"So am I, Grace. I loved Jeffrey like a brother."

He couldn't support them both, and he had chosen between them when he traveled halfway around the world to be with her. He must have known that decision would destroy his friendship with Jeffrey. Grace felt sorry for them both. It hurt her to realize that from now on, they would detest each other.

"I hate to leave you, but I have to return to the gypsum mine for a couple of days, damn it. While I'm gone, I'd like it if you'd think about...everything." His fingers played with the loose tendrils on her cheek. "If you really want to wait until after the seventeenth, then of course, that's what we'll do. That's what we agreed. But we owe Jeffrey nothing, Grace." His gaze hardened. "I think you can begin your new life without any guilt toward that bastard."

"I won't change my mind, Ian," Grace said softly. "And please remember that you and I haven't made any decisions yet." She touched his hand to soften her next words. "I can't commit to anything right now. I may not be ready to make a commitment before you..." She bit her lip and twisted her hands together in her lap.

"If that's how it happens, I'll accept your decision." A thin smile curved his lips. "I won't be happy about it, but I'll accept it. Meanwhile, please think about the possibilities we've discussed tonight."

They walked together to the front door of the hacienda then turned and gazed deeply into each other's eyes before Ian bent and brushed his lips gently across hers.

"I love you, Grace."

After she closed the door behind her, she leaned against it and blinked at the tears stinging her eyes.

In the last month she had wept more than she had in her entire life. It hurt to realize there were undoubtedly more tears ahead.

CHAPTER TWELVE

GRACE LONGED TO FALL into bed and sleep for twelve hours, but after reading a note she found on her pillow, she set the alarm for seven o'clock.

> Darling,
> Jeffrey phoned again tonight. He's insistent that I leave for London at once, and he's made the arrangements. I have decided to surrender rather than continue these telephone disagreements, which only upset us both. We need to speak in person.
>
> I do apologize for interfering, Grace. Clearly, all I accomplished was to create new problems and make matters worse. Be assured that I shall correct Jeffrey's impressions.
>
> You're very tired, darling, and you need your rest. Don't feel you need to rise early to see me off. We aren't saying goodbye, only au revoir.
>
> I love you,
> Mary

AFTER THE ALARM jarred her awake, Grace read Mary's note again, then pushed her feet into a pair of slippers and tied Jeffrey's old robe at her waist. Yawning, she splashed cold water on her face and ran a hasty comb through her hair.

She found Mary dressed and coiffed, smoking and sipping coffee in a wicker chair on the veranda, surrounded by her luggage.

"If I have half your energy and look half as good at your age as you do, I'll be well satisfied," Grace murmured admiringly. Bending, she pressed her cheek to Mary's.

Mary laughed. "All it requires is a couple of face-lifts, a few nips and tucks, and enough curiosity to get out of bed every day. Señora Valdez, that treasure, left a tray of coffee things near the petunias. But really, Grace, you didn't need to wave me off."

"I couldn't let you leave without telling you how deeply I appreciate your visit and how much I've enjoyed your company." Sitting beside her mother-in-law, she smoothed the old robe over her knees, then sighed with pleasure after her first sip of coffee. She would miss Señora Valdez's fragrant, strong coffee when she returned to San Francisco.

"Jeffrey is behaving like a total ass, I'm sorry to say. My son and I are destined to have words," Mary announced in a tight voice. "I'm rehearsing what I wish to convey even now. And, Grace dear, I *will* straighten out the trouble I've caused."

Grace held her coffee mug close to her chest and gazed toward the royal palms. "Ian and I danced only with each other, and we were dancing close. If Diane and Marcella hadn't phoned Jeffrey, perhaps someone else would have."

"The point is, no one did." She drew a breath. "I saw you and Ian dancing. I'm old-fashioned enough to believe the two of you skirted close to the line of propriety. But you didn't cross it."

"I'd agree with that assessment," Grace said softly. What happened later *had* crossed the line and she was guiltily aware of it, but she didn't feel she had to apologize for dancing.

"I always swore I would not be an interfering mother-in-law, but look what I've done. I'm thoroughly disgusted with myself." Mary grimaced. "As a result of my interference, Jeffrey has leapt from the dance floor to the bedroom, and I'm to blame." Her mouth settled along grim lines of determination. "Well, I'll take care of *that!*"

A twinkle of amusement sparkled in Grace's eyes. "I know that expression. I have half a mind to phone Jeffrey and warn him."

Mary patted her hand. "At the moment, I doubt it would improve your spirits to call London," she commented wryly. "Give me a week. Then I believe that son of mine will be properly contrite and begging to apologize. Or my name is not Mary DeWilde."

Grace laughed out loud. "Poor Jeffrey. I almost feel sorry for what's about to descend on him."

They watched a white limousine turn into the driveway and glide past the royal palms. Their time together had almost ended.

"Mary...what shall I do with Anne Marie's diaries? Their final disposition is too momentous a decision for me to make alone."

Mary hesitated. "Anne Marie's secret weakens with each generation," she said slowly. "Indeed, it will shock the family deeply if ever it's revealed that the DeWildes are not truly DeWildes. The revelation would undoubtedly raise a scandal. But the shock lessens as time progresses. The DeWildes have grown into DeWildes. Nothing will alter that or diminish it. Do you understand what I'm saying?"

"A rose by any other name is still a rose?" Grace asked, smiling.

"Exactly." Standing, Mary counted her bags of luggage before she opened her purse and touched the spine of a romance novel tucked inside for reading on the airplane. "I believe I have everything."

"You haven't advised me about the diaries."

"And I don't intend to," Mary replied crisply. She greeted the limo driver, indicated her luggage, then embraced Grace tightly, enveloping her in an aura of rose-scented fragrance. "Tell that scoundrel Ian goodbye for me. And stay in touch. I want to know when Grace reopens, and everything about the children, where you're going, what you're doing, what you're wearing. I want to know how you're feeling and what you're thinking."

"I love you, Mary DeWilde."

"I love you, too, darling." Mary glanced at the chauffeur standing beside the opened door of the limousine. "I want you to remember two things. If the divorce is a mistake... it's a mistake that can be corrected."

"And the second thing?" Grace whispered.

"We've discussed it already. Jeffrey will eventually come to terms with your not having loved him when you married. I'm completely convinced of this." Mary leaned back and gazed directly into Grace's eyes. "Your marriage will truly end not with the divorce, but on the day you begin a relationship with Ian or anyone else. That, Jeffrey will never forgive. Remember Maximilien and Max, dearest Grace. Remember my husband, Charles, who never forgave his father for trying to keep him out of the war. The DeWilde men find it *very* difficult to forgive, and they *never* forget." With those words, Mary turned and walked down the steps.

Grace pulled Jeffrey's robe around her body. She stood on the veranda, gripping her coffee cup and waving until the white limousine disappeared from sight.

AFTER GRACE COMPLETED her daily round of telephone calls, she treated herself to a long walk and then a swim.

Afterward, she let the sun dry her body, trying to recall the last time she had basked in the sunshine. Then, as now, she had found it boring to lie idle. And although the air was cool, it was hot enough in the direct sun to raise a sheen of perspiration, which she didn't like.

Sighing over the dictates of her own opinions, she rose from the towel and draped it over her arm before she returned to the house. Some people were fashioned to be sun-worshipers, others were not. She lacked the patience and the mind-set to deliberately waste time.

While she dressed in a loose shirt, slacks and sandals, she realized it would be something of a relief to return to Grace and her frantic schedule. The weeks in Nevada had sped past more swiftly than she had anticipated, yet she couldn't recall what she had done to fill the days. Certainly she hadn't accomplished anything of note.

Thanks to Ian's relentless efforts to entertain and cheer her, she had had enough of gambling to last a lifetime, had seen so many shows they blurred in her memory. She had dined in world-class restaurants, shopped with Mary, viewed the Hoover Dam.

And she had read all but the last few entries in Anne Marie's record of her long life.

What Grace would remember most about her six-week hiatus in the desert was Ian—and Anne Marie.

Wandering into the living room, she paused to listen to the silence in the house. With Ian and Mary gone, and Señora Valdez in town shopping for groceries, she had the house to herself. With no demands on her time and interruptions unlikely, this seemed a perfect opportunity to finish reading the diaries.

After making a pitcher of iced tea, she carried the tea tray into the library and settled into a comfortable chair positioned to catch the warm desert breeze.

The stack of pages remaining in the translation had dwindled. She would finish reading the diaries today.

Grace adjusted her reading glasses and immediately lost herself in the later years of Anne Marie's life. She read about the beginnings of World War II and Anne Marie's heartbreaking loneliness. From the window of her modest cottage in the village, Anne Marie could see Kemberly's west wing, and she spent her days watching and waiting for Max's wife, Genevieve, to call on her.

Genevieve DeWilde's kindness and gentle strength illuminated the diary pages and Anne Marie's solitary life. Genevieve was Anne Marie's lifeline to her son Max and to her grandchildren, grown now and old enough to be swept into the looming world disaster. Without Max's wife, Anne Marie's later years would have been unendurable.

After Maximilien's death, Marie had re-established tentative communication with her mother. But too many years had passed for the relationship ever to be easy or comfortable. Marie remained in Paris, a successful designer, and lived a sophisticated life that Anne Marie could not understand or wholly accept. The diary revealed that Anne Marie believed her daughter had borne a child out of wedlock and later adopted the child as a passing nod to convention. For years, Anne Marie continued to write to her daughter, but Marie responded only at Christmas. Eventually their communication ceased altogether.

It was Max's wife who remembered Anne Marie during the holidays and on her birthday. Genevieve who brought small gifts, photographs and news of the family. And it was Genevieve's tireless efforts that finally persuaded Max to agree to allow his mother into his presence for the first time in thirty-six years to celebrate the baptism of her first great-grandchild.

Jeffrey! A thrill of goose bumps rose on Grace's skin, and she reread the entry with interest and a feeling of heartbreak.

October 11, 1940. Bless dear Genevieve. She has given me the greatest gift imaginable! I was allowed to attend my great-grandson's baptism. Think of it! But the greatest gift was to be in the same room as my beloved son, to warm myself at the sight of him after all these years, to breathe the air he breathed.

What joy I have experienced this day! How often I have imagined it. And how confusing the reality. I remember my darling Max as a young man in his twenties, and despite the photographs Genevieve has brought me over the years, I was stunned to discover a man firmly of middle age.

But now I know how dear Martin would have looked at age sixty. And Maximilien, too, for Max resembles them both, tall and handsome and distinguished. I could not take my eyes from him.

I fear I surely disappointed Mary, the young woman Charles married. I scarce paid her and the infant Jeffrey a jot of attention, as I was so unnerved by the sight of my own son. Tomorrow I shall post Mary a note and blame my distraction on my age. She seems a sensible young woman, handsome rather than pretty. She will need great strength to endure the coming conflagration.

My heart aches to foresee Max's pain in the future. Charles will not forgive him for allowing his other sons into the war effort, but not him, though now he fights for the Free French Army. Max above all should know that the men in this family do not forgive easily. Sadly,

I predict this generation, too, shall have its estrangement and heartache.

But, oh, to see my darling Max after all these years! The joy fatigued me, too great to bear. He carries himself tall and straight like my Maximilien always did, and I recognized many of Maximilien's gestures. Certainly he has Maximilien's brilliance for business. With Max at the head of the family, DeWilde's has grown into an international success. The DeWilde name is synonymous with quality, elegance and fine gems.

And Martin, he has Martin's beautiful hazel eyes and fine brown hair. Genevieve says that my son is musically gifted and plays the piano like a virtuoso, but only when he is alone.

I see that he is the best of them both, my son. Handsome and gifted, an assured and brilliant man. He is part Maximilien and part Martin. They would be so proud of him, so very, very proud.

After the boy was baptized, our party returned to Kemberly. I was not certain if I was invited, but I went along as if I were. The baptism finished so swiftly, I wished to prolong the moments with my Max. This time may never come again.

There were so many, many things I longed to say to him, words I have rehearsed for thirty-six silent years. I wanted to tell him about Martin, that dear good man, and about my beloved Maximilien, whom I knew in a way that a son cannot. I yearned to ask if it was true that my darling Maximilien died with my name on his lips and if he forgave me at the end. I wanted so much to speak and to listen, to learn if Max sounds like Martin or like Maximilien. But my son kept a roomful of people between us. When I mustered the courage to attempt an approach, he moved away from me.

But—and my heart soars to speak of it—there was a moment. The day was long and the excitement of seeing him exhausted me. I had observed my great-grandson and feasted my heart on the sight of my son; I will nourish myself on this memory for a long time to come. I whispered to Genevieve that I had wearied, and that dear soul immediately summoned the car to carry me back to the village.

The driver assisted me inside and would have closed the door, but I said, and I know not why, but I said, wait. I peered up at the steps of Kemberly and Max stood there looking back at me. Looking... looking... exactly as I looked at him, filling my sore heart and replenishing my spirit with the sight of my only son. So, too, did he look at me.

It was as if time stopped for us while we gazed our fill, pouring memory into empty spaces. We were together in thought and heart as we had not been together since he was a child, standing at my knee, gazing into my eyes.

And in his gaze I saw the lost years. I heard the unsaid words. I saw regret and sorrow in my son's eyes. And perhaps love? Oh, surely I did not imagine a little love.

And then, my son offered me the gift of his voice. He said, so softly it was almost a whisper, he said, "Driver, take my mother home."

He called me mother.

Did you hear, Maximilien? Martin? My son called me mother.

I am not too old to weep.

SHADOWS CREPT ACROSS the library floor and lengthened toward evening. Grace stopped reading to have dinner, asking Señora Valdez to serve her fruit plate in the library. She ate sitting at the library table, not certain if the loneliness that depressed her spirit was her own or if she remained in the grip of Anne Marie's solitude.

Despite everything, tonight she badly missed Jeffrey. The Jeffrey of this past year was not the Jeffrey she had known throughout her married life. Her Jeffrey was warm and caring, a loving man devoted to wife and family. He was strong and powerful, and he'd always made Grace feel cherished, secure and safe. It would have astonished his friends to learn that he could be playful and very witty when he and Grace were alone together. She had always known that Jeffrey was at his best when the day ended and they were alone.

Lowering her head, she gently rubbed her forehead. Where had the years gone? The good, good years when Kemberly had rung with children's laughter and reverberated with the excitement of Jeffrey striding in the door, calling her name...where had those years fled? How had they passed so swiftly?

Had she enjoyed them as much as she could have? Had she appreciated those years? Had she experienced any inkling that one day she would wish with all her heart that she could turn back the clock and live that period again?

One of the questions frequently asked by journalists was, What has been the best time in your life?

Usually Grace's bright eyes sparkled and she let her energy and zest for life provide the answer. "The best time is now."

Lifting her head, she gazed through the French doors at the first stars appearing in the night sky.

The best time was no longer now. The best time had been when she was married to the man she loved, not the Jeffrey DeWilde of recent months, but the Jeffrey DeWilde whose hazel eyes glowed when he looked at her. Jeffrey, who had wept with joy at the birth of their children. Who had whispered with quiet conviction that it was she who made his life complete and worth living. Jeffrey, who knew at a glance if she was sad, angry or frustrated, or needed a few minutes alone. Jeffrey, who delighted in surprising her when she'd told him countless times that she didn't like surprises. Jeffrey, who after all these years could look at her in a certain way and make her melt inside and tingle from her toes to her throat.

That was the Jeffrey she missed tonight, longed for tonight. That Jeffrey would have understood the effect of Anne Marie's diaries. He would have taken her in his arms and loved her and kissed away her secret fears that she could end alone and lonely as Anne Marie had. He would have told her that her children were outgrowing their need for her, and that was how it should be, but he never would. He would always need her as she needed him.

In little more than two weeks she would sit before a dark-robed judge and swear that their differences were irreconcilable. She would state for the public record that their marriage could not be salvaged.

She would deny her heart's truth and swear they no longer needed each other, no longer loved each other. She wouldn't mention all the wonderful memories that haunted her tonight. To obtain her divorce, she would concentrate on the Jeffrey of the past year, not the Jeffrey who was so much a part of her.

She could not bear the possibility that she might never see him again after Ryder's wedding. The thought was unimaginably painful and alien.

"Señora DeWilde?"

For an instant, Grace stared at the doorway with unseeing eyes. Then she gave her head a vigorous shake. "Sorry. I was ... what is it, Señora Valdez?"

"If there's nothing else, I'll clear your dishes and then, with your permission, I'd like to leave early tonight."

"Of course."

Grace returned to her chair by the French doors. While she found Anne Marie's story fascinating, she would be relieved to put the emotionally wrenching pages away. She identified too strongly with Anne Marie's estrangement from her son, Max, and with Anne Marie's loss of the man she loved.

After the house quieted, she read of Anne Marie's eventual decision to return to Amsterdam. It was a courageous decision for a woman of advanced age to place herself at the very edge of the war raging across Europe. And she had done so despite Genevieve's pleading objections.

Oddly, it had been Max who facilitated Anne Marie's relocation. He and Anne Marie did not see each other after Jeffrey's baptism; Genevieve continued to be their only link. But it was Max who cut through the red tape of war to travel to Amsterdam and honor Anne Marie's request by purchasing the small house by the canal where Anne Marie and Maximilien had begun their married life together. It was Max who had the house refurbished and comfortably furnished, who hired a housekeeper and a driver. It was Max who arranged for Anne Marie's passport and transportation.

And it was Max who stood on the dock on a cold windy day and watched his mother's ship sail away from England. He did not speak to Anne Marie, nor she to him. There were no farewells. But Max must have known, as Anne Marie did, that mother and son would not see each other again.

March 6, 1942. A letter from Genevieve today, with photographs of Máry and Jeffrey. My, how the child has grown. He will be tall like my Max. The family has moved to a flat in London and permits Kemberly to be used as a military headquarters. All the news is of the war.

It is cold and damp today. I am weak from coughing. Hilta had her good husband move my bedroom to the ground floor so I do not have to climb the stairs.

Yesterday I passed the hallway mirror and stopped short. An old woman gazed back at me. Who is that fragile old woman? I asked in amazement. No, it cannot be me. Behind these dim eyes I am still Maximilien's young bride, waiting to hear his step at the door, waiting for him to laugh and catch me in his arms. I cannot be that sad, thin old woman. No, my cheeks are full and rosy, my eyes are bright and my bosom firm. There is laughter on my lips, and my steps are quick. Soon my life, my soul, my Maximilien will be home.

I instructed Hilta to remove the mirrors from the house.

April 12, 1942. I never used to notice the dampness from the canals. The doctor frets that my cough has worsened and advises a warm, dry climate. Even if I were strong enough to travel, I would not leave my snug little house. This house was my wedding gift. My ghosts are here.

They come to me at night, whispering in the shadows. Tonight the rooms are merry and alive with the past. I fancy I hear my darling Maximilien bounding up the steps with a surprise gift for me and for my precious Marie. He calls for me to come to him and pat his pockets and find the small token of love that he has brought for me. In the drawing room, Martin's nimble fingers play the sweet melody he composed for me. Each note is a rose plucked from the garden of his heart. Oh, I hear Max running in the door from school. "Mummy, I'm home! Mummy, come see!" Even Catherine is here. How can that be? She, who was never in this house, has come now, whispering forgiveness.

My dear ghosts gather around me, flooding my heart with memories. Oh, Maximilien. Do you remember our first day at the old Corn Exchange, when you and Martin strewed diamonds in my hair and lap? How we laughed that day! We were so young and so full of the future and our love for each other. And do you remember the night we took the children to the wharves to watch the arrival of Sinterklaas? We gazed at each other above their heads, so filled with wonder and happiness that we could not speak. Do you remember? Do you remember it all?

I'm tired, but sleep does not come. My chest pains me, and my ghosts are restless tonight. They dash about in the shadows, careless enough to almost show themselves.

Maximilien, beloved, I am so tired. And I have waited so long. I have waited my life away.

Come for me, dearest. Take me in your arms and let me come home. Let us find Martin and laugh and love one another as we once did. Let the waiting end. Let me hear from your dear lips that you forgive me for the tragedy I set in motion. I loved you always. I love you still.

This was the last entry in the diaries.

CHAPTER THIRTEEN

BEFORE GRACE TELEPHONED Rita or anyone else on her list of calls, she phoned London, dialing the minute she sat down, before she could have second thoughts. Her hand trembled as she sipped her morning coffee, waiting for Gabriel to answer.

"Grace?"

"Gabriel, when we worked together, it made sense for you to call me Grace. It no longer does. Please, I'd rather you called me mother."

He didn't comment. "How are you?" he inquired cautiously, his voice cool. As she had throughout this long year, Grace sensed that her son was searching for an excuse to politely hang up the phone.

"I'm frustrated, upset, confused. This is a very difficult time for me."

Gabriel's surprise was palpable. He'd expected her to answer as she usually did, shielding her children from her emotional upsets by saying something automatic—and inadvertently distancing—like, "I'm fine." A slight pause developed while he decided how to respond.

"I'm sorry you're upset," he said finally. "But you're the one who filed for the divorce." The pronouncement conveyed the clear impression that Grace deserved whatever distress she was experiencing. Her son had closed himself to any feelings of sympathy or genuine connection.

"Gabriel, I spent most of last night thinking about mothers and sons and about the destructive nature of secrets." Leaning forward over the library table, she spoke rapidly, wanting to say what she had decided to say before any temptation to change her mind overwhelmed her.

"You've asked repeatedly why your father and I are seeking a divorce, and I haven't offered a reason that you can understand."

"That's correct."

Again she sensed surprise, but unquestionably she had his full attention. Grace no longer felt that he was searching for an excuse to shorten the call.

"I apologize for being deliberately vague," she said softly. "I was taking a shortsighted view."

Grace had focused on Jeffrey's affair. If her children were ever to learn of their father's affair, and she hoped they never did, she believed it was Jeffrey who should tell them.

Last night she had finally realized that while she didn't feel comfortable revealing Jeffrey's secrets, she was free to tell her children of her own role in the disintegration of her marriage. And though she had touched on it last summer with Kate, she had yet to say anything to Megan or Gabriel.

Learning the truth would undoubtedly lower their esteem for her, but it would give them a way to explain the divorce to themselves. Gabriel, more than Megan and Kate, *needed* an explanation he could understand. If he didn't receive that explanation, he and Grace would never be close again. The estrangement that had begun when she left England would continue to widen and would one day become unbridgeable.

"I hurt your father terribly, Gabriel."

"I . . . if you would rather not go into this . . ."

He was like Jeffrey in so many ways. After a year of punishing remarks intended to wrest an explanation from her, he suddenly questioned if he truly wanted an intimate glimpse into his parents' lives and problems.

"A year ago, I confided to your father that I had not loved him when we married." There it was, bald and unadorned, so hard to admit. Grace glanced at her shaking hands, then continued. "I married Jeffrey because I was dazzled by the DeWilde name, fascinated by the prestige and fortune that accompanied it. I admired your father, I respected him and cared about him...but I wasn't in love with him. Learning this hurt your father deeply." She drew a long breath. "That's how it began, Gabriel. And things just... deteriorated from that point. Jeffrey was shocked and deeply hurt that he'd married a woman who didn't love him. He still is. He cannot accept or come to terms with it."

A tense and lengthy silence opened over the phone lines. Grace felt her heart plummet to her toes. Gabriel would be asking himself what kind of woman married a man she didn't love. Perhaps he would condemn her as a grasping fortune hunter. A painful headache drummed against her temples. She had always wanted her children to admire her, to love her. After this conversation, she feared that her son would not.

On the positive side, and the reason why she had made this call, her secrets would no longer insinuate themselves into Gabriel's life. Lack of understanding would no longer poison his thinking or perhaps cause him to secretly torment himself, wondering if Lianne might one day leave him for no apparent reason, the same way it seemed his mother had left his father.

"*That* is the reason why you and Father are getting a divorce?" he asked finally. Incredulity thinned his voice.

"It's not the sole reason, Gabriel," Grace answered carefully, "but it's the primary problem that your father and I cannot resolve. Jeffrey cannot forgive me."

Gabriel's outburst of laughter was so unexpected, so utterly astonishing, that Grace removed the phone from her ear and gave it a shake as if the equipment had failed.

"I'm sorry, Mother. I apologize for laughing. I realize it's a totally inappropriate response, but . . ."

Mother. Gabriel had called her Mother. Grace went limp. Suddenly boneless, she leaned back in the library chair and closed her eyes. To her amazement and completely contrary to her expectations, she understood at once that she and Gabriel had turned a corner. Eventually, they would find their way back to each other. Moisture dampened her eyes.

"That is the most ridiculous reason for a divorce that I've ever heard!" Anger infused his voice. "Everyone who knows you and Father knows you adore him. This is crazy. The one thing that Megan, Kate and I knew as absolutely certain when we were growing up was that our parents loved each other. What in the name of God is Father thinking?"

"Wait, Gabe. How would you feel if you discovered that Lianne didn't love you when she married you? That she married the DeWilde name and fortune?"

"Hell, I'd be happy and thankful that she married me no matter what her reason was!" He laughed again. "If Lianne married the DeWilde name instead of me, then I must possess more than my share of the DeWilde charm, because I know she loves me now. There are some things about love that can't be feigned." He paused. "I'd guess that you fell in love with Father very soon after the marriage. You must have, or he would have known."

"Yes," Grace whispered. She hesitated. "You don't think less of me for marrying a man I didn't love?"

"It isn't the most straightforward thing you've ever done," he said after a pause. "I wouldn't list it on my résumé, if I were you."

His dry comment surprised her into laughter. "Oh Gabriel. I didn't expect to laugh during this conversation." His teasing reassured her as nothing else could have.

They talked for another thirty minutes, easier and more comfortable with each other than they had been since she left England. Grace reminded him of Jeffrey's early history with his own father and how Jeffrey had felt abandoned first in favor of the war and then, after Charles returned, in favor of the business. Jeffrey viewed Grace's confession as confirmation that, once again, someone he loved had chosen the business over him.

"I think it's fair to say that neither your father nor I want a divorce. But we can't live together, either. We've tried to overcome our difficulties, but we haven't been successful. So... Gabriel, it's time for both of us to move on with our lives."

"This is the saddest thing I've ever heard." There was no laughter now, only deep sorrow.

"Yes," she agreed in a low voice.

"Mother? Do you intend to have this conversation with Megan and Kate?"

"We've never treated you children differently. I talked about it a bit with Kate last summer, and now that I've explained it to you, I feel obligated to explain to Megan."

"It's not my place to advise you...."

"But?" she asked, smiling, seeing his handsome face in her mind.

"I would suggest that you not call Megan or speak any more about it to Kate. Megan and Kate don't understand why you and Father are getting a divorce, but they've managed to remain neutral." A hint of discomfort and embarrassment entered his voice. Gabe had not been neutral. "They're upset and saddened by all this, but they accept your reasons are private in a way that I couldn't manage to do. It doesn't seem necessary to give them an explanation that makes Father look like an ass."

"Denigrating your father is not my intention," Grace objected sharply. "I've avoided this conversation because I believed it would make *me* look like an ass, as you put it. Frankly, I expected you to condemn me out of hand for marrying your father before I loved him. I was ashamed and embarrassed to tell you. I did so only because I believed you needed and deserved some explanation. You were right about that, Gabe, and I was wrong. But it never occurred to me that you might think your father's feelings are foolish. They are not. If your father's reaction seems unreasonable to you, I deeply regret that. Please remember that your background is different from his. Whether or not you understand, his pain and his response are valid for him. I expect you to respect that."

"You've given me a lot to think about, and I'm grateful that we had this conversation. But I strongly urge you to reconsider repeating it to Megan and Kate. You'll only upset them, unnecessarily in my view."

Grace stiffened in alarm. "The whole purpose of this call was to strip away secrecy and confide my part in our family's difficulties."

"Sometimes keeping a secret is the kindest choice," Gabe said gently. "And sometimes it isn't beneficial or helpful to treat all children the same. We're not the same. I needed to hear all of this, Mother, but Megan and Kate don't."

They talked for another ten minutes, then Grace hung up the telephone with a slightly dazed expression. Influenced by Anne Marie's diary, she had reached the reluctant decision to telephone Gabe and peel away one secret. It had never occurred to her that Gabe would dismiss her confession as being as irrelevant as Grace had always believed it to be.

When the phone rang, she picked it up quickly, thinking Gabriel might be calling back. But it was Walter Kennedy.

"We're all set, Grace," he said confidently. "We're scheduled for eleven o'clock, two weeks from Thursday. Two of Mr. DeWilde's attorneys will be present, but we've agreed they will not ask any questions while you're on the stand. They'll be present primarily to verify the property settlement documents we'll present, and to make sure there aren't any surprises."

Grace shifted to gaze toward the pool, shimmering in the sunlight beyond the French doors. "There won't be any surprises, will there?"

"No. It's taken a great deal of negotiating, but both sides are finally in agreement on all points. You'll take the stand, Grace. I'll say something such as, It's true, is it not, that...and you'll answer yes or no. Don't volunteer any information, don't feel compelled to explain or enlarge. The questions have been agreed to by Mr. DeWilde's attorneys and are designed, in accordance with the wishes of both parties, to keep as much personal information out of the public record as possible."

"Thank you, Walter," Grace murmured, "for making this as smooth as something this painful and difficult can be."

"You'll be in and out of court in about thirty minutes."

Grace blinked. "Obtaining a divorce requires only thirty minutes?"

"If you ignore the hundreds of hours outside of court," he said dryly. "But yes, the actual court proceedings are brief."

"And afterward I can leave Nevada?"

"You can catch the next flight out, if you like. You'll be a free woman."

They spoke for another hour, reviewing the questions Walter would ask, then Grace slowly hung up the telephone. The elation she'd experienced after talking to Gabe had vanished like smoke. After considering the list of telephone calls she still had to return, she crumpled the paper in her fist. There were days when she resented spending so much of her life talking on the telephone.

Steeped in the depression that had overtaken her during Walter's explanations and instructions, she left the library and followed a brick path that led to the corral. She was leaning against the rail, watching Señora Valdez's sons work with the Ingrams' Arabians, when she heard Ian call her name.

Whirling, she watched him stride down the path toward her, sunlight gleaming in his hair like silver. Running forward, she threw herself into his arms.

"Ian! You came back early."

"Hello, good-looking. Now, this is the kind of greeting that warms a man's heart." He grinned down at her.

She gazed into eyes that were startling blue in his tanned face, eyes that loved her, then she dropped her head on his shoulder and burst into tears.

THE FOLLOWING DAY, Señora Valdez packed a light supper for them, and Grace and Ian rode the horses into the low hills to a grassy picnic spot beside a creek swollen with the late spring runoff.

Ian tethered the horses while Grace spread a cloth over the ground and laid out a platter of cold lobster, a bowl of pasta salad, homemade bread and a variety of tempting side dishes. She opened a bottle of Chablis, which was still cool, and filled two glasses, then assembled two plates of food.

When Ian rejoined her, he lowered himself beside her, and the two of them enjoyed the feast Señora Valdez had prepared for them.

"You never mentioned why you returned early," Grace commented at length. "I didn't expect you until Friday."

Ian finished a last bite of the lobster before he answered. "This may sound a bit silly, darling, but I had a revelation while I was tramping around the gypsum mine. Or maybe it was merely sunstroke. Sunstroke and revelations share some of the same symptoms." He smiled when she laughed. "God, I love the sound of your laugh."

"Tell me about this big revelation."

"There I was, standing in the desert, hot and dusty and wishing I were with you. Suddenly a voice filled my head. 'Ian, you ass, what in the hell are you doing here?'"

"I believe I asked the same question weeks ago," Grace commented dryly.

"When no reasonable answer popped to mind, I returned to the operations building, rang Paris and instructed Henri, my first vice president, to send young Monsieur Arras out here at once to take my place." He took Grace's hand, stroking his thumb across her palm. "I didn't come to Nevada to bury myself in the desert. I came here to romance the love of my life."

"That's what you told the bank's vice president?" Grace asked, smiling.

"The first part, not the last. Then I tossed my briefcase and laptop into the Lincoln and drove back here." Leaning toward her, he refilled her wineglass. "I've made some decisions, Grace." Raising his head, he studied her face, more serious than Grace had seen him in a long time. "I'm going to retire immediately. I'd rather spend what time I have traveling, reading great books and seeing friends than shuffling paperwork at the bank."

Grace blew him a kiss. "Excellent!" Her voice was huskier than usual. It was so hard to think about him dying, let alone listen as he planned his final days.

"I'm leaving for Paris the day after your divorce is granted. And, Grace, I want you to come with me. Being an optimistic sort, I've already purchased our tickets. If you agree, we'll leave on the three o'clock flight to New York on the seventeenth. We'll depart for Paris on the morning of the eighteenth."

Startled, Grace stared at him. She placed her wineglass on the ground beside her. "I haven't decided about us, Ian," she said at length. "Even if I had, I can't leave for Paris on the spur of the moment. I have responsibilities and obligations in San Francisco. Tomorrow a construction crew will begin repairs at Grace. They should finish about the time I return. I'll need to organize an ad campaign and reopen the store. I'm going to be frantically busy for several weeks."

"I thought you said Rita Mulholland could handle everything."

"I'm sure she can. But it's my store, my responsibility. Besides which, I promised Ryder that I'd attend his wedding on the twenty-sixth. I'll be leaving for Australia the instant I know everything is taken care of at the store. I'm sorry, Ian. But I can't possibly go with you to Paris."

He fell silent, staring down at his plate. After a minute he looked up and met her eyes. "Do you love me, Grace?"

"I've always loved you," she answered softly.

"But could you love me as a husband? Could I make you happy? Could you love me as you loved Jeffrey?" When she didn't immediately reply, he began picking up the remains of their picnic and packing the items into the basket. "Do you remember the Christmas we skied in Gstaad? There was one evening when many of us were in the lodge. We all thought Jeffrey had driven to Bern to handle a business matter. At the last minute the matter resolved itself and he didn't go. I'll never forget your face when Jeffrey unexpectedly walked into the lodge. The radiance of your smile lit the heavens. I watched you, and I thought I would give everything I owned to have a woman look at me like that. To have *you* look at me like that." He paused, examining her expression. "Could you, Grace? Could you love me that much, that deeply?"

"I don't know," she whispered, looking at him. "I know that isn't the answer you want to hear, but...I just don't know. Maybe if we had more time..."

"All right, that's fair." He smiled at her and patted her hand. "I'll take you any way I can get you, darling, whether you love me as much as I love you or not. But you can't blame me for wanting it all." Having cleared the picnic from the cloth, he stretched out and rested his head in Grace's lap. "I'm sorry to pressure you, Grace, but there's an unfortunate necessity for haste. I need to know where you and I are going."

"I know," she said, placing a hand on his cheek.

"What you decide will affect the decisions I need to make. And, darling, I need *your* decision very soon."

Grace leaned against the trunk of a pine, gazing toward the horizon. From this moment, she suspected the smell of sage and horses would always remind her of Ian and of being here with him.

"From what you've said, I assume you plan to return to San Francisco hours after your court appearance. Is that correct?"

"I'll appear in court in the morning and leave for San Francisco in the afternoon."

"Then, could we agree to this? Will you call me the next morning, here at the hacienda, and give me your decision? Is that enough time for you to decide?"

They both knew it wasn't. But time was the one thing Ian could not give. Suddenly the irony of the situation overwhelmed Grace. She had married one man without loving him, now she was seriously considering doing the same again.

She loved Ian, yes, but it wasn't the kind of love that she felt for Jeffrey. If she joined Ian in Paris, it would be for reasons she hoped he would never discover.

They sat in companionable silence, Ian's head in her lap, her hand stroking his cheek, listening to the lazy drone of insects and the trickle of water tumbling over the rocks in the creek bed.

"I miss Jeffrey," Ian said quietly. He clasped Grace's hand and placed a kiss in her palm. "Damn him. The next year is going to be very difficult without Jeffrey to lean on occasionally."

There was nothing Grace could say. Even if she could have summoned an appropriate response, the lump in her throat would have prevented her from speaking.

"I never imagined anything could damage the friendship between you and Jeffrey. I'm so sorry," she managed to say at last. "I feel responsible."

"Don't," Ian said emphatically. "None of this is your fault."

"Here we sit amid the wreckage of a forty-year friendship and a marriage of thirty-two years. That hurts to think about."

Lapsing into silence, they watched the sun sinking toward the low brown hills. "Shall I drive you to the courthouse on the seventeenth?" Ian asked eventually, shifting his head on her lap.

"I think that's something I need to do myself. I appreciate the offer of support, but frankly, Ian, I'd rather you weren't there for the proceedings. This is something I must do alone."

They left before darkness set in, riding back to the hacienda beneath a flaming sunset of scarlet and orange.

But before they mounted the horses, Ian drew her into his arms and kissed her deeply and with heart-breaking tenderness.

There were so many things he might have said to her. He could have asked her to marry him regardless of how she felt, could have asked her to give him the one thing he wanted to make his remaining time happy. He might have pointed out that he was asking for only one year of her life against the rest of his. He could have reminded her that he had always been there for her, and until now, he had never asked anything in return. Ian knew her well enough to press all her buttons, to subtly manipulate her with guilt or pity or compassion.

But he loved her. He said none of those things.

DURING THE FINAL TWO weeks before Grace's court appearance, she and Ian established a routine. Each had lengthy lists of phone calls to make every morning, so they didn't meet until lunch. Then they spent the rest of the day together and didn't part until well after midnight.

They swam, played tennis, rode the horses. Several times, they drove into Las Vegas for dinner. They decided the number seventeen had been removed from the roulette wheels, as seventeen never won when they placed chips on it. They shrugged, and Ian said one could not read omens into the random drop of a roulette ball.

By unspoken agreement they did not discuss Ian's illness or Grace's divorce, nor did they address the future. They laughed over the past, smiled at stories that had been told and polished through years of retelling. They discussed art and books and films. They shared memories of youth, and one night, they talked seriously about God, religious dogma and the possibility of an afterlife.

When they kissed good-night, their lingering kisses were tender and sweet. Electricity flashed between them, along with curiosity and urgency, but they held their passion in check. The wait was nearly over.

And then it was Wednesday night, and tomorrow Grace would drive the Ingrams' car into Las Vegas to the court-house. She would enter the courtroom a married woman and leave as a single woman.

"I've changed my plans," Ian murmured, holding her close, his lips against her hair. "I canceled my flight to Paris."

Grace wrapped her arms around his waist and rested her head on his chest, listening to his heartbeat.

"When you ring me Friday morning . . . if you tell me we have a future, then I'll fly to San Francisco. I love you, and I don't want to wait until you're free to come to Paris. I'll come to you."

Grace tightened her arms around him. On Saturday morning she could wake with Ian's handsome head on the pillow beside her. Right now, that was an appealing thought.

"When you return from the courthouse, I'll drive you to the airport," Ian said, kissing the top of her head.

"I've arranged for a car and driver."

Gently, he tilted her face up so he could examine her eyes. "Are you pulling away, Grace?"

She considered the question. "I don't think so," she answered, returning his gaze. "It's more that I know tomorrow will be difficult and I'll need some private time to deal with the finality of it."

"I'll be here waiting for you. I wish you weren't leaving immediately. I wish you'd allow me to take you to dinner.

I'd do my damnedest to make you laugh and look forward instead of backward.''

"I know you would. Thank you. But it's time for me to leave,'' she said gently. "I'll need a few hours alone after I return from the courthouse.'' She touched his lips with her fingertips. "When I'm fit for company, I'll come to the guest house and find you.''

CHAPTER FOURTEEN

GRACE AWOKE BEFORE the alarm rang. Leaning against a pile of mounded pillows, she twisted Anne Marie's diamond-and-sapphire ring on her finger and watched as darkness shaded to light outside the windows.

This was the last morning that she would awaken as Jeffrey DeWilde's wife. Her final morning as a married woman. Moisture brimmed in her eyes, and a single tear fell from her lashes.

Today the path of her life would divide. She would veer down a road she had never wanted or thought she would take. The new direction pointed toward a variety of possible futures.

One future was built around Ian Stanley.

Other possibilities hid behind a bank of mist that she could not yet penetrate.

Another possible future curved into a cul-de-sac with Jeffrey's name on it.

Was that truly a reasonable and valid choice as Mary had insisted it was? To divorce Jeffrey, then wait for him to regain his senses and return to her? How long should she wait for him? For the rest of her life as Anne Marie had done?

"I have waited my life away," she whispered, repeating Anne Marie's lament. She turned the sapphire-and-diamond ring on her finger, watching the gems sparkle and flash in the morning light.

Letting her head fall back on the pillows, she gazed at the ceiling and wondered what Jeffrey was doing now. Did he remember that this was the day? Did he know what time the proceedings would take place? Was he thinking about her? Had he spared a thought for all the years they had loved and laughed and worked side by side? Did any of it matter to him anymore?

Grace stayed in bed until the sun was well into the sky, not rousing from a depressing lethargy until she heard a light knock. When she opened the door, she discovered a tray on the floor containing a coffeepot, a plate of hot croissants and a vase filled with flowers from the veranda pots. "Thank you," she murmured, but Señora Valdez had tactfully withdrawn.

When it was time, Grace carefully laid out the clothing she would wear to divorce her husband. She had purchased the cream-colored linen suit in Las Vegas on a shopping trip with Mary, although she had not told Mary where she intended to wear it.

When she returned from the courthouse, she would fold the suit into a trash bag, along with matching high heels and purse and her undergarments. She would carry the bag to the incinerator behind the hacienda and push it deep inside. Then she would place her jewelry into a small package she had prepared yesterday and mail it to Lenore Cleef to be auctioned at the next charity bazaar Lenore chaired.

She did not want a single reminder of this day to remain in her life.

At nine-thirty, Grace squared her shoulders, walked to the garage and slid inside the car. For a long moment she gripped the steering wheel and sat very still, staring through the windshield at the garage wall. Then she breathed deeply, backed out of the garage and drove through the desert sunshine to the courthouse.

AFTER THE PROCEEDINGS, Grace could remember very little of what had transpired. Thick sheaves of paper were entered into the record from both sides of the aisle, and she recalled that at one point, all the attorneys had converged before the judge to confer in low voices. Dimly she remembered sitting in the witness chair, with Walter standing in front of her, looking handsome and relaxed while he asked Grace the questions they had reviewed together.

The only surprise came when the judge halted Walter's presentation to lean toward Grace and inquire if she was all right. His concern startled and bewildered her until she suddenly realized silent tears were running down her cheeks.

Now it was over. Standing, she watched as Jeffrey's attorneys pushed papers into their briefcases, talking between themselves. Neither of them glanced toward her.

Walter took her arm and pressed it against his side, then he guided her out of the courthouse, leading her gently as he might have led a blind person. "Do you have time for lunch? We'll have a drink and celebrate."

Celebrate? She stared at him in confusion. What was there to celebrate? Could anyone truly "celebrate" the destruction of thirty-two years of marriage?

She managed to decline and thank him for the offer without screaming or unraveling before his smile. "My flight for San Francisco leaves at five. I still have some packing to do," she said, wondering if she was babbling.

"I'm sure you'll be glad to get home and sleep in your own bed," Walter remarked, smiling as he opened her car door.

She was having great difficulty following his conversation. She wasn't going home. Home was Kemberly. And she wouldn't sleep in her own bed tonight. She would sleep in a new bed, with no memories attached. A lonely bed. Not the bed she wanted.

"Thank you," she said abruptly, thrusting out her hand to shake his. She needed to get away from him, away from the shadow of the courthouse. "I deeply appreciate everything you've done, and your consideration in all matters."

"I admire you, Grace, and I've enjoyed the time we've spent together. I hope the future is everything you want it to be."

"I'm sure it will be," she said, certain now that she was babbling, uncertain of everything else.

"I'll send along the paperwork in a week or two," Walter said, stepping back from her car door. "Drive carefully."

She remembered his caution, but she didn't remember the drive back to the Ingrams' hacienda. When she realized she was parked in front of the veranda, sitting in the car clasping the steering wheel, she stared in astonishment at the flowers nodding from the pots. She could have sworn a magic beam had transported her from the courthouse parking lot to the hacienda. She didn't remember one thing about driving here.

Moving like a sleepwalker, she entered the hacienda and walked directly to her bedroom, where she peeled off her clothing and stuffed it into the incinerator bag. She dropped her diamond earrings, a sapphire lapel pin and her least favorite wristwatch into the box on the bureau and sealed the package.

Then she froze. She had forgotten Anne Marie's ring. And her wedding ring. Extending a shaking hand, she stared at the rings sparkling on her fingers. No. She could not give away Anne Marie's ring or her wedding ring. But she removed them both and dropped them into the purse she would carry on the plane.

Naked, she stumbled into the shower and stood beneath the spray, crying helplessly, rubbing her bare ring finger.

A marriage she had believed would never end had ended.

From this moment forward, she would inhabit a different world that she didn't understand or fit into.

Never again would the words "my husband" roll easily off her tongue. "Our" was now "my." There was no longer a "we." The next time she said, "That reminds me of Venice!" the man she said it to wouldn't have the faintest notion what she was talking about; she had lost thirty-two years of shared memories.

What was hardest to accept was that never again would anyone understand her as Jeffrey did, because no one except Jeffrey knew all the small, often seemingly insignificant events that had gradually transformed her into the woman she was today. She had been wrapped in a cocoon when Jeffrey married her. Jeffrey had nurtured the cocoon, and through love and encouragement, he had coaxed forth a butterfly. New friends—new men—would find it difficult to imagine that she had ever been less than a self-assured and confident woman. They wouldn't know that once she had been shy and uncertain. No other man, not even Ian, could see her entire personal history as Jeffrey did.

Numb, she toweled her hair and body, then stepped into Jeffrey's old robe and buried her face in the lapels. For a long time she stood very still, striving to inhale his scent from material long since permeated with her own fragrance.

The last thing she wanted now was to speak to anyone. It was habit that made her pick up the ringing phone, a reflex action that she instantly cursed and regretted.

"Gracie."

Abruptly her knees collapsed and she sat down hard on the edge of the bed. Doubling over, she pressed a shaking hand to her forehead and closed her eyes.

"Oh, Jeffrey." Her whisper was choked and scarcely audible.

"Gracie, are you all right?" he asked in a low, anguished voice.

"No." Right now she could not imagine ever feeling all right again. Helpless tears leaked past the fingers she held over her eyes. "I'm so tired of crying. But the tears just won't stop." Her voice sounded a hundred years old.

"Damn it! This is so wrong."

"I know."

"I love you, Grace. I've always loved you. I always will love you."

"I love you, too," she whispered. She was strangling. Dying. The old cliché was untrue. People could die from broken hearts.

He swore, then she heard a crash and the sound of breaking glass. She was too numb to wonder at Jeffrey actually smashing something. For a long moment neither of them spoke. They held the phone to their ears and listened to each other's silent misery.

"I want to apologize for the offensive things I said the last time we talked," he said finally, speaking in a voice so low she had to strain to hear. "I was out of line. And I was wrong. I know you and I know Ian. I know neither of you would—"

"Please, Jeffrey, don't. I understand."

And on reflection, she did. Jeffrey had lost a beloved wife and a friendship he had valued above all others. His pain had congealed around the poison of jealousy and ugly accusations.

"Grace . . . God, I don't know what to say."

"There's nothing to say."

"I never wanted it to go this far. I'm sitting here in shock, unable to believe that we're divorced. Gracie, for God's sake, we're *divorced!* How in the hell did that happen? It's unthinkable. I keep wishing we could go back and do things differently. Wishing that . . . damn it!"

"If I just hadn't told you! Oh, Jeffrey, I go over and over it in my mind, replaying that night so it ends differently."

"I had an *affair*. My God. It's unimaginable. I'll regret it for the rest of my life, and I swear to you, I don't understand how it happened. I'll never understand it. No wonder you can't forgive me!"

Closing her eyes, she leaned her cheek against the soft, worn lapel of his robe. "I forgive you," she whispered.

His silence was so long, so painful, that for the first and only time since she had known him, Grace was glad she could not see his face. His expression would have shattered what remained of her heart.

His heartrending whisper raised a flood of tears in her eyes. "Thank you, Gracie. Thank you."

Holding her breath, praying, she silently urged him to tell her that he could forgive, too, that he didn't care that she had married him without loving him. What mattered were all the years that she *had* loved him; what mattered was that she loved him now.

But he couldn't speak the words. Jeffrey was a DeWilde, and DeWilde men held their anguish close to the heart. When forgiveness came—if it came—it would be complete and total. But that moment lay somewhere in the future, if ever. Jeffrey could not forgive her yet. Perhaps he never would.

Grace realized she was on the verge of flying to pieces. And she didn't want to appear weak before him.

"Goodbye, Jeffrey," she whispered. There was nothing more to say.

"Will I ever see you again?" He sounded bereft and lost, bewildered.

"We'll see each other at Ryder's wedding, remember?"

Already she dreaded the encounter, could not imagine being near Jeffrey as anything other than his wife.

"And after that?"

Grace could not answer. Before they were together again, Jeffrey would have to find his way to forgiveness. She would have to consign herself to loneliness and a commitment to wait for him. She didn't know if either of them was willing or able to do what was required. "Goodbye, Jeffrey. I can't talk more now. I love you."

"I love you, too."

Quietly, she hung up the telephone. Ironically, this was the first conversation they'd had in a year where they hadn't argued. The realization made her feel sick inside. Standing, she walked into the bathroom, kneeled and threw up until her stomach was as empty as her heart.

WHEN SHE HADN'T COME to the guest house by three-thirty, Ian searched for her at the hacienda. He found her sitting in one of the wicker chairs on the veranda, dressed to depart, her luggage waiting on the steps.

When Grace met his gaze, she saw the disappointment and anger drawing his expression. "I'm sorry, Ian. I didn't want to talk to anyone. This is the worst day of my life."

Kneeling beside her, Ian clasped her hand and stroked her fingers. "You're cold." If he noticed that she had removed her engagement and wedding rings, he was tactful enough not to mention it aloud.

"Am I?" The thermometer on one of the veranda posts read seventy-one degrees. But her fingers and toes throbbed as if they were frostbitten.

"Do you want to talk about it?"

She turned her gaze to the lane of royal palms. "No."

"Grace, please. Don't leave like this. Stay one more night. We'll have dinner somewhere quiet. We'll talk about happy things, good things. We'll make plans for the future. We'll drink your favorite champagne and laugh and be silly. Grace?" Still kneeling beside her, he peered into her face. "Darling, say you'll stay."

A gray limousine turned into the long driveway and glided toward them.

"I'm sorry, Ian, but I need to be alone. I have a lot to think about. Please try to understand."

He pressed her hand to his lips, but he didn't argue, a consideration for which she felt profoundly grateful. When the limo drew up to the veranda steps, he stood and helped Grace to her feet. Smiling, he looked down at the tailored navy suit she wore above dark stockings and matching navy pumps.

"When I think about you, I always picture you wearing high heels. When I stayed at Kemberly, I could predict your mood even before I saw you just by listening to the tap of your high heels approaching. The tempo spoke volumes."

The limo driver glanced at her luggage and lifted a questioning eyebrow. Grace nodded.

"I love you, Grace. Give me a chance to make us both happy."

Gently, she placed her hands on his cheeks, framing his face between her palms. "You're a dear, good man, Ian. You're my best friend, and I love you. Thank you for being here for me. I could not have gotten through this terrible time without you."

His hands tightened on her waist and a look of alarm narrowed his blue eyes. "This sounds suspiciously like goodbye."

She hadn't thought she would smile today, but she did. "No," she said softly, placing her fingertips against his lips. "No matter what the future holds, you and I will never say goodbye."

His expression relaxed into a smile. "About that future..."

She actually laughed. "You're relentless."

"Utterly," he said, pulling her into his arms and embracing her tightly. "Are you actually going to make me wait for your decision until tomorrow morning? Are you that cruel?"

When she pulled back to look at him, he was smiling. But his eyes were serious. "I don't mean to be cruel, Ian, just very sure."

"Pretend the driver isn't watching, and kiss me."

Grace lifted her mouth to his and they kissed, deeply, lingeringly. The emotion between them shook her. When their lips parted, tears swam in her eyes. "I don't want you to die," she whispered. "I can't bear it."

Gently, he brushed a tear from her cheek with the back of his hand. "Marry me, Grace. When you ring me tomorrow morning, tell me you'll marry me." Emotion thickened his voice.

At the foot of the veranda steps, the limo driver cleared his throat and glanced at his wristwatch. "It's almost four, ma'am."

"I'll be right there," Grace said, still looking into Ian's eyes. She kissed him hard, trying to tell him with her lips and body what he had meant to her in the past and what he meant to her now.

Then she ran down the steps and slid into the car. Pressing a handkerchief to her lips, she twisted on the seat and looked back at him, standing on the veranda, until the road curved away and she could no longer see him.

THE AIR WAS STALE INSIDE her condominium. For a moment Grace stood just inside the door, surrounded by her luggage, and gazed at furnishings that had become alien during her six-week absence.

The straight lines and uncluttered surfaces seemed stark and impersonal. High-tech gadgetry that previously had delighted her now seemed glaringly out of place and a little daunting. Her home reminded her of a magazine layout, too burdened by perfection to actually be lived in comfortably.

The telephone rang, breaking the silence and jarring her. In the study, her answering machine picked up and she heard her daughter Kate's voice.

''Welcome home. When you feel up to it, give me a call. I love you, Mom.''

Mom. Grace smiled. Her youngest daughter was sounding less English and more American with every passing day.

Taking off her jacket, she walked into the study and glanced at the answering machine. While she was in Nevada, the phone had rung over to her office at Grace, but the ring-over had ended this morning. Already she had a dozen calls, none of which she intended to return until tomorrow. Her children and friends would understand. She didn't care about the others.

After opening a few windows, she carried her luggage into her bedroom, pausing to study the room. Jeffrey wouldn't like it, she decided. It wasn't a frilly room, but it was feminine. Even a casual observer would have known at once that this was a room designed for a woman who lived alone.

Suddenly she hated the room. She hated her condominium. She hated San Francisco, hated her bare ring finger, hated starting over, hated her age, hated making decisions for a future she couldn't embrace.

Reaching blindly, Grace picked up a bottle of lotion and hurled it at the wall. Shaking, she stared at the thick, viscous liquid slowly dripping down the wallpaper, at the pieces of broken glass on the carpet, then she covered her face with her hands. She could not remember the last time she had done something so futile and idiotic, so out of control.

Going into the bathroom, she ran cold water over a washcloth and pressed the cloth against her hot face.

She had to hear his voice. Her resistance lasted only as long as it took to change into her sleep shirt and a bathrobe, then she sat on the bed and dialed London, even though it was the middle of the night there.

Jeffrey answered on the first ring.

"Were you sleeping?" she asked in a low voice.

"No." They listened to each other breathing. "Damn it, Gracie, what are we going to do?"

"I don't know." She watched the lotion seeping down the wall, leaving an oily stain behind. "Ian wants me to marry him."

They had always told each other everything; it didn't seem strange to tell him this. It did seem strange that she couldn't tell him that Ian was dying.

The silence continued for a full minute. "Ian loves you," Jeffrey said finally, speaking in a flat voice. "He'll do everything he can to make you happy." Another long silence followed. "Is that what you want, Grace?"

"I don't know," she whispered, twisting her finger around the phone cord. "I have to decide tonight."

"Tonight?"

"There are reasons... why I have to decide immediately." Suddenly she felt exhausted. It had been a long, painful day, the most emotional day of her life. Lowering her head, she said something that she had not said since she was in her early twenties. "Jeffrey?" she whispered. "Tell me what to do. What shall I tell Ian?"

"I can't make that decision for you," he said finally.

"Yes, you can."

Never had two more miserable people attempted to have a conversation. Suffering as she knew Jeffrey was suffering, Grace closed her eyes and struggled to breathe.

"Do you love him?"

"Not like I love you. But I've always loved Ian. You do, too."

"Grace, I need time. I want to tell you to forget about Ian Stanley, that back-stabbing son of a bitch. I want to tell you to wait for me, to give me time to work this out. I want to beg you not to do anything that will make it impossible for us." He paused, and she imagined him angrily pushing a hand through his hair. "But I don't have the right to say any of those things."

"How much time, Jeffrey?"

"Lord, I wish I knew."

"Another year? Five years? Ten? Forever?"

"You married a DeWilde, Grace. You didn't marry me."

The lotion, thick and pink, had almost reached the carpet. She watched the progress with dulled eyes. "I could wait my life away," she said, wondering where she had heard that phrase, "and in the end, you still might not forgive me."

Anguish infused his whisper. "I would if I could. God, Gracie, you must know that. I love you."

"The DeWilde men don't forgive easily, and they never forget," she quoted softly, watching the lotion soak into the carpet.

"I'm sorry, I didn't hear you?"

"I have to hang up now."

"Grace?"

He was going to tell her not to marry Ian, she heard it in his voice. But as he had stated, he no longer had the right to advise her. She'd been foolish and wrong to ask his opinion.

"Good night, Jeffrey." Gently, quietly, she hung up the phone. And she didn't pick it up when it rang two minutes later. She sat on the side of her lonely bed and counted eighteen rings before the silence returned.

She had a great deal to think about. And not much time.

GRACE DIDN'T ATTEMPT to sleep; she knew she wouldn't. After unpacking her luggage, she ran some laundry, checked the personal mail that had accumulated, then she opened the box that contained Anne Marie's diaries and the thick manuscript translation.

For a moment, she held one of the diaries against her chest, thinking about Anne Marie's long, eventful life. The joy, the heartache, the tragedy, the loneliness of her later years.

As in any life, there were unanswered questions in Anne Marie's story. Grace wondered, as Anne Marie must have, what Martin had said in the letter he wrote to her before he committed suicide, the letter Maximilien had intercepted. And most important, had Maximilien ever forgiven her?

That was the question that most troubled Grace's mind. When Maximilien lay dying, had he regretted the lonely years apart from his beloved wife? Had he cursed himself for denying them an opportunity to live out their years together? In the end, had it really mattered that he had not sired the children who loved him?

Slowly, her thoughts moved to the present. Would Jeffrey follow in the footsteps of his great-grandfather?

If Grace did as Jeffrey asked, if she waited and hoped he could resolve his conflict, would she end like Anne Marie? Far from home, waiting her life away while she grew older and lonelier?

Could she live in a state of suspension? Could she bear it? Did she love Jeffrey DeWilde that much?

Or would the next year be better spent trying to make a dying man happy? Was her loving friendship for Ian deep enough to throw away any chance of reconciling with her husband?

These were the questions that tormented her as the night slowly seeped away.

There was another question, as well. Because she had immersed herself in the diaries during the most painful period of her life, and because of the parallels between her life and Anne Marie's, her decision about the final disposition of the diaries was a difficult one to make. Yet she had to make it.

The impact of Anne Marie's secrets had diminished over time, but the fact that the DeWildes carried no DeWilde blood was still powerful enough to shock the family at its core. And the diaries were so much more than a revelation of family secrets. They were a chronicle of one woman's private pain. They had never been intended to be read by anyone but the writer.

Oddly, Grace sensed that Gabriel, who knew nothing of the diaries' existence, had provided the answer. "Sometimes keeping a secret is the kindest choice." The kindest choice for Anne Marie, and for the DeWilde family, was to draw a veil across the past.

Near dawn, Grace lit a fire in the hearth in the living room and held her hands to the flames. The air was damp and cool at this early hour. Unlike the blazing dawns of the desert, morning in San Francisco rose pale and watery.

For an hour she sat quietly, occasionally rising to place more logs on the fire, letting her thoughts drift in no particular order. Jeffrey walked through her memory, and so did Ian. She recalled moments of intense joy with each of them.

And then it was time. Ian would be sitting beside the telephone, awaiting her call. He answered on the first ring.

"Ian..." She watched the flames leaping in the grate. "This is the hardest call I have ever had to make...." The flames blurred behind a film of moisture.

She heard a low sound as if the breath were flowing out of his body. "I think I already knew," he said finally, his voice soft.

"Jeffrey and I have so much history together," she whispered helplessly. "We have children together. Our lives are so tightly interwoven that I'm not sure where Jeffrey ends and I begin. I'm not ready to let go of that. I can't do it yet. I love both of you, Ian. But Jeffrey is my husband, and you are my dearest friend."

"I'll settle for whatever you can give, Grace. I just want to be with you."

Tears swam in her eyes. "You deserve someone who can love you wholly and without reservation, someone with no regrets, no baggage. You deserve better than I can give right now. Maybe if we'd had more time..."

His pain charged the silence. Grace lowered her head and wondered how many times a woman's heart could break. How many heartrending silences could she endure and still survive?

"Grace..." he said finally, his voice hoarse. "Will you come to me at the end?"

"Oh, Ian." Tears drowned her voice. "No matter what my circumstances are, no matter where I am or what I'm doing, I'll come to you. I'll be there for you, as you have always been there for me. I'll be at your side, my dear friend, until the last."

"Thank you." He paused, and she imagined him gazing out at the desert sunshine. "That makes it a little easier, knowing I'll see you again, knowing you'll be there." He drew a breath. "Don't cry, darling. Don't cry for me."

She couldn't answer. Tears choked her, blinded her.

"Really, you look so terrible when you cry. Your eyes are probably swelling right now, and your nose is getting red. You're making those dreadful little sounds."

She laughed through the flood soaking her cheeks. Her heart was shattering in her chest. "Sweet talk is not your strong suit, Ian Stanley."

For her sake, he, too, managed a laugh. "Apparently not. Listen, darling, I really have to run. A bevy of curvaceous show girls is pounding at my door, begging to accompany me to Paris. Should I take one of them home with me, do you think?"

"Absolutely." She was strangling. Her chest hurt and her stomach cramped in pain. She could not bear this. "Choose the sassy one with the longest legs."

"My thought exactly." He paused a moment. "I'll always love you, Grace. One of the great joys of my life has been knowing you."

"And I will always love you, Ian," she whispered. Tears streamed down her face. "You've made my life richer, happier, better than it would have been without you."

"Darling?" he said, speaking so softly that she almost couldn't hear. "Hang up now, before I say something that will embarrass us both."

"Goodbye, Ian. I'll be there for you. I'll come to you."

"Goodbye, darling. Be happy."

Gently, she placed the telephone in the cradle, then covered her face in her hands and sobbed. One of Anne Marie's diaries slid off the sofa and fell to the floor at her feet. When she was finally able, when she had cried until no more tears would come, she bent and picked up the diary.

It had fallen open, and Grace scanned the page before she leaned forward in pain and covered her eyes.

"Oh, Ian, I shall miss you all the days of my life," she whispered hoarsely. When the years weighed heavily, and she too heard her beloved ghosts whispering in the shadows, one of them would be her dearest Ian.

After a while, she moved to the floor and sat near the fire in the grate. It would take a long time to burn Anne Marie's diaries and the translation pages. And it would be painful to watch the smoke of family secrets drift up the flue.

Taking a handful of loose pages, Grace extended them toward the flames, then paused.

She could not burn the diaries. She could not do that to Anne Marie, or to the DeWilde family. Lowering her head, she pressed a hand to her forehead.

Destroying Anne Marie's diaries was not Grace's decision to make. As of yesterday, she was a DeWilde in name only.

Letting her head fall backward, she stared at the ceiling, blinking rapidly.

Right now, she didn't like Jeffrey DeWilde. She deeply resented that he didn't want her enough to halt the divorce but wouldn't release her, either. Irrationally, she was furious at him because she had chosen him over Ian, and because he didn't know that Ian, who loved him, was dying and needed him. The fury of her emotions made her body shake.

And yet she loved him. If Jeffrey DeWilde had walked in her door right now and opened his arms, she would have run to him with joy in her heart.

"Please, Jeffrey," she whispered, unconsciously paraphrasing Anne Marie. "Please, forgive me for the tragedy I set in motion. Don't wait too long. Let me come home."

Seeing Jeffrey's face and Ian's in the flames, she held Anne Marie's diaries to her chest and quietly wept.

Weddings By DeWilde

continues with

WILDE MAN

by Daphne Clair

Also available this month

Here's a preview!

WILDE MAN

"WHY ARE YOU SO scared?" Dev said quietly.

Maxine's eyes fixed on him. "Scared?" She willed scorn into her voice. "Don't be silly!"

"I work with fear," he said. "Mine, the animals I take away from their homes and habitats, the people who see predators as monsters. I know it when I see it. And I see it in you. I don't want to hurt you." He sounded calm and quiet, as he had when he'd talked to Delilah. Maxine thought fleetingly, foolishly that she wished he'd stroke her as he had the crocodile, soothe her with his big, gentle hands.

This man talked the most feared creatures on earth into trusting him. And then he caged them. Oh, all for their own good, of course. But they were caged nevertheless. He was downright dangerous!

A shiver ran through her body. "If you don't want to hurt me," she said starkly, "you'll leave me alone."

Dev looked at her quite soberly for a long time, and then he gave a nod. "I never go after a frightened creature unless I have to. Sometimes it's necessary, of course, to protect them."

Maxine swallowed. "I don't need any protecting, Mr. DeWilde Cutter. I can look after myself very well. And I'm not frightened of you," she added belatedly.

At last he smiled a little. "Never thought you were."

She didn't want to ask him what he meant by that.

Because she was afraid to hear the answer? Brushing aside the uncomfortable thought, she turned abruptly and pushed open the door and started walking away from him.

When he caught up with her, she said briskly, "I hope you've given some thought to being sensible about the DeWildes' offer."

"Can't you give it a rest?" Dev asked plaintively.

They walked by an open concrete compound where a frilled lizard, a shade smaller than Archie, scurried along a big log and froze, hoping to remain unnoticed. "Have you had a chance to discuss it with your mother?"

"You think she'll agree, don't you? Jeffrey's probably trying to talk her round now. My mother's too soft for her own good, but it won't make any difference, you know. I'll fight it all the way."

"*Why?*" Exasperated, Maxine turned on him. "For her sake? But if she's willing to compromise—"

"Because I feel guilty!" Dev said harshly. "And this is one way of making it up to her, that's why!"

"Making what up to her?"

"The fact that I hate my name," he growled. "That ever since I was six years old I've refused to answer to the name she gave me."

MILLS & BOON®

Weddings ✤ Glamour ✤ Family ✤ Heartbreak

Since the turn of the century, the elegant and
fashionable DeWilde stores have helped brides around
the world realise the fantasy of their 'special day'.

Book 11: ROMANCING THE STONES—Janis Flores

Nick Santos was close to solving the mystery of the missing
DeWilde jewels, but Kate DeWilde was proving to be a major glitch
in his progress. Falling for his boss's daughter had put a definite
crimp in his investigative style—doing as she asked would mean
kissing the case of a lifetime good-bye...

Book 12: I DO, AGAIN—Jasmine Cresswell

Michael Forrest represented everything Julia Dutton wished to
avoid in a man—but his high voltage sexuality was irresistible. Was
Julia brave enough to commit to a man who offered only a few
short months of ecstasy? Meanwhile, the missing DeWilde jewels
were coming home to Jeffrey—via his ex-wife. Would the collection,
his family and his marriage finally be whole again?

Coming to you in March 1997

MILLS & BOON®

Weddings By DeWilde

If you have missed any of the previously published titles in the Weddings by DeWilde series, you may order them by sending a cheque or postal order (please do not send cash) made payable to Harlequin Mills & Boon Ltd. for £2.99 per book plus 50p postage and packing for the first book and 25p for each additional book. Please send your order to: Weddings by DeWilde, P.O. Box 236, Croydon, Surrey, CR9 3RU (EIRE: Weddings by DeWilde, P. O. Box 4546, Dublin 24).

MILLS & BOON®

Four remarkable family reunions,
Four fabulous new romances—

Don't miss our exciting Mother's Day Gift Pack
celebrating the joys of motherhood with love, laughter
and lots of surprises.

SECOND-TIME BRIDE   Lynne Graham

INSTANT FATHER   Lucy Gordon

A NATURAL MOTHER   Cathy Williams

YESTERDAY'S BRIDE   Alison Kelly

Special Promotional Price of £6.30—
4 books for the price of 3

Available: February 1997

MILLS & BOON

Next Month's Romances

♡

Each month you can choose from a wide variety of romance novels from Mills & Boon. Below are the new titles to look out for next month from the Presents and Enchanted series.

Presents™

JACK'S BABY	Emma Darcy
A MARRYING MAN?	Lindsay Armstrong
ULTIMATE TEMPTATION	Sara Craven
THE PRICE OF A WIFE	Helen Brooks
GETTING EVEN	Sharon Kendrick
TEMPTING LUCAS	Catherine Spencer
MAN TROUBLE!	Natalie Fox
A FORGOTTEN MAGIC	Kathleen O'Brien

Enchanted™

HUSBANDS ON HORSEBACK	
	Margaret Way & Diana Palmer
MACBRIDE'S DAUGHTER	Patricia Wilson
MARRYING THE BOSS!	Leigh Michaels
THE DADDY PROJECT	Suzanne Carey
BEHAVING BADLY!	Emma Richmond
A DOUBLE WEDDING	Patricia Knoll
TAKEOVER ENGAGEMENT	Elizabeth Duke
HUSBAND-TO-BE	Linda Miles

Available from WH Smith, John Menzies, Volume One, Forbuoys, Martins, Woolworths, Tesco, Asda, Safeway and other paperback stockists.

New York Times bestselling author

JAYNE ANN KRENTZ

Legacy

A story of two unlikely lovers

Honor Mayfield thought that her chance
meeting with Conn Landry was a stroke of
luck. Too late she realised she was falling for
someone who was seeking to avenge a legacy
of murder and betrayal.

"A master of the genre...nobody does it better!"
—Romantic Times

MIRA®

**AVAILABLE IN PAPERBACK
FROM FEBRUARY 1997**

"Mortimer has a special magic."
—Romantic Times

CAROLE MORTIMER

*Their tempestuous night held a
magic all its own...and only she
could mend his shattered dreams*

Merlyn's Magic

AVAILABLE IN PAPERBACK
FROM FEBRUARY 1997